THE BATTLE

FOR

CRESTED HILL

TERRY LURSEN

TEL PUBLISHING

HUNTERSVILLE, NC

For further information, please contact TEL Publishing
terrylursen@gmail.com

THE BATTLE FOR CRESTED HILL

This is a work of fiction, a dream allegory. All of the characters and events portrayed in this book are fictional, and any resemblance to real people or incidents is purely coincidental.

Copyright © 2016 by Terry E. Lursen
Cover Design: Stephen Lursen Art
Etching Artwork: Stephen Lursen Art
Published by: TEL Publishing

ISBN: 978-0-9910989-5-8 - Hardback Version
ISBN: 978-0-9910989-6-5 - Softcover Version
ISBN: 978-0-9910989-7-2 - ebook Version

All rights reserved. No part of this publication may be reproduced, stored in a retrieval system or transmitted in any form or by any means, electronic, mechanical, photocopying, recording or otherwise without the prior written permission of the copyright owner.

Scripture taken from the New King James Version ®. Copyright © 1982 by Thomas Nelson, Inc. Used by permission. All rights reserved.

All maps and etchings Copyright 2016 by Stephen Lursen Art

Library of Congress Cataloging-in-Publication Data

Lursen, Terry E., 1957 –

the battle for crested hill

Library of Congress Control Number: 2016907088

Acknowledgements

Thank you to the Great One, the giver of life and the giver of courage. For I know whom I have believed and the courage you give is the courage I receive to press on with the gift you have given. I pray You are honored.

Thank you to David Simon of www.koshercopy.com for being a friend and reading through this wonderfully strange and adventuresome story. You have helped me to edit with the wit that was needed, the spiritual aptitude that was necessary and the guidance of a spiritual man that was practical and prudent.

Thank you to the critique group of Gena, Jim, Richard and Erica who, although we didn't get through much together, you taught me some very important lessons in writing and how to be tough on myself and the little bit of skill that lies within these pages. Erica, you helped me most of all. Thank you, you are a good teacher. I had forgotten how much Piers Plowman and Geoffrey Chaucer have influenced my life.

Thank you to John Bunyan who has influenced me as well in his extraordinary writing, "The Pilgrim's Progress". Your suffering in the flesh and in the Lord proved to me as gain and I pray that these writings will be gain to someone else who needs to be free from the Darkend Road.

Thank you to my son, Stephen Lursen, of Stephen Lursen Art, who continues to deliver such amazement to my spirit as to figure what I need when I need it. Stephen, you are a gifted and most fantastic artist. I'm very proud of you and am grateful that you continue to help me as you do in my writing journey.

Thank you to my family, my wife, Jane, my adult children Jessica, Stephen, Cara and Christian, and even little Leiana, who have listened to my stories, my readings, my dreams, my allegories, my poems, my rantings, and my shenanigans for years. The opportunity that life has brought us to have finally found a resting place for some of these stories, dreams and visions is quite remarkable. I pray for us all that we learn from the past as these writings attempt to teach us to remain on the Lighted Pearl Pathway all the rest of our lives. I love you all immensely.

There comes a time when a demand is given and you're told what to do and if you don't do it, then the demand sits waiting out the window for you to decide to obey and until you do, you'll have to do something else in the meantime.

Saying, "I will obey and I will go," and then not doing it, is basically lying to the one who has given you the command. But, it is also lying to yourself in that the words that you speak don't match your within or your walk. The within has to be activated to submit and follow the demand first, otherwise, words will flow like streams in a desert. You don't know where they come from and they're basically useless because they lack substance and meaning. They soon dry up from not having a constant flow in the midst of the heat.

Do what you've been told to do by the Great One and stick to it until the task is completed. No one likes to be called a schlup, particularly when it's true...

Table of Contents

Mount Illumine
The Crested Hill
Atlas Stone
The Carb
Prominens Stone
Ementior's Stand
Battling Trees
Plain of Alongore
Thicket of Cadgwith
Plateau of Decree
Voice of the Friend
Two Boulders
The Great Mount
Western Slopes
Forest of Black Tree
Four Wandering Preachers

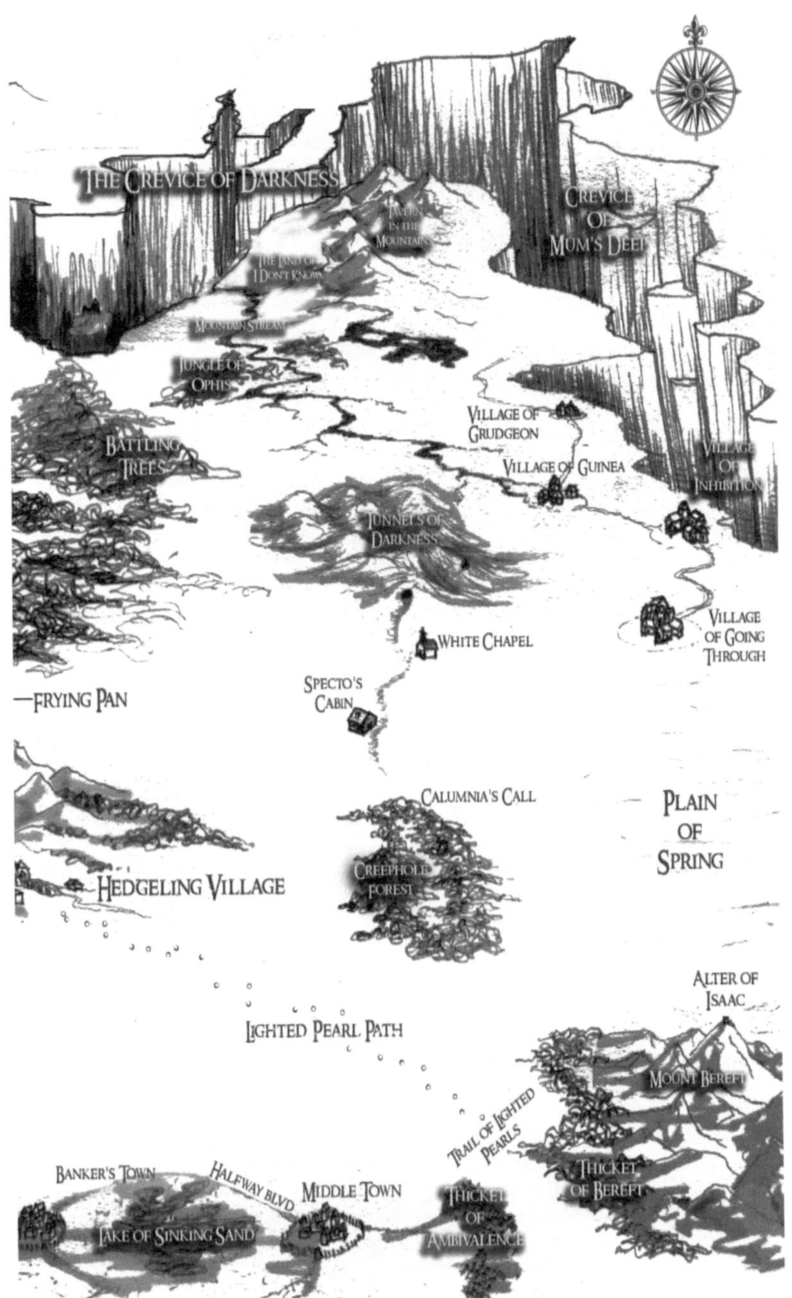

The Crevice of Darkness
Crevice of Mum's Deep
Tavern in the Mountains
The Land of I Don't Know
Mountain Stream
Jungle of Ophis
Village of Grudgeon
Village of Guinea
Village of Inhibition
Battling Trees
Tunnels of Darkness
White Chapel
Village of Going Through
Specto's Cabin
Frying Pan
Calumnia's Call
Plain of Spring
Hedgeling Village
Creephole Forest
Alter of Isaac
Lighted Pearl Path
Mount Bereft
Trail of Lighted Pearls
Banker's Town
Halfway Blvd
Middle Town
Thicket of Ambivalence
Thicket of Bereft
Lake of Sinking Sand

The Battle for Crested Hill

Prologue

It is in times when men think they are good, that they lie sleeping, being rest assured that whatever it is they have accomplished in their short lives is surely going to take them to wherever it is that they are supposed to go. Hardly a man knows his wherever he is to go and so it was with this fallen fellow as he lie sleeping on his pillow of beginnings that his real task was coming before him. He had lived a life thus far believing that Will was with him, being his best friend, and that Will was his guide, but Will was the most confused of men if there ever was a state of men to be confused. This is where many folk of educated stature find themselves on the wheresabouts thinking they are something, but are far from it. It is what it is is hardly ever true for things are not always what they seem. It was said of him that he had wisdom beyond his years, but in this short life of his, he was proving what the Great One had said long ago and that was that wisdom is known by her children. So, if this fallen fellow was of any type to be wise, it was only in his mind, for his children were beginning to tell the truth on him in no uncertain terms. He had left another task undone, yet he believed he was obeying the Great One all the while. Self-deception tends to work that way. The Great One shied away from telling him to do anything else for now, because of his own particular proclivity to his very personal way of thinking. Was it because he didn't listen to the Great One or was it that he simply refused to obey Him? Is obeying listening? Is listening obeying? The poor poke thought thoughts that were one thing, thinking that his thoughts were the thoughts of the Great One, but were not. And, as it is with most thinking men who think immature thoughts, thinking they're something that they certainly are not, he thought he was mostly doing right things and so he unwittingly walked with confusion as his guide instead of wisdom. And, instead of allowing the Great One to lead the way, he found himself following the path to fallenness.

This fallen fellow is the spirit of a certain man and this story takes place in the Realm of the Spirit where all the real battles take place. He was not like all men, but was like those men who are truly alive, having been made alive by the Great One. Other men think they may be alive in this world and are restless without spirit, but are, for the most part, more concerned with worldly things as worldly things are very, very different to one or the other. It might be viewed as selective focus, or it may not. It may be viewed as being called, it may not. Regardless of the point of view, not all men are alive, but those who are have this spirit that has been quickened and it is the spirit of this particular man that we are dealing with here.

He was approximately twenty-eight years of age, having made a complete circle already in his adventures, but was far too young to have done so. He had left what he thought to be his beginning just a few years hence, but in his quandary of thinking that all spiritual leadings were right, he found himself among other friends that were way too kind to tell him the truth to the true state of his being. He was lost, not in the eternal way, but lost in a most undefinable way, the way of uncertainty. His reality was not reality, in the sense of being real, as he was to discover through revelation. His reality was his actuality, of those things that can be touched, tasted, heard and seen. For the spirit of a man to go after these things would most presumably seem to be corrupt, yet he didn't think there was anything wrong with his way of thinking. It was always some else's thinking that was not quite right…or so he thought.

He was on the wide road of uncertainty, but didn't know it and that's probably why there are those who have sympathy for this fallen fellow who didn't even know his name. This is that which brings us to a particular night of his sleeping.

As he slept, he found himself on a very wide road and was approached by a terrific Spirit. Of which kind, he was uncertain, as to whether this spirit be dark, or this Spirit be light. The Spirit was not unkind to him, but wanted him to do something that he was not willing to do. This fallen fellow had a tussle with the Spirit who would not let him go. Since the fallen fellow had had a history of wrestling to get his own way, he automatically agreed, without a word spoken, to wrestle this thing through. As he wrestled and tussled with the Spirit, not one of them could get the best of the other. Their arms flailed about one another, pulling and grabbing, letting go here and grabbing there until they rolled and rolled to what most would call a stalemate. As the Spirit would have none of that, he revealed his anger with the fallen fellow and threw him off of him, however, the fallen fellow landed on his feet in a readied position.

The Spirit winced at the thought of himself and this uncommon fallen fellow continuing in this endeavor to see who could win in this wrestling match. The Spirit knew that this fellow had too much personal will to give up and submit, so he decided to allow this fallen fellow to live out his behavior on his own. This poor fellow had learned nothing of the Spirit's right voice and the Spirit's right moves. In his righteous anger and unrelenting disappointment, the Spirit simply raised his left foot high and flung it at the fallen fellow's right inside knee.

This particular knee had been severely injured many moons ago in the flesh, upon his first invitation and introduction to the Spirit's voice. At that time, this was just to see if the young fellow would give in and sacrifice anything, beginning with his flesh, that, and if anything else. The young fellow discovered what the Spirit knew…that he could, he would and he did. He was made alive that night. But, after a few years of following in wistful obedience, the young fellow had failed to remain in recognition of the true voice of the Spirit and was unwittingly leaning fully upon the voice of his own personal Will or, in the case of deceiving deceptions, voices entirely different from that of the true and right Spirit. Uncertainty teamed together with Will and formed a conflicted union of agreement that sounded eerily like the true Spirit, but was not. The true Spirit knew for certain He could wrestle away this conflicted agreement from the fallen fellow, but would not, for the poor poke had a mind of doing things his own particular way.

As the fallen fellow, unexpectedly received the most terrific blow from the Spirit's left leg and foot onto the inside of his right knee, he was crushed in pain and immediately flew to the widened dirt road writhing in pain, just as he had a few years ago in the spirit of his birthing. As the fallen fellow cried aloud in pain, having said nothing back to the Spirit as to the why of the matter, he simply hung his head down in pain and shame knowing the why, but not relinquishing the power of his own strength and will and accepted the power of his own powerlessness to change. He lost his battle with this terrific and powerful Spirit and soon realized that he had been flung back to his beginning all over again.

The last thing he heard as the Spirit left his sight was the Spirit turning back to him and calling out a word that was horrifyingly loud and frighteningly formidable. "GIGOT!" the Spirit angrily called out to him revealing the disposition of their relationship and the utterance of his true identity. The Spirit left as He came, faster than light! But, His terrific voice made an indelible impression upon the fallen fellow who was hither to be known as "Gigot".

This fallen fellow, who everyone in the spiritual realm called "Gigot," knew for certain that this was no unkind Spirit. He also knew for certain that he had been told his real name and it was this name that he has gone by since the time of his sleeping until now. This became the time of his beginning again, of starting over as the likes of a little child. If Gigot had ever followed Uncertainty, he would certainly follow him now, as the Spirit's anger was kindled that night and he would leave Gigot to follow Uncertainty until the arrival of the day of reckoning and the day of his awakening on the narrow road that answers the Whatever's, the Wherever's, the Whoever's and the Why-ever's that all men seek to know.

Another twenty-eight years passed and the circles of movements had taken their turns once again, but this time it was in the form of words rightly spoken from the Watchman, the Hanged-man, the Prayer man, the Evangelist and the one he admired most, the Beloved Husband. As time had passed, these five men of the ancient writings had come back as good friends do, to re-tell their stories as they had told him twenty-eight years hence. For twenty-eight years, he just didn't understand what they were saying as he was under the uncanny influence of Uncertainty. In that duration, he listened to a blend of Truth, Uncertainty, Willful Wantonness and as these mixed together in his ears and in his heart, the blend caused him to behave like a man who lacked Understanding. It is amazing to realize the things that certain men must overcome, but over time, the veil was being lifted from the eyes of his heart and the ears of his spirit. Bit by bit, in the slow essence of the release of purity through the men and their writings of old, the Spirit of the Great One found Gigot finding himself on the Road of Return and turning right onto the Road of Right Thinking. It was this Road of Right Thinking that led him to the place of his reckoning…the steps that led to Mount Illumine. Gigot was finally able to look up from himself and see that he was the Prodigal, if there ever was one. You know the one…the one that the Great One had talked about so many moons ago and the one that Gigot himself had taught so many people about…he had been so confounded that he just didn't get that he was talking about himself.

It is here that we continue our story, with Gigot, at long last, learning to submit to the right voice of the Spirit of the Great One as His voice is very particular and quiet and unlike any other. The Spirit of the Great One spoke through the men of the ancient writings with right thoughts and right thinking as they had been given the task of being his only friends. Gigot had been left alone with the men of the writings to be led to and through the Realm of the Spirit beginning with the bottom of the backside of Mount Illumine where he worked with his whole heart and his whole strength and his whole mind to climb to the top moving forward onward leaving Uncertainty and Wantonness behind and accepting the knowledge of the men of the writings that Faith and Truth is about him and within him. It is here that Gigot is beginning to realize that the Great One is with him and holds his heart in his hands.

"Gigot," the Spirit of the Great One spoke in a still, small voice, "Climb to the top of Mount Illumine, for it is there you will be instructed on how to get to the Crested Hill. It is there that the battle will begin to be waged to regain what you have lost to the Darkness and the lords of the Dark through all the many years you have given over to uncertainty and selfish pride. You know this is true."

The Great One, alone, leads Gigot up the backside of Mount Illumine to the very top, high above the Plain of Alongore, to see the land of his past and his present and presents the call to battle.

Gigot, humbled by His Presence within and without, hung his head in honor and wiped away the wetness from his eyes. "Yes, I hear you, my Lord."

Aged men realize that lost time is not merely lost time, but also lost opportunity while they carry their bags of regret. Not all men know Regret in their latter days as other men do for they do not recognize his name. Still, there are others who walk closely with Regret, listening to his voice until their time has ended. For these, Regret brings about a tiredness and a loathsomeness to those who do not realize that they do not have to do what they have chosen to do. If they would only release their bags of toilsome regret in order to hear the right voice saying, "Walk this way," they could release, forgive and find peace. It was this that Gigot was beginning to see with his own ears in the presence of the Great One.

The lords of Darkness had come in their many shapes and traits through the years and Gigot had been confounded by the many. Strength within and strength denied had become his motto for it was proven over and over by the way that he lived until progressive failure beckoned his call upon his mind to invade with dark tones of oppression, depression, deceit and despair.

"Gigot, in this land of new beginnings, the moon only sets and rest only comes when you learn what you are to learn in obedience and if you do not grasp it into your being, you will continue to move and to fight until you do learn to hear and obey my voice. As you have reached the top of Mount Illumine, you see that this is not the place of rest, but the place of revelation. There are those whom I have set to guide you on your journey from here. Be the man that I Am in you. Be of good courage and do not fear. Take the charge, for the battle is long, but the victory is Mine."

I

The Plain of Alongore

Torrent had shown up with his legions on the broken Plain of Alongore. At long last, Gigot finally arrived at the top of Mount Illumine having recognized the voice of the Spirit's call to come and do battle.

"It's good to see you here, Gigot. Torrent has taken everything up to the middle ground and is quite obstinate indeed. Had the Plain not been broken, he might well have taken it all. Are you battle ready?" Lortnoc asked.

Lortnoc and Sendink were visibly excited that Gigot was there with them on Mount Illumine, but Lortnoc was uncertain that he was truly ready for the fight. This was Gigot's first delve into real combat at this level. Gigot had been under training for many years under the Great One, yet sitting atop Mount Illumine, his failures were evident as they raged before him on the Plain of Alongore.

The barren wasteland below was filled, teaming with crazed warriors of darkness and doom. The Plain trembled at their weight and shook to the height of Mount Illumine where the three warriors sat upon their horses of war. They were covered in mail with their breastplates of armor, helmets and shields.

"I believe you should be asking the Great One regarding your doubts, Lortnoc, " Sendink professed, "Gigot wouldn't be here if he wasn't ready. Be who you were called to be and we shall do the same. Gigot has a purpose here in this Realm. He will not fail." Sendink's words penetrated Gigot as Lortnoc agreed.

Gigot had listened to the two as they readied their horses anxious for the fight. Even their horses revealed their masters' thoughts with each other. Gigot thought himself to be in tune with Lortnoc and Sendink as a result of understanding and growth. He could see the valid point of Lortnoc, but he knew he was no longer the passive, uninvited and defrocked fighter he had come to be. The Great One had seen to that.

"I suppose I do not have to ask who our enemy is today, do I?" Gigot inquired of the two.

Lortnoc merely glanced at Gigot with his wry smile knowing that Gigot intimately knew their common enemy for he had observed his handiwork for moons and moons beyond.

"How are they so many?" Gigot wondered in amazement.

Sendink moaned as he responded, "Gigot, it's been awhile."

Gigot shuffled in his saddle, stiffened his back, bit his lip and took a breath knowing it to be the truth and that he was personally responsible for this onslaught.

"Torrent is crazed and beside himself. His legions are many and you know his path of destruction is wide and replete with vast confusion," Sendink revealed what they all knew to be true and what they had seen in the plight of war that so constantly raged.

"I'm seeing something from this Mount that I've never seen before. This view is disturbing. His forces seem to be multipying on the fringes. Where are they coming from?" Gigot probed.

"Multiples of replication, yet not the same kind...but are still a maniacal threat. Each one comes at will with a very different skill, yet all have the same purpose to distract, deceive, divide and destroy. Their common interest keeps them together. They seem to enjoy the battles, albeit foolishly waiting to be defeated. They breathe the air of stupidity in this wasteland. You know, the kind of air that makes one do something for no apparent reason. The air is filled with it. That's part of the reason why we're here," Lortnoc responded unashamedly and continued, "Gigot, why do you think you are here? Now...in this moment?"

Gigot hesitated to answer immediately as he was learning to prepare a thought rather than depend on the immediate. Usually his immediate was replete with anxiousness and arrogance or a mixture in-between where doubts arise to entertain the mind and mistakes awaited him with each new step. Gigot contemplated the question.

He could sense the power of his horse beneath him, knowing that he had been a gift of the Great One. This beast named Faith was battle ready and experienced, yet Gigot sat atop the beast as one who was now to be the leader instead of the led. Within, he mulled the now...the "why now and in this place Eternal?" He contemplated, for in Time past he had seen a milder place, yet had been bewitched and found the price paid was far too extravagant for the bewitching again.

He no longer doubted, but rested in the fact that his placement in the fray revealed his intended purpose. He rested with Lortnoc's question as the steed formed the recourse. Within themselves, they all knew the anser to the 'now' and Lortnoc's brow heightened at Gigot's repose. It was his will that willed the now where there is no fear of loss or defeat. It was his will that finally said, "Now," and they all knew that the willing will was what the Great One had desired in him. All passivity and inertia of times past had proven to be his undoing. Now was in his will.

As the three braced themselves on their horses of war, there was no fear of the tumult that awaited them. They believed. They knew the battle was won before they flinched. Still, the battle had to be fought nonetheless. This would become the beginning of the battles for Crested Hill. They all knew its outcome, yet the battles had to be fought all the same.

The real question was not in the 'why now?' but in the 'why did it take so long?' As they perched atop their horses, they shared the same thought. Gigot gulped knowing the answer of the right question and drew a breath without a sigh for they all knew there would be no more regret from this moment on. No, this day of battle would not rely on a lesser foe to defeat them and allow the wanting to wait for another moon. They knew that even regret had a power all its own and Gigot would no longer allow its power to rouse suspicion over success.

Lortnoc's wry smile was comforting as he said, "Embrace the victory Gigot. This moment of war has come and the glory of the field of battle waits in the heart of the Great One. He has chosen you to wage this battle yourself. We will be here, in you, within and without, for He is here with us. You know that is true."

Gigot looked over the barren wasteland of the Plain of Alongore filling to the brim with his enemy and as they raged, they raged with one another in their depravity. It was as though their own dark blood was their sustenance as well as their life and their stench. Gigot focused on the center looking for the leaders and observed their uncanny resemblance to the many faces he had seen before. His eyes winced with fervor from the rising, heated vapor of brewing death.

As he focused on the leaders and their skill, Epaga, Yesege, and Olyon, other leaders of the Great One, arrived quietly to the side of Sendink. Epaga, who most resembled the Great One, rode his horse before them and stopped in fron of Gigot with a strength that imbued them all in one accord. His eyes fixed upon Gigot's determined figure.

Epaga said, "The moment has come and the moment is long. So goes this battle, this moment, on this broken Plain that you know all too well. This battle is yours, Gigot. Take courage and do not give up, do not give in. Know that we are in you for this moment of battle. Do not give up, do not give in. Take the Plain of Alongore and listen to no one along the way."

Epaga took to Gigot's side, displacing Lortnoc to the right. They had become one in the strength of Epaga and Gigot moved forward waiting for the command. He straightened himself on his horse named Faith and as he pulled his sword, he braced his feet in the stirrups. Gigot moved five paces forward, raising his sword high focusing on the face of Torrent below. Faith was ready, strong and great, a fearless Friesian with a coat of black brown, a long mane and eyes as intense as his maker. He had been measured to be the right horse for the right occasion and had been made ready as a gift of power from above.

In one accord, Epaga, Lortnoc, Sendink, Yesege and Olyon breathed together the breath that propelled Gigot down the flight from Mount Illumine. Gigot flew forward downward atop the fearless Faith. As they raced onward, Gigot kept his sword pointed forward. A tormenting stench rose from the depths of the wasteland to Gigot's nostrils as the fumes of death always do. This vapor of death rose from below as fast as Gigot flew down the Mount to confront him with the power to steal his breath. However, these forces of Darkness had not encountered the power within Gigot that drove him to their presence, for this, their moment had come.

Torrent had waited for this clash for he had survived past the many phases of the moon. Torrent thrived in the deceit and power he had without. He knew more would come to the Plain to ultimately take the Crested Hill and all the more they came to meet Gigot in the mist of death. Arrows screamed by Gigot as he rode to the waiting warriors below.

Suddenly, Significance appeared alongside Gigot to his left, as he strove valiantly down the Mount. Great Need appeared on his right. They rode fast together towards the scornful rage.

Significance, with his haughty attire, had no intention to distract, but secured enough of Gigot's attention to yell, "I made it! But, why did you leave without me? I'm not quite ready for this, my sword is being cleaned and shined and all warriors good and great must have need of a brilliant and shiney sword by their side. What will the others say if I am not with you in our moment of victory? Others need to know what it is that we're doing here, they need to understand the significance of what I'm, I mean we are about to do! This soon to be victory will be our reward and soon all men will look to me to carry them through in their battles as well! You should be Proud!"

In time, Gigot had been driven by the voice of Significance, but here, Gigot shuttered at his presence and the ushering in of his desires. Gigot would have none of it, not in this moment. Resolve moved him forward in spirit to continue moving forward, downward, onward to the kill. Great Need pressed a little from the right. He drifted a little behind as his horse began nipping on the beast under Gigot trying to use Faith to keep up.

Great Need exclaimed, "Slow down, Gigot, my horse is not as fast as yours. We had no food or drink this morning and we are faint of heart! Let's stop and rest and think this through. I need water before we do battle and I don't think I'm up to this task. Please Gigot, stop and think! What about…"

Gigot, unwavering, refused to acknowledge Great Need or Significance, nor did he slow or look back. They became no more.

As Gigot flew through the mist, the darkened stench of death was choking, but not to Faith. Faith pressed ever onward, downward cutting through the heavy vapor of death with more fervor than before. Gigot and Faith became one in movement and thrust. The arrows, though many, were deflected by his armor. His helmet, breastplate and his shield that he bore on his right arm and shoulder were made of uncommon mail and strength. The shouts of the throng of legions screamed in fire and gore as Gigot approached the landing below. Through the vapor of death he rode Faith unwavering, determined, focused, resolved until he appeared at the bottom of Mount Illumine ready to meet his foe on the broken Plain of Alongore.

He rode through the darkened mist not seeing anything before him as the thickness of the vapor was thicker than blood. In the flashing moment he arrived at the bottom of the hill, all of the shouts and screams disappeared into the no more. The arrows fell lifeless into a vapor. He breathed heavily as his horse so readied for battle breathed all the more, heaving from the diving course. Once arriving on the Plain of Alongore, he abruptly halted the beast flowing to his right and stopping to see the plain barren with no foe in sight.

In this moment of battle on the Plain, he sat breathing in the incoming air. The vapor of death was dismissing. As he sat there upon the beast, the air to breathe became more and all the more he realized that his foe had vanished in the presence of Faith. In an instant, they had completely disappeared, yet as his eyes to see the what was real, he peered in the distance. There, he saw one with a sword in hand, a tall one, with his sword held downward into the heart of a fallen Nimp, the kind of spirit that comes only from the lord of the Dark.

He moved Faith forward towards the tall one. The closer he came to the two, the slower he moved. He could smell the breath departing from the fallen Nimp. These were faces he'd seen before, faces both good and evil, yet unrequited until Gigot had decided to arrive.

The tall one and the fallen one were there on the broken Plain, alone. No more Torrent and no more warriors of death. As Gigot continued closer, he could see that the face of the tall one was one of his own. He recognized this warrior as though looking into a mirror and seeing himself as he once had been. On Faith, he rode towards the warrior. The tall one did not move, nor did he withdraw his sword from the heart of the fallen one, whose chest still rose for breath to breathe one last breath.

Gigot arrived and sat on his horse before the man recognizing his face as his own and yet inquired all the same, "Who are you and who is this one fallen breathing his last breath to breathe?"

The tall one tilted his head and smiled a smile of relief, saying, "I am Will, at your service. And this is the Presence of Passivity, the one who cast his spell in this place more than a few moons ago."

Passivity spoke as he stretched his arm to Gigot, "Gigot, do not let me die this dying breath, I beg your mercy. Let me live to breathe your breath once again. We've been friends for so long and I'm certain you can't live without me."

Gigot got down from Faith and walked towards the Presence of Passivity. In mercy, his spirit was moved. He knelt down by the head of the fallen one, whose armor had been pierced through by the sword of Will. Gigot moved his right hand towards the helmet of the Passivity's Presence. This is the one who he had trusted as a friend of the spirit of his own being. Yet, from Mount Illumine, he realized that the Presence of Passivity was not a friend at all, but an enemy of the worst sort. Will thrust his sword through the heart of Passivity and let it stay.

"No...no more," Gigot spoke shaking his head rejecting Passivity's plea. And with that, he closed the frontal shield of the Presence of Passivity's helmet only to hear the final draw of breath. Gigot looked up at Will and realized that in these moments, a part of his past lay before him, dead to rise no more.

"Gigot, we will to do this together," Will said pulling his sword from the Presence of Passivity.

"Together, yes, we Will" Gigot responded.

Looking up in the far away distance towards the top of Crested Hill, Will said, "We have to take the ground...all of the ground. We have only just begun. Your life, your destiny awaits you atop Crested Hill. That mount and all of this ground you see here and in-between you gave up in time, but in the Realm of the Spirit we're here to recover it and your resolve must continue moving forward. Kardio and No'us must be set free."

Gigot stared curiously into the distance and then looked at his opened hands before him in wonder. "Am I the only one responsible here?"

Will raised his brow and said, "Still, you do not see? You must see, I know that you do," Will snickered at Gigot's sense of ignorance from the knowledge of all that had just occurred as well as who was actually responsible.

The air that had moved in was clean and had cleared out the choking stench. Breathing in the clean air, they both stood resolute together bearing their swords in their sheaths knowing the battles that lie before them and around them. This was not just a battle for the Plain of Alongore, but all of battles were for the ultimate contested mountain of Crested Hill. It was Crested Hill that had to be taken completely for all of the land between here and there had been inundated with the seemingly unlimited forces of Torrent, the Mendacium, their leader, the lord of the Dark, known as Ementior, the Lord of the Lie, and his lord Ophis, the Snake King, the great deceiver who believes he can appear as anyone or anything even to the appearance of the Great One himself. Just then, a rider, riding fast and carrying a white flag came from the distant Plateau of Decree. The rider rode the same kind of horse as Epaga and looked the same with a few extravagant differences which bore him apart from the true Epaga. Epaga's horse's bridle did not have a black onyx stone implanted in its forehead. Still, the resemblance was uncanny and the closer he came the more he resembled the likeness of Epaga. Will stood determined as the rider approached.

Gigot seemed confused and was walking towards the rider with the white flag.

"Gigot! What are you doing?" Will shouted.

Immediately, upon the arrival of the rider with the white flag, Resolve appeared before Gigot and merely looked at him with a disdaining look and then disappeared. Gigot turned to Will, who by now had walked forward towards the rider intercepting his presence before Gigot.

"What do you want?" Will demanded.

"I come in peace, isn't it clear?" The rider responded innocently and with a great deal of pretense. "You have the ground, we've willingly given you the Plain of Alongore. Now leave us alone in peace and we'll not trespass on the Plain again."

"Alongore..." Gigot remissed, sighing heavily and dropped his face before the rider. Gigot suddenly realized what the Plain of Alongore was for it had been broken long ago and he grew tired immediately for Resolve had disappeared from his presence.

"Who are you?" Will demanded, pulling his sword from its sheath.

"I am Deceit...but you knew that didn't you? Everything here is uncovered, is it not?"

"You gave us nothing that was not rightfully ours to begin with. You fled, that's true, but not because you chose to," Will exclaimed decisively.

"Oh...no, that's not true. It is true that we left, but we understand Gigot's plight," Deceit continued with his eyes fixed on Gigot. "Gigot is tired from the battle for he has done much in this, his moment of victory."

Suddenly, another rider came riding with a white flag of his own from the Western Slopes. This rider, Will knew for certain. It was Divide and he was riding in fast.

Gigot's eyes had grown weary and had become transfixed on Deceit. He did not see Divide coming from the left flank. Divide was coming in so fast that he made his approach to Gigot and Will in less than a moment. Will stepped to his left to intercept Divide, leaving Gigot exposed to the face of Deceit. As Divide made his entrance to their position, he immediately dropped his flag forward revealing the point of the spear the flag was attached to.

Will ripped his sword forward and raised it upward deflecting the tip of the spear as Divide passed through the lot of them. Before Will could turn, Deceit had gripped Gigot's neck and was ready to break him. In Gigot's face, Resolve appeared and defiantly spoke the "No!" that he needed to speak and both Deceit and Divide disappeared into the no more.

Gigot dropped to his knees not knowing for certain what had just occurred, thinking through the foreboding moments. Will ran to him kneeling before him face to face and said,

"Gigot, will you join me? We will to do this together. You have to stop listening to the voices from without. They are not the voices from within. Do you hear me?"

Gigot raised both brows as if he were trying to come awake from a sleeping stupor.

"Gigot!" Will shouted.

Gigot raised both arms and stretched them out to Will's shoulders, looked him straight in the eyes and said, "I'm here, you know what I've done and the ground I've lost. I'm ready, but I'm not. I was on the Mount. But now, I'm confused…and tired."

"You're not tired, Gigot…you're distracted. Focus here…in me. We are all we have and all we have is all in the Great One. Listen to his voice and only his voice! Understood?

Will pointed upward past the Plateau of Decree and on towards the Crested Hill and said, "That's the only way we can take everything leading to the Hill…ok?"

Gigot looked Will square in the face and with a very determined looked said nothing. He simply breathed. He faced the Plateau of Decree, looked back at Will, bit his lip and mustered, "OK."

In the moment of agreement between Gigot and Will, Epaga, Lortnoc, Sendink, Olyon and Yesege, appeared before them as they had been with Gigot atop Mount Illumine. It became clear to Gigot that they had been with him the entire time, yet unseen. They brought an indescribable encouragement to Gigot and Will. Nothing was said for nothing needed to be said. Their presence meant everything for their strength became the strength in Gigot and in Will that moving to the place they needed to be.

II

The Plateau of Decree

Epaga looked Gigot straight in the eyes and said, "Take Courage, Gigot, we are here with you. Believe that we are in you. You are not alone."

Epaga directed Lortnoc alongside Gigot and said, "Lortnoc will be going with you and Will moving forward, understood? You must take the ground from the Plateau of Decree to the Western Slopes. The ground will not be taken in time for it was not given up in time. You have heard it said, "Now is the time," but there is no time of now here in the Realm of the Spirit for here we are out of time and the demand of now comes only from the spirit who is known as Ementior. That spirit is clothed in light, but is not light. His dwelling place is the place of darkness, not the darkness that you have seen for that is only a shadow of the true. His darkness is having been removed from the high place to the dwelling place you know as the In-Between. You cannot see in his darkness, so beware of the light that comes in shadows. Light that is true light bears no shadow; it is and can only represent itself in truth. I say this with Sendink by my side for you came to see the darkness as it is when you were deceived by Deceit."

Gigot received all that Epaga was saying, receiving it into himself knowing that his spirit was speaking the truth from knowledge in the High Place. Epaga knew Gigot as did they all. In time Gigot would have allowed humiliation to comfort him by the fact of being found out, but now, there was no hint of humiliation. He was no longer a part of him on the road to the Crested Hill. Gigot remained silent and listened intently to the instructions of Epaga,

"The roads you have traveled you will see again because these are the roads and the grounds given over to the Dark. You will see faces you have seen before, but you will see them as they really are as here in this realm, they are revealed and cannot be veiled. You will hear the voices that you have heard in your past and as you have been told, you must remain with us. We have overcome, do not give up; do not give in. Take the ground, Gigot. You know my voice and the voices of the ones who go with you for they are the same. Again, listen to the voices within, for that is the ground to be gained. Do you understand?"

"I hear and I understand, Epaga," Gigot affirming the repetition.

Epaga, Sendink, Yesege and Olyon vanished from his sight and the three of them, Gigot, Lortnoc and Will set their faces towards the Plateau of Decree. It was late and the moon was setting over the mount as a sign of yet another message given and another lesson learned. Gigot pondered Epaga's words with Will as Lortnoc remained silent listening to their spirit. It seemed good to them to understand that since there was no time, there was no need for urgency, so they would never call on him again. Time did not dwell here, so how could now? Gigot was seeing the plight of his past for many of his decisions had been made with urgency pushing him to the brink and yet it was now who had been the real culprit in working with urgency to force Gigot's hand in so many opportunities to fail.

Gigot laughed with Will at his old saying, "Hurry up and wait," and he could see where that saying, as ridiculous as it had been, had become a sense of lifestyle…never content and always insisting on the next urgent move. It seemed that urgency and now had never been his friends, but had only been sent to take advantage through anxiety in the dark. Oh, how he had dwelt with now by his side and for the first glance he could see folly in following the demanding now that had a spirit of its own as a tiger set to pounce upon a prey

In time past, now had almost gotten Gigot killed by two different violent men on two different occasions. In another circumstance, now had insisted its way so much so that Gigot had given a man a heart attack. It was that intense spirit of a raging tiger that drove him at times and at others, Passivity had had his way. How is it that he could see these things where he stood in these moments and yet, in those times past, he had been driven by the spirit of now and didn't realize the depths of what he was doing?

Will and Lortnoc listened to Gigot's revelation and agreed with his assessment. They were well on the road to the Plateau of Decree by the revelation of Gigot in their hearing.

"What else have I listened to?" Gigot pondered with Will. Will looked back at Lortnoc as Lortnoc's attention was elsewhere given to a stranger approaching from the lowest part of the plateau. The spirit floated and moved quickly to them as they halted their horses and readied their hands on their swords. Gigot recognized the spirit dressed in fine white linen arrayed with fuchsia in her long brown hair. He smiled a curious smile at her with the wrinkled brow of the lack of understanding.

He recognized this spirit and knew her voice as the voice of the one in whom he had called Friend. She had multiple voices and spoke with softness in each one. Gigot's attention was drawn to her one voice and then the voice of the other. She was speaking and not saying any words, but Gigot heard all that she said and was made excited and uncomfortable to see her.

Lortnoc moved forward in the road to place himself before Gigot intercepting her guile. Lortnoc was not amused and merely tilted his head to the right, raising his left eyebrow and as Friend had seen that same look before in Gigot, she knew that her voices were being questioned. Lortnoc sarcastically asked, "What say you…Friend?"

Friend responded, "I am here to guide you along your way through the Land of Decree, where words are spoken and revealed to be true to all that hear the voices of all that is spoken in this realm and in the next." She was enticing and her voices were so beguiling that they had the intent to melt the ears of the listener in oneness with her voices.

Will raised his shoulders and straightened his back, shook his head and said, "You can't be serious…"

"Oh, but I am, you doubting one," she said as she smiled her smile of a very intimate kind of friendship. They could sense a sensing of passivity rising about them. She had come closer now to Lortnoc and Will as to get closer to Gigot on his horse behind them. She raised her left hand outward towards the face of Will and with the back of her hand drawing it downwards to caress the face of Will.

"It's been so long," she insisted intimately, wiping the bottom of her mouth with her thumb as she had so many times before as she had stood in the doorway, pleading with him to come to her.

"Gigot…you know me, I have always loved you and have always been your Friend." She set her eyes towards Gigot imploring him to come closer, but could see the spirit of Resolve through his face and her expectancy turned cold. Her face went to a pout and then a frown.

"Gigot!" she implored and at once a flush of wind burst forth behind her as her voices had called more spirits in brilliant colors from beyond. The power of her erotic sensation was powerful to enjoin their likenesses as one. Her spirits rose from the ground on an equal plain with their eyes. She moved gracefully, yet intently to entice once more with her painted gaze.

Lortnoc had had enough of this despicable ruse and roused his horse to move forward against her, "This is enough, we've heard you before, we've heard you all before. You…be gone!"

In a flash, she vanished and departed with the wind that had brought her forth and as a wisp, only the scent of her embodiment was left in the air where they stood. Gigot and Will had breathed her scent before and knew it all too well, but here, as Lortnoc breathed it with them, they breathed it no more and it vanished as well with the passing wind.

Lortnoc, recognizing this spirit, this so-called 'friend' turned to Gigot and asked, "Gigot, we know the question is not 'Why now?' but "Why did it take so long?' With that being the case, do you know the answer?"

Gigot scrunched his chin, knowing that they all knew the answer and said, "The flesh is weak, isn't it? I know how desperate my condition was in my flesh and I didn't quell the overriding power over what my flesh desired to do regardless of how I thought or what I truly believed."

Will looked at him with a winced look and said, "You know that I have been weakened and will continue to be until we take the Crested Hill. Do you think or believe you had anything to do with that?"

"Alright, I see where this is going…I'm responsible for this and I know it and just so you know, I say that from the standpoint of this…this Friend, humility and from humiliation's view. I see and am continuing to see what I allowed, or what you and I allowed, and Lortnoc knows that we chose to disavow his help all the while. Through it all, Passivity's Plea was enjoined in such a way as to the adverse. You know and I see how we gave in."

Lortnoc remained quiet as they continued along the trail that seemed to be more enclosed by the brush the further they trekked along. There was a watery mist in the air. The deeper they trudged through the trail the deeper the forest became. The trees were damaged by some storm and many of them were black from being burned and rotting.

"We let this go, didn't we," Will looked at Gigot, knowing that he was feeling Gigot's remorse, acknowledging his part of being a co-conspirator in all that they had chosen to undertake.

As they walked along, they used their swords to cut through the brush, thick with leaves and vines that tended to cling to the breaks in their shields. As they were climbing up towards the plateau, there was so much work to clearing the trail of the vines covering the dead, black trees for the vines seemed to have a mind of their own…clinging to them every step of the way. The work of the climb simply made it harder.

Lortnoc went back to the conversation, "Gigot, you know you believed something that you lived out in your flesh, do you recognize what that was?"

At that point, it began to rain…hard, with sheets of pouring rain so much so that they could not see in front of them. They ran underneath the shrouded trees and huge leaves to protect themselves from the onslaught of the pouring rain. Sharp pellets of hail pelted the trees above and shot through the trees tearing the leaves apart, leaving the three of them exposed to the sharp pellets. They took further into the forest, moving away from the trail to get some type of relief from the chards of the stinging hail.

"We're here because we chose to defeat flesh," Gigot shouted to Lortnoc as he stood facing an onslaught of hail pinging and slamming against his armor. He turned and faced the west wind with its missile-like hail pounding their position. He took more than a few steps forward away from Lortnoc and Will and the pounding of the hail became fiercer. Gigot's armor was being pelted relentlessly as though the closer he walked into the storm towards the pathway of the trail, the harder the storm raged. As the winds picked up past gale and into storm, Gigot stood unmovable and unrelenting. Lortnoc and Will crouched beneath the giant leaves. The hail was coming in through the forest close to forty-five degrees and Gigot was thrown back by Will as Will jumped in front of him. Gigot heard a thump go through the armor of Will. Will's breastplate had been punctured to the extremity of his heart and he was bleeding out through the breaks.

"NO!" Gigot screamed, but not at the sight of Will, but at the storm and the storm ceased with foreboding darkness all around.

Lortnoc moved to Will's aid and pulled with all his might on the shard of hail that had pierced the breastplate of Will. Will inhaled and then exhaled with all his strength to push the shard outward as Lortnoc fell backward with the razor sharp shard in his hands. Will had no other strength left but to fall back on the ground while blood poured profusely from under the breastplate. Gigot ran to Will and knelt beside him as Lortnoc regained his composure with the two of them realizing that this war would create casualties, yet they did not know how, when or who. The heart of Will had been punctured to the extremity of his heart and he was bleeding from the point of the shard. Lortnoc shoved his hand through the break at the bottom of Will's breastplate and placed a finger into the puncture in Will's chest.

Will was still breathing, but had passed out from the shock.

While Gigot was watching all of this occur from his kneeling position over Will, his eyes met Lortnoc's across the body of Will. In between the meeting of their eyes, Epaga appeared and looked them both in the eyes and said, "Gigot, is this happening or has this happened already?"

Gigot knew that his heart had been broken moons ago, but he had not acknowledged it. He had decreed life forevermore over his spirit and had decreed health over his flesh and the flesh of his loved ones. But decreeing a thing that does not exist does not make it exist. Only the Great One can do that. Gigot had believed Torrent's lies rather than living in Faith and Truth. What he should have done was join himself in agreement to Faith rather than allowing Will to use his tongue to speak things foolishly as though he were the Great One himself.

As a result, his heart was broken and he had died to it without recognizing the depth of the death to his heart. It was here as Will breathed his last breath that Gigot was seeing what he had done and he let Will go because in the past he had let Will go in exchange for Passivity's Presence.

Crested Hill was gaining clarity and in the knowledge of what was and was to be, he saw that the death of Will had become more of a choice than a casualty of war. He had allowed the heart of Will to die, albeit in the midst of battle, his heart had died nonetheless. Sorrow appeared and as Gigot cried, Sendink appeared as well.

In the midst of Gigot's sorrow, the Great One appeared in Gigot's spirit and said,

"Gigot, why are you allowing Will to die?"

"I caused this, I know it," Gigot cried.

"Gigot, come out of yourself and answer me."

"Will is responsible for all of this, isn't he? I believe I caused it, but it was really Will, wasn't it? Giving in…giving in to the battles, the loss, the loss of Crested Hill, allowing the Presence of Passivity…this was all Will's doing wasn't it? If Will dies here, then he dies, doesn't he?"

Gigot had not seen Torment arrive as he had so many times before. Torment was brewing his brew over Gigot's head and he was none the wiser. The accuser took to the spirit of Gigot and Gigot attempted to stand, stumbled, yet dumbfounded, rose realizing that in the true presence of the Great One, all is revealed and nothing is hidden. In the moment of realization, Torment vanished.

Gigot knelt before the body of Will in the spirit of the Great One.

It was one thing for Will and Gigot to work together as one, but there was more to Will than Gigot realized. Crested Hill was the property of Will and it had been taken over by Ementior's Torrent, the Plain of Alongore had proven that.

"You were here to strengthen Will, not the other way around. Will made these decisions long ago and the decisions that he made, some were wise and others were quite foolish…to your demise. He realized this and in the knowledge of his realization, only his heart moved him for the ground he had given up was actually the greatest gift he had been given. In time, he despised his self to death, but that was not to be. Gigot, he saw this and called on you and that is why we find ourselves here on the Plateau of Decree. Interjected thought is not inward thinking. He came to realize this late, but not too late for all is not lost. As I stated earlier, time does not exist in this Realm. He gave his life for you, Gigot. The storm raged because you both allowed it. You have a tendency to turn the eye away from the gales and the storms and so did Will. But you see here with seeing eyes for here, nothing is hidden and all is exposed."

Epaga continued in the Great One's Spirit, "Gigot, Will is not dead, but is sleeping a sleep of rest. The moon has set for you have seen and are seeing that it is your voice that speaks of what is real and what is not. Dwell in the Faith that you have been given and speak the truth for it is here in you and with you. There is consequence in delay and consequence in urgency."

Epaga took a breath and continued, "You will journey to the Western Slopes. The life that Will continues to give for you is for you both and when Crested Hill is taken, it will be done for you both as you will see. We will guide you through the thicket back to the trail on the long plateau and we will continue to guide you to the Western Slopes where all is unstable and a treacherous decline. As I have said, do not give up, do not give in. Your battle is for life. You cannot do this on your own, as you have attempted to do, so trust, you are never alone."

Will breathed.

A rest came over the three as they rested in the knowledge that a moon had set from the learning of that which is spoken for hearing ears hear and seeing eyes see...finally.

III

The Trail Leading to the Western Slopes

Gigot found himself rested on the trail leading from the Plateau of Decree to the Western Slopes. The rain had ceased and the darkness was clearing even more. No one else was there except the stillness within that told him, "Go this way." Lortnoc and Will had gathered all of their belongings and had saddled up their horses ready to go. Endurance had arrived during the rest and they all appreciated him being there in their midst.

"You do remember that all of the ground taken is all of the ground that was given up in time?" Endurance inquired. The three looked at each other and then looked at Endurance and they all started laughing.

"So, we are the mindless number, is that it, Endurance?" Will said coaxing him to reveal the manner of the repetition of his statement.

"We just need to remember, that's all. Everything we'll see along the way, we've all seen before, but in a different realm, that's for sure," Endurance said as he looked ahead around the winding bend.

As he spoke, a band of Preachers showed up along the trail. Endurance and Lortnoc rode out to meet them ahead of Gigot and Will. The Preachers were walking along the long trail and Gigot wondered at how they must have arrived at such a place with no horses to their names.

"Hello, hello…" they all cheered. There were four walking Preachers all giddy that they had come upon a group that had four horses.

"How's 'bout lettin' us use your horses for a Spell? We've been on this journey for so long and we are plum tuckered out," the hopeful one said in the mist with his slow drawn out tone.

"My, yes, we've been traveling doing the Great One's work and none of us has been given a horse as of this particular moment," said another in a rather smug, yet educated sort of way as he pulled out his silver pocket watch to watch it glisten in the light. "I say…we certainly deserve a horse to travel about upon, do we not? Why, we'll turn around and travel in your direction, it doesn't matter much to us which way we go, if you'd just let us use your horses. You see the value of my importance among these great men of renown and how my personal theological pontification is merely a drawing point to woo the masses with deep thought and spiritual heights… why…uh-um," he choked on his words as he gathered his coat to his chest.

Lortnoc and Endurance looked back at Gigot and Will as Gigot and Will maneuvered to get in a parallel line before the four Preachers. One of the Preachers who had a dark, oily complexion and played with a bouncing ball as he walked up to Gigot asked in his rich, raspy voice,

"What's this horse's name?"

"Faith," Gigot responded.

The Preacher simply looked back at his three comrades as they laughed with one another and said, "Listen! That's my name, my name is Faith!" and the other Preachers laughed at Gigot.

"My name is Love," said the smug one.

"My name is Hope," said the man with the slow, drawn out tone.

Preacher Hope said, "This is Tried and Longing. He's not a part of us, but we let him serve us nonetheless."

Tried and Longing explained, "I took to going along with these three because of who they said they were. I've studied and studied and I've done all that my fathers' told me to do, but I didn't quite measure up to some of them. So, I went out on my on to do the Great One's work and this is where I ended up. I figured if these Preachers were Faith, Hope and Love, then I couldn't go wrong, but all we've done is wander aimlessly along this trail without any horses and the moon has yet to set upon us and I'm tired."

The Preacher named Faith cleared his throat with a mighty, "uh-hum," interjected and said, "Look, we've done some preachin' in our time and preached our preach. I told people to have faith in me because I was speaking on behalf of the Great One. The more they listened to me, the more of my faith I gave to them. I had the biggest church in town and when that wasn't big enough, we made other churches so that others could come and listen to my voice so we could all share the same faith that I had, rather, that we had together. Why my faith is in all kinds of people all over the land. The Great One should be proud of me now and give me a horse like that one. Now is my time, especially since it has my name, it must be mine!"

As Preacher Faith reached out to grab the bridle of Gigot's horse Faith, Faith bit him on the hand real hard and made the man fall to his knees in pain.

"Now, now, now, let's don't start getting ourselves in a tizzy," said Preacher Love in his deep sophisticated voice. "I always tell my people that the way of the Great One is the way of love. We just need to get along as the Good Book says. Do unto others…you know that one, don't you? I say, what did you say was your name, young man?" he said looking at

Gigot.

"My name is Gigot, Preacher Love," Gigot said with a doubting voice.

"Now, Now, Now, don't go doubting my sincerity, young man, you may want to doubt my ways, but never doubt my motives, cause my motive is always L-O-V-E," he said as he tilted his head back and forth with the letters of love moving closer to Will's horse.

"Love, Love, Love, that's what I'm about, isn't that right, young man?" he said to Will winking as he moved closer with his eyes fixed on Will's horse.

It seemed that Preacher Love could mesmerize his people with his smile, his eyes, his heart, his love, and his own personal salesmanship and then, as most find out, he could get anything out of them that he wanted. Here, he wanted Will's horse and he believed that he could mesmerize the horse right out from under Will with his deep theological thinking, but he had another thing coming from Will that he had not anticipated.

As Preacher Love continued to speak on the goodness of love, the right-thinking of love and the right acting-out of love, he lunged for Will's horse, Truth, in such a way as to reveal his own imperfection of greed. Greed turned Preacher Love quite green as he lunged for Will's horse as Truth reared on its hind legs and then came down with a resounding thump on the feet of Preacher Love.

"Ohhhh," he cried out in pain, "you broke my feet, you shameless creature! You broke my feet…" The other Preachers helped him out of the way and laid him to rest on the side of the trail writhing in pain. Torment and unknown pain showed up as they had opportunity and Preacher Love enjoined them as he had need of more company in his own self-pity implying that anyone who could not love Preacher Love as he so insisted, they must be filled with hate and a hateful disposition. Preacher Love believed that his love was the love that all men needed, or, so he thought.

"How could you treat me with such hate?" Preacher Love screamed and yelped along with pain and torment.

Preacher Hope had begun to massage his feet to determine the level of the breaks in his feet, but Preacher Hope had to acknowledge that Preacher Love's feet weren't actually broken…bruised, yes, green, yes, but not broken. It seemed that pride had gotten the best of Preacher Love's greed because his mesmerizing had always worked on other folk. But it wasn't working here.

Tried and Longing knelt before Gigot, Lortnoc, Will and Endurance and entreated them to allow him to go wherever it was they were going. Lortnoc revealed, "Tried and Longing, where we are going you cannot go. This work that Gigot and Will have to do, they have to do it themselves in the power of the Great One."

Preacher Hope then interjected with his winsome smile and sweet, long drawl and said, "People, now, now I just know that we're all brothers here. Even though we're not headed in the same direction, we are on the same road with the same purpose and that is to do the work of the Great One. Well, my Good Book tells me who I am. I am Hope!"

He continued on with his teeth glistening in the sunlight making his smile all the brighter, "It also tells me that without hope, the world is lost and going to an eternal separation from the Great One himself. That's why these fine gentlemen needed me to go along on their journey and that's exactly why you need me, too, to go along on yours. Now, I've walked many a mile…"

At this point, the four, Lortnoc, Will, Gigot and Endurance found themselves looking at each other with winced eyes and raised eyebrows at how Preacher Hope smiled through every word that he spoke. Will found himself scratching his head in wonder as Preacher Hope's words reached out as tentacles to tether the four to himself as he preached his words about how much they needed hope in their lives.

"As I was saying, this is my Good Book and you need to hear the words that I speak for they will bring a comfort to your souls. You are somebody, can I get an ame-en?" Preacher Hope inquired.

"You need to stop," Lortnoc stated emphatically to Preacher Hope, "You lack self-control, among other things."

In that moment, Preacher Hope had maneuvered himself over to the horse of Endurance and was scratching the forehead of the horse and telling him how great and magnificent a creature he was.

"You are magnificent and great, yes you are. You are a creature born for adversity, a creature born for life eternal, a creature in need of ho-ope forevermore…" Preacher Hope said enticing the horse to kneel before him even as Endurance continued to sit upon the steed.

The more that Preacher Hope smiled, the closer he got to the bridle of the horse. He was caressing the horses forehead with strokes of pure hope when all of a sudden, the horse sneezed a mighty sneeze all over the face of Preacher Hope.

Preacher Hope fell back away from the horse and exclaimed, "Well, I ne-va…"

And with that, Endurance's horse looked over to Faith and whinnied.

Defeated, the three Preachers crawled over together to the side of the trail. Tried and Longing remained kneeling before the four in the middle of the trail.

He said, "What is it that I need? I've done all that I've been told to do and I've left all as well. I have nothing but these clothes you see here. All has been left behind for the work of the Great One."

Endurance pitied Tried and Longing for he saw something of himself in him and asked, "Why are you doing the work of the Great One? Did He command you to do this?"

"Well, I suppose so. Yes, I think so…maybe. That's what my great Preacher back home told me. He said that the Great One had his hand on me and that I was going to do a great and mighty work for the Great One. So, I set out on my journey and left all behind just for him. I gave all I had to my Preacher cause that's what we were told to do…me and the others."

At that point, the four, Gigot, Lortnoc, Endurance and Will could hear the voices of the others coming around the bend of the trail. It was the others that Tried and Longing was talking about. They, too, had left all behind to the Preacher known as the Great One who used to say he most resembled the Great One himself. They all resembled Tried and Longing and seemingly had been told they all had the same purpose in doing the work of the Great One, yet none of them understood that the Great One that Preacher Great One was referring to was none other than himself. Sorrow, Poverty and Great Need accompanied them on their journey and Gigot and Will were at a loss of what to do or what to say.

Weakness appeared and tended to them like a mama dog to her pups and they all seemed to appreciate the care that Weakness gave. Sorrow, Poverty, Great Need, Despair and Guilt surrounded the others and they were all crying in the midst of the spirits.

Just then, Preacher Love and Preacher Hope got up and said with one voice, "You're responsible for these poor people. Can't you hear their cries? They have Great Need of you to help them and the best way to help them is to help us help them. We both know the Great Preacher known as The Great One for he is a friend of ours. We can meet their Great Need by giving them all of the Faith, Hope and Love they deserve. Won't you just give a little to help the little ones in Great Need?"

"Give a little what?" Will stammered, as each of the three Preachers whipped out offering plates from behind their backs.

Gigot choked on his breath.

Lortnoc looked at Gigot and said, "Gigot, I know that it is true that you have encountered each of these in time past, but they are not here, they are the ones that you did not help in their time of Great Need and the ground you gave was the Great Need left undone. Some of these you could have helped, but the others were the need of their friends and preachers who saw their own need as greater than the true need of the younger. Weakness wallows in Great Need and Great Need will always be around to take the ground of the minds and hearts of men who passively follow men who deem themselves great in the eyes the Great One."

Acknowledging this, Gigot breathed in their direction with the breath of help, but they had all vanished. Gigot and Will knew where they had lost and where they had given in. They should have said something more and done something more in the time past when Great Need arose, but they didn't. It was in these moments that Epaga arrived and they were all reminded of what true love is for true love is holy.

Epaga elaborated, "Preacher Love sounds like true and holy love, but is not, for there is no obedience and doing in Preacher Love's love. He is much ado about talking as is Preacher Hope, for they love to sound as sounding brass or a clanging cymbal, but do not know the difference between holiness and hypocrisy. The clothes they put on are for appearance and not for truth. Holy love is from the heart of the Great One himself and he instills that holy love in the ones He has chosen. Holy love is born out of holiness and it sees and hears from the seat of holiness and not from the seat of Great Need. When a man is filled with holy love, it cannot remain still, for holy love is active and giving, not lacking and wanting. If a man comes to you saying that he has the love of the Great One inside of him and yet he, by his own desire, desires what you have, that is not holy love because it does not take, but gives. You know the Great One by what he has done and what he has given, not by what he has taken. It has always been a choice of the follower and not a demand. There is no taking from the ones whom the Great One has called to himself. That is the role of the usurper who deceives with a great and mighty deceit to deceive even the chosen ones if they do not remain in the Great One."

Gigot and Will observed and heard all that Epaga said and they knew it to be real and true. They had come to realize that they, too, had left all, but had not left it to a man. Some, they had, they had left to many Preachers along the way and yet they thought they had left it to the Great One. But now they were uncertain. One thing they did know, though, was that Passivity's Plea had played his part in their parting of all that they had given. That would never happen again for this they learned from the knowledge of how Passivity's Plea works with the Preachers who enjoin permissiveness as their partner rather than the Spirit of the Great One himself. They were also beginning to see how Preachers and others reveal themselves by their fruit. Wisdom is known by her children. Fruit and children and the sowing of seeds, it seems, have a great deal in common.

IV

As It Is

Once again, learning was learned and rest was forthcoming. The moon set and Gigot and Will were given a rest from their travels before they hit the Western Slopes. Gigot fell into a dream once dreamed from long ago and in the dream he found himself walking along a familiar trail and every once in a while he would approach an even familiar wall. The wall started out about knee high and was made of singular stones that someone of great strength had pieced together. Gigot didn't know enough to go over the wall, so he simply followed the wall until it ended and continued along the trail. The trail led in a wide circle in a roundabout sort of way and as he would make the same turn, he would approach the very same wall, but each time the wall had been built higher. It seemed he was experiencing the wall in a vicarious fashion as though someone else that he knew was watching and building as he walked about the trail. Again and again, he simply followed along the wall until it ended and then he would proceed to follow the trail around its turns and turns and end back at an even higher wall.

Finally, he decided that he'd had enough of circling along and was tired of the walking the same trail and seeing the same, but taller wall. He decided by the time he got to the end of the wall, instead of proceeding along the trail as usual, he would go around the end of the wall and look to see if there was someone on the other side who was building this massive stone wall.

So, as it was, that by the time he got to the end of the wall, he went around the deep corner and to his surprise there was a man sitting at his desk writing. He was surrounded by paper, paper and more and more paper. He got the unction to go and see who this writer was and as he approached the writer, he noticed that as a finished piece of paper would leave the desk of the writer's table, another block would be added to the wall. Astounded at this magical feat, he stood there for a bit watching the wall being built around him and the writer, who had paid him absolutely no mind.

Bit by bit, paper by paper, block by block, the wall was built higher and higher and as it went higher, it encircled Gigot and the writer as an igloo. The writer intermingled his thoughts with Gigot's thoughts and as Gigot stood there in amazement, he could see the words from the eyes of the writer as they were being written on the page. The writer's head was forcefully looking down as he steadied his eyes upon his page and wrote and wrote with a vengeance.

With each completed page, another block would be added to the already encircled wall about them. It was getting dark from the wall being built as the light was being shielded from their midst.

In the darkened moments of being enclosed about by the wall, Gigot knelt down in front of the writer to see who he was and as he knelt further down, he got the attention of the writer. In a flash, they saw each other face to face and eye to eye and he realized who he was.

The writer merely stared at Gigot as he wrote his final words upon the only remaining paper. As the final piece of paper was completed and the final block put in place, there was just enough light left to see that there was an inscription written on the final block that would in turn encapsulate the walled circle into darkness. The inscription read a question and the question spoke aloud in complete darkness to Gigot as he was reading these words, "Who is writing your story?"

And the dream ended.

After the dream, he thought he had awakened as he was led further into the darkness that had been created by the entombment. He came to realize that he was being moon shifted. While Gigot was supposed to be resting and sleeping, the dark would creep about stealing shadows from the light of the moon. He watched as the darklings were building for themselves a kingdom that they believed was light itself, but was not. Gigot could see them building by their mangling about the countryside cutting and stealing the shadows of things from the light of the moon while they believed no one was looking. They were taking the shadow of a tree and placing it there on their side of being, while others were stealing the shadows of all kinds of flowers and placing them here on their side of being.

As Gigot walked about their darkness, unbeknownst to them, he shadowed their every move. Perchance if one turned around, he simply moved into their shadow. They did not see him, but they could sense him and hear him breathing. As one darkling proceeded to rip away the shadow of a large tree, Gigot spoke.

He asked, "Why are you stealing the shadows?"

The darkling shook with Fear and Fear recognized Gigot.

"What are you doing here?" Fear asked.

"That's what I just asked him," Gigot responded.

"Who?" Fear asked.

"This…that darkling, what are you doing?" Gigot asked again unafraid of Fear as darkness dwelled around them, there was nothing else to fear.

"Time only changes in the light, so what we do we do in the dark because we're out of Time. We're making ready for the Dark One, building him a kingdom of shifting shadows," Fear responded.

"Haven't I seen you before?" Gigot inquired, "I've seen you in the light of day, haven't I?"

"Always, my son, always. If you've ever looked into the mirror, you've seen me. If you've ever looked at an enemy, you've seen me. If you've ever looked into the face of a…"

"Stop it, I see you!" Gigot demanded.

"You've also seen me in unsuspecting humans when perchance they invite me to join them," Fear continued, "I am made to live in the Dark, so I bring what I'm joined to with me here to dwell. Even if it's only a shadow of a thing, then that it is fine, too. I am made without form, but here you see me well. Would you like to stay here? I promise I won't bother you here. It's only in the light in Time that we like to bother. We like to toy with humans and get them to do the irresistible things…but, of course, you know that, don't you?"

Gigot grimaced at what Fear and the Darklings knew as they gathered about to listen.

Fear lifted his finger to his lips and licked his forefinger and held it up to the Darkness so that it might bring a shadow from the light of the moon and it did. Although he had no form, his shadow did, even the wetness from licking his forefinger glistened in the shadow of the moonlight.

"Irresistible things, yessss," Fear laughed and the Darklings laughed with him.

"We like to, hmmm…let me see…what we call…" as Fear leaned towards Gigots face, he whispered, "intermingle."

Fear smiled a ghastly smile and the rest of the friends who had gathered about jeered as more and more Darklings encompassed the two of them.

"We affectionately call ourselves, 'The Intermingling Society". We like to do well in the community presiding over the communities with confusion, so that the unsuspecting or rather demonstratively suspecting would be, or, could be used and toyed with…just a tiny bit!" Fear twisted his two fingers together and rubbed the tips of his fingers together to mocked the idea of the little bit as he turned about face to the Darklings and he lifted his arms wide revealing their true demeanor.

"Then, after we use them, we discard them. They're refuse waiting to be what they are, waste. Wasted lives, wasted souls. But you know what I mean, don't you, Gigot?" taunting Gigot with scorn.

And the dream ended.

V

Moments Out of Time

Gigot awoke tired from the rest to the noise of an extra-large swamp rat, a newt of enormous proportions. He was rummaging through the brush looking for something to eat. Will was there, but the other companions had gone on ahead to allow Gigot and Will to get the rest they needed. Gigot boarded Faith and Will boarded his horse, Truth. The moment they hit the trail leading downward to the Western Slopes, along came a messenger with news of a great feast that was occurring at the home of Wealth and his Beloved Fiance` Finance.

The messenger spoke up and said, "All are invited to this glorious event. It is the Feast of Kings at the prestigious home of none other than Mr. Wealth himself. Come one, come all to the Feast of Kings at noon today just ahead up the hill where all men dream to dream their dreams of brighter days ahead."

Gigot looked at Will and said, "I believe we may know this man, this Mr. Wealth. What do you say we go to this Feast of Kings and see what we can see?"

"It seems to be on the way," chuckled Will. "Hunger has come upon me and I could use a feast right now."

The messenger smiled his smile of fortuitous gladness and said, "Come, follow me, I'll take you there myself."

The messenger was on foot and had no horse, but that, he didn't seem to mind. He was a jolly soul, fleet-footed and quick. He could run as fast as a horse anyway and as he ran alongside Gigot and Will, he changed his hat and his name. The closer they came to Mr. Wealth's estate, the greater the smile became of the messenger whose name had changed to Mr. Marketer. Mr. Marketer was his real name and his fleet-footed feet could keep on running as he talked the whole way there.

"It's just right here, right here on the left," Mr. Marketer said with the greatest of enthusiasm. "Have you ever been to Mr. Wealth's estate?"

Will turned to Gigot, who by now was becoming leery of the whole opportunity, and frowned as Gigot was frowning and said, "Indubitably, we have been to some Mr. Wealth's estate, and most likely have contributed to it…but possibly not this one. I do believe that any Mr. Wealth is any Mr. Wealth, wouldn't you say, Gigot?"

"Yes, indeed, Will, you certainly speak the truth," Gigot conceded.

"Oh, but nay, and nay three times, I say," said Mr. Marketer, "Mr. Wealth is the wealthiest of the Wealth clan. You may have met his kinsmen, Mr. Banker, Mr. Credit or Mr. Greedy Businessman. We certainly pay homage and respect to this fine family for they are so deserving of all our gratefulness. They have done the world so much good. They create, they build, they finance, and they are thought to be some of the greatest helpers to all mankind. Why, without them, I don't know what the world would be like without the likes of them. They are givers and helpers and servants of the people both great and small. There isn't anyone they wouldn't help in their time of need."

"Yes, I do believe you believe what you say," said Gigot, "But let me ask you this and would you please answer me truly?"

"Why, yes, indeed," said Mr. Marketer, "everything I say is required to be the truth, why I could have written that Good Book myself if it hadn't been written before my time."

Will chuckled within himself at the response of Mr. Marketer when to their surprise they found themselves surreptitiously at the doorstep of Mr. Wealth. Mr. Marketer was ringing the doorbell and ignoring the thought of answering any of Gigot's questions.

Mr. Wealth's butler came to the door immediately with a smile and a grin, quickly looking over Gigot and Will faster than a fleeting foot can fly. With a haughty smirk, the butler said, "Right this way, we've been expecting you. I believe your friends have already arrived for the Feast of Kings."

Will looked at Gigot as they both winced and said, "Friends? I didn't know we had any friends on this part of the Trail. I guess Lortnoc and Endurance have planned to meet us here."

Enticed by a former Desire, they went into the great hall. Mr. Wealth, Mr. Banker and Mr. Credit simultaneously greeted them as One. They both smiled their smiles of great pleasure and Mr. Banker said, "Hello, kind gentlemen, welcome to the glorious home of Mr. Wealth. It is with great pleasure we welcome you both to this fine estate. We've been expecting you! Please allow me to introduce myself. I am Mr. Banker, the most renowned banker in all the land. There isn't a soul for miles around that hasn't done business with me. And this fine gentleman to my right is Mr. Credit. He is my right hand man. He is the one whom we delightfully call the greatest helper in all the land. Mr. Credit, please meet…"

Mr. Banker was certainly sure of himself and stuck out his hand for a handshake and a greeting of equal quality.

Will shoved Gigot's arm forward and awoke him from the trance that Mr. Banker had put him in. "Oh, I'm Gigot and this is Will, we're certainly glad to meet you!" Gigot said with a smile and a hearty handshake.

In the moment of the handshake, Gigot saw what he had seen before. He had known these two spirits in the days of time past. They were the ones who gave him and Will all the money they needed to buy their houses and all of the whatevers their soul desired. Then they gave them some more money to buy more whatevers and to open businesses in order to fulfill all that they felt they needed whenever they felt they needed it. Gigot remembered Passivity's Presence always lurking around them then along with all of the money they had borrowed to move their lives along as they saw fit.

As they shook hands with Mr. Banker and Mr. Credit, Indebtedness appeared between them as a silky, glue-like substance and they couldn't let go of Mr. Banker and Mr. Credit's handshakes. Indebtedness was spiritually melding their hands together as they shook and shook, all four hands together that became six with Indebtedness' cemented bond.

The more they shook, the more they shook and the mansion of Mr. Wealth began to shake with the power of Mr. Credit's movements. Just then, Ignorance, Stupid and Gullible walked into the great hall to the shaking gentlemen. They laughed at one another and saw the fun they perceived was going on and desired to shake along with them.

"Come one, come all," Mr. Marketer said, "Come to the Land of Wealth and Prosperity! All of the land, all of the houses, all of the whatever's your little heart desires can be yours for the taking and we'll help you get what you want today, right now, you need to get what you desire right now!"

Gigot and Will both knew that they had been here before and all of the shaking going on was making them both look delirious and dizzy. They saw the messenger named Desire sitting on a king's throne over in the corner of the great hall smirking and smiling all the while.

"I see that you're becoming Delirious and Dizzy," Mr. Wealth expounded as the mansion erupted with the greatest of shaking, filling Mr. Wealth with the most rapturous of happiness to see these two fellows falling in line once again with his wooing.

"Ah, yes, let me introduce you to my most favorite and greatest of all clients…Mr. Fool, meet Gigot and Will, they'll soon be Mr.'s just like you and me, isn't that right?" Mr. Wealth extended his right hand of agreement again to Gigot and Will and at the same moment, his one right hand had become two as Mr. Fool, Ignorance, Stupid and Gullible started laughing at the prospect of meeting two more friends in need.

Will slapped Gigot's extended arm down and let out a scream, "NOOOOO!"

And with that exclamation of defiance, Mr. Wealth, Mr. Banker, Mr. Credit, Ignorance, Stupid, Fool, and Gullible all vanished in an instant with only the vapor of Indebtedness still lingering and Desire casting a shadow over them as he departed.

In an instant, Gigot and Will found themselves where they had left themselves by the roadside of the Trail to the Western Slopes. They were panting and reeling from the experience. Gigot and Will sat to rest by the way with their horses waiting alongside them. Along slithered Indebtedness with a swank and a hissing swagger like he owned the road. He slithered over and sat down alongside the two of them. Curiously, they rested and watched Indebtedness move above them on the slope and then slide down, squeezing himself in-between the two of them saying, "You know, you just can't get rid of me that easy, now can you?"

Gigot could see Will slump down the side of the slope a bit to make room for Indebtedness as Indebtedness had grown a little fatter since the last time they'd met. It seemed that there was no way of getting rid of Indebtedness quickly and as soon as they both came to that realization, two of Indebtedness' friends, Guilt and Consequence showed up asking if they could come alongside and rest with them all.

"Is that ok with you?" Guilt asked.

"It's ok with me, if it's ok with you," Consequence chided in.

Humiliated, Will chided back, "I guess I have no choice in the matter at this point, do I?"

"Oh, I wasn't talking to you, I was talking to my friend, Indebtedness," Guilt replied.

Consequence chuckled out loud, "Ha, ha, he, haw, don't you just love us being here with you all?"

Gigot was churning on the inside from the presence of Guilt and Consequence knowing that Indebtedness was not going away any time soon and he realized that as they all began to slide down the slope while resting by the way of the Trail to the Western Slopes. They had arrived at the low point of the Western Slopes with the burden of Indebtedness, Guilt and Consequence to weigh them down heavier than their thoughts could carry them.

Their horses, Faith and Truth, stood on higher ground and watched them slide slowly down the slope as though the slope had turned to sludge. They were all sliding under the tremendous weight of Indebtedness as he grew fatter by the moments spent with him, but it was a slow slide from the thickness of the sludge.

Faith turned to Truth and they whinnied for the attention of Gigot and Will. Will and Gigot had gotten stuck in the sludge that was darker and thicker than fudge. So, the two horses threw out their leashes attached to their bridles and caught Will and Gigot before they slipped further down the slope of sludge.

Indebtedness caught eye to the leashes unfurled and tried to catch on to the legs of both Will and Gigot, and they both at once jerked, pulling away from the grip of Indebtedness. Guilt was holding onto Indebtedness with all his might and slid further down the slope of sludge into the no more.

Consequence, however, had never let go of Will and had him by his leg armor and had a pretty tight grip fairly assured of his salvation. The two horses pulled and pulled the three up the sludge as Indebtedness and Guilt had fallen out of sight off the cliff.

Gigot and Will were sweating profusely from the pulling and tugging from Fear and Travail. Stress made it all breathtaking. Consequence didn't pay Stress any mind as he had his own responsibilities to deal with.

Faith and Truth had pulled Gigot and Will to safety and as Gigot and Will laid down on the slope exhausted just above the sludge. They breathed a breath of release, yet believed somehow that Consequence was here to stay as a result of their former times.

Stress, Fear and Travail disappeared with the breathing of relaxation and rest as Endurance and Lortnoc appeared from around the bend.

"Consequence," Endurance entreated, "We all know why you're here and that you are a most deserving chap indeed. Surely Goodness and

Mercy are following Gigot and Will now and you are not welcome here."

Consequence was shaking his head and said, "Not so, dear Endurance, I know you too well for you and I have had our differences and here we are again. I'm stuck with these two as they are the most deserving of me. I cannot let go of them. We are eternally attached."

Lortnoc raised his brow and spoke, "Consequence, in the realm of time and space, you have many attachments, but not here. Here, you are as a thought, a breath…a stale wind. And, although you believe you have a right to not let go, the power here is far stronger than you or anything you can hold!"

"A threefold bond is hardly broken," Consequence said as he joined his arms locking them in-between Will and Gigot as Will and Gigot were at a loss as to how to get rid of Consequence.

Endurance and Lortnoc placed their hands on their swords and as they prepared to pull them from their sheaths, Will seemed to be strengthening from an internal energy rising from within. He propounded, "Consequence, I know that you are attached and we owe you a great debt that has to be paid in time and space. But that is not where we are. We are not attached to you here. You have no hold on us here. Go to Indebtedness and leave at once! Be gone!"

And with that, Consequence disappeared leaving Lortnoc, Endurance, Gigot and Will alone on the Trail of the Western Slopes.

"It only takes a moment, doesn't it, Lortnoc?" Will pondered as he was beginning to see the power of truth.

"It actually takes less than that Will," Lortnoc replied, "…far less."

They all got up and proceeded around the bend on the Trail of the

Western Slopes. They got away from the sludge and mire of Consequence and soon happened upon a man whose back was straight and narrow and carried with him a great smile.

Will entreated the man whose back was straight and carried with him a great and wonderful smile and asked, "Who might you be on this terrible Trail of the Western Slopes and how is it that you carry such a great and wonderful smile?"

The man said, "Why, hello! My name is Grace Walker and I'm about the Great One's business on this terrible Trail of the Western Slopes. My smile I carry with me everywhere I go as a reminder of the joy that is set before me in this realm and the next."

Yesege, who had appeared, smiled and concurred with the man who called himself Grace Walker.

"Hello, my Friend," Yesege called out to Grace Walker. "Why don't you tell Will and Gigot the Testimony of your great and wonderful smile?"

Grace Walker, always the one to speak of his testimony of his great and wonderful smile agreed with Yesege and said, "Once there was a Poor Man who dwelt as a Royal Subject in the Land of the King and even though he was a Royal Subject who dwelt in the Land of the King, he had committed a great and terrible Sin that became as a Burden to him and to those all around. The Poor Man knew of his great and terrible Sin so much so that his Burden became great and he carried this Burden on his back for all to see. After having carried the weight of the Burden of his Sin, he carried his Sin and the Burden thereof to the Great and Mighty King who was known in the Land to be a King of Judgment, Mercy and Grace."

"Knowing this, that his Burden was too great to bear, he submitted his Sin and the Burden thereof to the Great King in confession and repentance.

His remorse was great and was loathsome to himself even unto death for what he had done to the Great King in His Land. The Great King, who happened to know all things, knew of his great Sin and the Burden thereof, and said to him,

"Poor man, I know your heart and confession. I know that you have repented this moment in the ears of my heart. You are forgiven of your great and terrible Sin and the Burden thereof and I will remember it no more. Go and Sin no more!'"

"As in Time and Past Time, the Poor Man who had been forgiven and relieved of his great and terrible Sin and the Burden thereof, tried to walk among the people of the land. Yet, there were those who had permission to go in and out of the Land of Time of the King and they who knew of the Poor Man's great and terrible Sin, but did not know the what and the why and the how. They said to him, "You have committed a great and terrible Sin, therefore you must carry it on your back as a Burden for all to see that you committed this heinous act in the Land of the King. We will be around to help any and all to remember what you did and how unworthy you are for we are here to see to it that you carry this Burden all the days of your life."

"The Poor Man agreed with his accusers for he knew them to know the truth as they saw it yet they did not know, nor did they understand the edicts and verdicts of the Great and Merciful King. In his agreement with the accusers, the Poor Man picked up his Sin and the Burden thereof every day and its weight, he wore on his back. The weight of the weight was sore and trying and heavy enough to bow the back of the Poor Man so much so that he walked around with a bowed back."

"As was the case in the Land of the King, the King in his moments saw the Poor Man among the peoples of the land and inquired of the Poor

Man as to why he walked about with a bowed back. The Poor Man replied, 'Oh, Great and Merciful King, full of Judgment, Compassion and Grace. I dwell here as a Royal Subject in your Great Land and I know for certain that you released me of my great and terrible Sin and the Burden thereof, but I had cause to not forgive myself and the others that travel about in and out of your great land, who do not know nor do they understand your edicts and verdicts thought it best for me and others around to remember my great and terrible Sin and the Burden thereof so much so that I should pick it back up again and carry it on my back so as not to ever forget that I committed such a terrible and heinous act."

"So, in my agreement with my accusers, I have continued to carry it every day of my life."

The Great King, full of Mercy, Compassion and Grace observed the Poor Man and said, "Poor Man, what was it that you did that was so great and terrible, I do not remember what it was?"

The Poor Man, ashamed of his great and terrible Sin and the Burden thereof was too ashamed to say. Then, it occurred to the Poor Man that if the Great and Merciful King, being full of Judgment, Compassion and Grace and who also knew all things, but did not remember what the Poor Man's great and terrible Sin was, then why should he?"

In that moment, the great and terrible Sin and the Burden thereof disappeared from the back of the Poor Man and he straightened his back as all of the other peoples who dwell in the Land of the King have straightened their backs.

The Poor Man replied to the Great and Merciful King, "Oh, Great and Merciful King, full of Judgment, Compassion and Grace, if you do not remember any great and terrible Sin, or the Burden thereof, then I certainly don't either."

"Then, the Great and Merciful King smiled and gave His smile to the Poor Man and gave him a new name and called him, Grace Walker."

"He who stands before you, Will and Gigot, is that man who once bowed his back as a Poor Man who carried the weight of his Sin and the Burden thereof on his back for all to remember. But in this moment, I stand before you as Grace Walker with the smile of the King of the Land. The Great One is the Great and Merciful King full of Judgment, Compassion and Grace. For those who stand before Him full of confession and repentance, he knows their Sin and He is willing to forgive and He remembers it no more. Go in peace and be encouraged as you travail the Western Slopes for its ways are as oil and its foundation is as sinking sand."

VI

The Western Slopes

Will and Gigot were enthralled by the tale of Grace Walker and so bid a hearty and glad farewell to him and began once again on their journey to the Crested Hill by way of the Western Slopes. They were beginning to realize that with each new victory, the sight of the top of Crested Hill was becoming clearer. They had not realized just how clouded the mountain had been, but with each new moon, the fierce cloud covering and grave storms that surrounded the mountain in thick darkness was slowly dissipating.

In the distance around a hill on the Slope, a traveler traveling at an extremely slow speed was making their way towards them, but at a pace that seemed to gnaw at them to the point that they wished he'd just arrive. 'How was it?' they conjectured that they could see this Stranger who seemed to resemble someone they both knew from so far away.

As the traveler approached, he was a she and she was carrying a slender pole with a white flag attached. However, she was on foot and moving at a very slow pace due to her pacing about five paces with each step that she took. She was dressed in a Queen's robe of garnet and blue and she called herself Elissa of Carthage. She was absolutely stunning in all her regalia as she was searching the hillside and the Western Slopes for her husband and her gold. She wore a gold insignia on her robe that favored the look of a W and asked Will and Gigot if they might help her find her husband and her gold. She was in a terrible way from the thought of losing her wealth and her husband and didn't know what to do.

As they were standing there listening to her story, one of her servants named Worry arrived and then there appeared two more of her servants, Distraction and Anxiety.

She said, "Oh, it's been so long and too long that I have missed you all. Oh my, where, oh, where have you been?"

Distraction and Anxiety both hemmed and hawed a bit and refused to fully admit their whereabouts of their unseen moments and seemed to be confused about how they actually found their Queen Elissa. They could sense her servant Worry and they were drawn to her by the scent of her perfume.

"Oh, my," Queen Elissa stirred with her favored servant Worry, "What will we do without my husband and my gold?"

Anxiety moved closer to her as to console her in her turmoil and throughout the entire experience of watching and listening to them, Will and Gigot had found themselves standing on the shore of a sinking sand lake bed and the longer they stood there, the more they realized that they had begun to sink. Queen Elissa's servants Worry and Anxiety seemed to be growing in stature right before their eyes and they were becoming antagonized within at how heavy her burden must be and how long she must have been carrying it. Distraction moved closer to Will and Gigot not knowing where he stepped as his weight began weighing down on the sinking sand.

Anxiety observed Distraction sinking and simply stood on the shore frightened. He did nothing to help his fellow servant. Anxiety understood a part of Distraction's weight problem and had to confess to his Queen Elissa that they might have known a little of the whereabouts of some of her gold. Anxiety moaned in the direction of Distraction. Distraction was sinking deeper into the lake of sinking sand all the while drawing Will and Gigot down the slope of sinking sand along with him.

Anxiety yelled out, "Distraction! Throw me the gold that you have under your garment and all those layers of robe."

Distraction turned red with embarrassment, looking towards his Queen and said, "Oh, great and wonderful Queen, it was Anxiety and myself who have been guarding your gold, keeping it safe from Thieves and Liars."

Distraction was sinking fast in the sand from the weight of the gold and began to throw bars of gold towards his Queen Elissa and Anxiety. Queen Elissa didn't know whether to be angry or joyed, but was in such a tizzy as to Distraction's fate as he was sinking fast into the sinking sand. Will and Gigot could offer no help to any of them as they were stuck in the sinking sand themselves alongside the shoreline of the sinking sand lake.

Distraction opened his robes fully and threw with all of his might, bar after bar of bright gold. He was sinking still, just not as fast as before. Anxiety paced at the edge of the sand with Worry in fright and fear and basically did nothing as Distraction sank further into the sinking sand. Without any more of the gold bars left, Distraction continued to sink. Worry covered his Queen Elissa and just as she suspected, her servant Distraction continued to sink all the way up to his neck. In Desperation, she began pacing along the shoreline in tandem with Anxiety and Worry, as Desperation guided her footsteps. Will and Gigot stood affixed themselves in the slow sinking sand as Distraction's weight not only had weighted him down in the lake of sinking sand, it had pulled Will and Gigot down along with him, but at a much slower pace.

With all of the gold that Distraction had carried in his robes, it occurred to Will to ask Anxiety what he might be carrying underneath his layers of robes and garments.

"Anxiety, pray do tell us what you have under your many layers of robes? Do you carry anything that might help your fellow servant and friend?"

Anxiety, afraid to reveal what he carried under his many layers of robes looked at his Queen and his Queen remanded him with an awfully stern look. He sheepishly opened his robe and out fell gold, ropes, chains and shackles.

Queen Elissa looked at all that he carried under his many layers of robe with shock, "Why do you carry so many things underneath your robe? And, why are there so many layers? You have on more garments than I do!"

Queen Elissa examined the shackles that had dropped from Anxiety's weight and realized that they were the same design as the jewelry she wore. Her necklace and bracelets were identical to the shackles and chains that dropped beneath Anxiety's robe. Queen Elissa was confused.

Anxiety merely took on a sheepish demeanor and looked back at his Queen with a most inquisitive look because he didn't really know the answer to her question. Meanwhile, Distraction was face up in the sinking sand and the only part of his body that was left above the sand was his face so that he might breathe a few more breaths before he sank completely in the mire.

"Help me, help me, someone, help me!" Distraction cried vociferously.

Anxiety was afraid and did not know what to do as the Queen began to pace along with Worry again.

"Why were you walking around with my gold? All of you had me believing that my gold had been lost and you had it with you the entire time!" Queen Elissa said exasperated. "You must take me for a fool!"

"Now, that's right, chide him for all this trouble he's caused us!" Worry said to the Queen.

"Trouble? Trouble I've caused you? Why if it wasn't for me being me and me being who I am, she wouldn't even need you around!" Anxiety lurched at Worry with both hands wanting to strangle him.

Distraction was spitting the sand out of his mouth and yelled, "Help me! Save me! Do something!"

Will and Gigot watched the folly of it all from their sunken place in the sand. Gigot looked back and forth from Anxiety to Distraction and then, back again, and the last time Gigot saw the face of Distraction, his face had changed into someone he recognized from his past. He was someone he thought to be important. He knew this man, although the man did not know him, and that's all Gigot could think about.

"What is his name?" Gigot thought to himself.

All of a sudden, yellow jacket bees swooped in around Anxiety and as he flailed his arms about to protect himself from the bees, he inadvertently threw the rope out in Distraction's direction. But, it was too late, as Distraction smirked at their stupidity, gurgled, and sank fast to be seen no more.

Will and Gigot were continuing to sink in the sinking sand as well. However, they were closer to the shore than Distraction had been. Anxiety and Worry, still jumping and flailing about from the bees, pondered with what they might do to at least save Will and Gigot, but they couldn't come to any agreement as to exactly what that might be out of fear of doing something that might bring harm to them or disrepute to their Queen. They were more concerned for themselves with the yellow jackets.

Will and Gigot looked at one another sensing Anxiety's stress and Worry's demeanor weighing them down faster into the sand. Just having them around was debilitating.

Recognizing this, they became silent and relaxed. In their silence, Gigot's thoughts became clearer. So, he looked to his right and there stood his horse Faith with his stone cold face as though to say, "Now…you see me?" Faith was close to the sand as he could be without touching any of the grains of sand. Faith whinnied and raised himself up high on his hind legs and with a mighty pounce down, threw the reigns down forward beyond his face. Gigot caught the reigns and as Faith pulled backwards, Will latched onto Gigot and they were both pulled to safety. Gigot and Will both lay on their bellies wincing from embarrassment as they had gotten caught up with Distraction, but they knew in their hearts that Distraction was merely that and didn't even exist.

"Did you recognize who Distraction became, or who he really was in that moment?" Gigot asked Will.

"Yes, I saw that, but I didn't know if it was real, or not." Will responded.

"Not, I suppose!" Gigot was learning.

The two gathered themselves to their knees, cleaning themselves off of the wet grains of sand and as they rose, their eyes met the eyes of their horses standing before them. Faith and Truth were there throughout the entire ordeal, but stood there watching as their masters watched Distraction, Anxiety, Desperation and Stress. A rather uncanny revelation came to Gigot and then to Will as their eight eyes met, that the whole thing was not their problem. Realizing this, they turned and found that Worry, Anxiety and even Queen Elissa and her gold had vanished.

Gigot and Will mounted their horses and allowed Faith and Truth to lead them along the shoreline of the lake of the sinking sand. Faith and Truth had no concern for what lie beneath the surface of the lake and knew exactly where to step along the Way.

The path was narrow along the shore of the lake and its Way profound which made it easier to stay on the path, leading to the thicket that lie before Middletown on their way towards Mount Bereft.

VII

Towards Mount Bereft

Gigot and Will traveled on towards Mount Bereft and kept its shadowy and cloudy atmosphere in view as it was a tremendous mountain that they had to go around in order to get to Crested Hill. As they continued on, their way became more clouded the further they traveled. It seemed as though they were walking through a wet fog…thick, yet smoky, with the aroma of a burned carcass of some sort. They covered their faces to their noses so as not to breathe in too much of the wet, foggy smoke as it was nauseating their senses. The trail led downward a bit into a slight valley with tall bushes and briers on each side of the trail.

When they finally did come to a clearing, they observed a middle-aged man; a very average looking fellow dressed in work pants and boots on his lower half and he wore a tuxedo, dress shirt and bow tie on his upper half. His name was Ambivalence and when they happened upon him, he was sore afraid of their presence.

Ambivalence lived on Halfway Boulevard in Middletown, just on this side of Mount Bereft. He lived in a tiny cottage just at the bottom of the upward motion of the hill. He didn't venture much upward onto the side of the Mount, but found himself spending the majority of his time going far enough away from his cottage, but still within eyesight of the greyish, yet bluish colored hut-like cottage. He had a hard time getting nowhere or anywhere, depending on the day or the time of the week. At times, he honestly could not remember if he was coming or going or where he had been…if it was yesterday or some other time in the past.

He constantly worried about the future and what it may bring to pass. He would dream of good things to come and yet, in very certain terms, his certainty would fall to ashes as he thought about his past constantly reliving the things he had done, or not done, and bewildered himself if he might re-do his past in his future. He coughed a lot, just in case he might get sick, and did so for preventive measures. His coughing, however, eventually made his throat sore and then he would down quite a bit of water to soothe the ache that he had created by all of his coughing. Once healed, he'd get back at it again, the coughing, that is, just to keep his lungs cleared of any and all obstructions whether imagined or real.

It was just on the edge of the thicket where he believed himself to be hiding from the sight of Will and Gigot as they spied him spying them from just within the spiny, prickly bushes garnered with purple leaves.

"Who goes there?" he inquired of the journeymen he'd never seen before…or, had he, he couldn't remember with any certainty?

Will and Gigot, sitting upon Faith and Truth, peered through the brush and wondered at who they saw, all dressed to the tees in his tuxedo crouched down and peering, thinking he was unseen.

"Who goes there?" Will questioned.

"You can't say what I say, can you?" Ambivalence, still hiding in the thicket and still believing he was hiding unseen.

"I asked you first! Who goes there? Answer me truly and tell me why you're here!" Ambivalence demanded.

"Come out from behind those bushes," Gigot stated kindly, wincing his eyes towards the not so camouflaged protector of the thicket.

Ambivalence rose to his feet with his hand on his sword as if to threaten them with the use of it if they took one step more.

Will and Gigot, sitting atop their horses Faith and Truth, merely glanced at one another bewildered at the man who was dressed for a party on the top and dressed for work on the bottom and brandishing a sword whose handle was quick, yet the sword had obviously been broken in two.

"Are you going to use that thing on us?" Gigot inquired peacefully.

"I will if I have to, that's up to you. There's a lot going on around here lately and I've had to protect myself with this and with that and if I have to kill you, I will. Don't put me to the test."

Truth whinnied at Ambivalence as if to laugh at him and Ambivalence took two steps to the right for Light was on his right. Then, he took two steps back into Fear leading him to take two steps to his left for Darkness was on his left. He was preparing an early exit through the brush if Will and Gigot even looked as though they were to dismount.

It seemed as though that Ambivalence's thinking came by way of the relationships he had known in the past and he simply had grown not to trust anyone. He had never known anyone who ever did what they said they would do. He figured that if all people had were their words and their deeds and what they said did not match what they did and what they did, didn't match what they said, then why would they do all the talking they were doing, or talking. It befuddled him to no end and that's what brought him to his inconclusive indecisiveness regarding people and almost all things that he had come across. Distrust and Fear had become his only friends and even they weren't reliable most of the time.

Gigot and Will needed to rest and even though they could sense Ambivalence's uneasiness, they began their dismount from their horses. Ambivalence took another two steps back and then his right leg moved right and his left leg moved left and he found himself not being able to move either way from his self-guided bewilderment on what to do or where to go next. He just couldn't seem to figure out if Will and Gigot meant him any harm, or not, and so he just stood there hyperventilating in Fear with his legs parted to the point where he could not move right or left.

Gigot saw Fear and gently said to Ambivalence, "We mean you no harm."

And with that, Ambivalence breathed a sigh of relief and moved his legs closer together before he lost his balance. Gigot and Will both raised their brows in curiosity at this awkward fellow and then smiled at him in friendship.

Ambivalence searched deep within himself for his smile, for he had not smiled in a very long time and he could not remember where it was or if he still had it. He searched and searched quickly within himself for his smile, but Fear was hiding it behind his Past. As Gigot and Will stepped closer to him their smiles grew and he saw himself in the reflection in their eyes. At that moment, he saw his friend Fear in the reflection and then looked down at their smiles and looked up at their eyes and he immediately realized he had to make a decision. He scrunched his forehead and turned his head to the left in Darkness and then to the right in Light and decided with all that was within him to smile and not allow Fear to tell him to turn back into the Darkness. Immediately, Fear left him and his frown automatically turned upside down.

Gigot stretched his arm out to greet Ambivalence and said, "I'm Gigot and this is Will, we come in peace."

Ecstatic, Ambivalence dropped his sword and lunged for Gigot and wrapped his arms around him gladly exclaiming, "I'm Ambivalence, friend, I'm so glad to meet you!"

He hugged and hugged Gigot with all of his might and hugged him tightly as he searched within to find the trust of another that he had lost so long ago. The tighter he hugged Gigot, the more he could sense this welling up within of a thing that he had not felt for many moons. What he was searching for was belief in another's words and when he realized what he was searching for, he believed Gigot's words that they meant him no harm and so trust catapulted upward from his belief. Gigot looked at Will and laughed and as tears of joy were rolling down Ambivalence's cheeks, Ambivalence lunged for Will and hugged him all the same.

"Oh, Friend, my Friends, my new Friends, won't you come and dine with me for lunch and we'll serve up a feast, we will, oh, yes, yes, indeed!" Ambivalence shouted joyfully.

Laughing with Ambivalence, Will said, "Certainly, certainly, we will stay with you for a while, we need to rest and eat, we're both starving for real food."

"Real food, well, that is what we shall have today!"

Ambivalence's heart was changing before their eyes and it was in his words that they saw Encouragement appear by his right side. Through the appearance of Encouragement, Will's horse Truth walked over to Ambivalence and nudged him with his nose. Tears welled up from within Ambivalence's within and when Truth touched him, he could see himself in the reflection of Truth's eyes. He no longer saw Fear or Distrust, or felt Consternation by his side. He did not see Unbelonging or Uninvited behind him, no, for what he saw when Truth touched his chest he could sense his own being-ness of what he had been created for. In a moment, Ambivalence got lost in the eyes of Truth and watched his reflection change. He began to see himself for what Truth saw him to be and he no longer saw himself as Ambivalent, but deep within the Spirit of Truth, he heard Truth speak to him and give him a new name. Faith stepped alongside Truth and as Ambivalence could see himself change in their eyes, he hugged them both and gave himself to their call.

"Your name is Purpose," the Spirit of Truth spoke into Purpose's spirit.

"Faith, I give to you," the Spirit of Faith implored to his spirit, "Your forgetfulness will no longer be of the things of the Right and the True and of where to go and of what to say, but you will now be able to cast all Fear, Doubt and the Sins of the Past into the Sea of Forgetfulness, where true forgetfulness belongs."

Purpose stood there in between Truth and Faith with his head bowed and his arms around the foreheads of the two horses. His tears of joy flowed from his deep within and he fell to his knees in honor as he sensed the Presence of the Great One in the Spirit of Truth and Faith.

Gigot and Will knelt as well with Purpose in the Presence and for the moment in the day, they were as One in the Spirit of Truth and Faith and none of them had a need.

As the three of them knelt in the Presence at the feet of Faith and Truth, Encouragement filled them to the brim with all that they needed in the moment.

"What say you, Purpose? What do you say about going with us on our journey to Crested Hill, we need a stalwart man like yourself to aid us on our quest?" Will asked.

"Indeed, I will. I will, indeed." Purpose stated gladly, "But first, let me change from these old clothes and put on some new ones that are right for the journey."

"Do as you need to do, but know that our journey is rugged and troublesome and from what I have heard of Mount Bereft, it will be dangerous," Gigot shared hinting at what type of clothing he would need to put on.

Purpose flew with excitement to his cottage straightway and ran to his back room while Gigot and Will helped themselves in the kitchen to the vegetable stew that was prepared on the stovetop. There was warm bread in the oven and they heaped bowl after bowl of vegetable stew and warm bread until they had had their fill. Purpose came in and joined them as he was dressed and ready to go on this pilgrimage to Crested Hill. Purpose had never been able to see Crested Hill from his vantage point because of the wet, smoky fog that covered Mount Bereft. But, as they walked together out of the cottage, fully prepared for their journey, the wet, smoky fog of Mount Bereft was clearing and the Light of Pearls was glimmering in the distance as if to say, "Walk this way and do not veer to the right or the left, for the Way is here and the journey is long."

The three of them stared into the gaze of the Light and its Way was hidden in their hearts so that they would not lose sight of the Way of the Light, nor take another wrong turn to Distraction or Doubt.

Not only was the Way clearing, but in the clearing of the wet, smoky fog, the three began to see the truth of Mount Bereft for it was no Mount of any size after all and after all of the talk that they had all heard of the steepness and the treacherousness of Mount Bereft, they saw that all of the talk had just been that…talk. In the Light, Mount Bereft was not what it had seemed from the Darkness of the wet, smoky fog, but was a beautiful hillside meadow brimming with grass as a knoll and teaming with Life and not Death. They looked beyond the grassy knoll and kept their eyes on the Pearl Lighted Path.

Gigot and Will had found Purpose and with Encouragement to set them on their way the three of them bonded them together as One, being united on this stretch of the journey to capture Crested Hill from the foes of the beyond and the outer influences that had created the Darkness in the first place.

VIII

Slaying Isaac

As the Pearl lighted pathway lit their way onwards, Gigot and Will rode Faith and Truth. Purpose proposed to walk together with them in some sort of unity in mind and spirit. As the path widened and was made clearer by the lighted pearls, a sense of peace overcame them all and they could see the mount of the Crested Hill becoming clearer to their eyes as their approach to the great mountain was strengthened by their inner resolve.

A strong comradery was being built upon by their presence together. It was as though Gigot had just found the one lost friend that he had been searching for all of his life and Will felt the same. They had so much in common it was laughable. As they trudged along the path, Purpose inevitably would find himself so enthralled in the conversation between Gigot and Will, he would finish each of their sentences. Purpose was becoming so confident that he was being allowed to lead the way along the Lighted Pearl Pathway until they happened upon a tremendous thicket. Thickets had always seemed to be a home to Ambivalence, who had now become Purpose, with all of his hiding and such, but this thicket was proving to be a distracting discourse through the path they thought they had been following.

They all sensed the downward flow of the path, but each trusted Purpose to guide them in the way they should go. The further they traveled, the fewer the lighted pearls there were until the lighted pearls were so sparse they saw them no more, all they saw was thick thicket.

Will's looks to Gigot were quite profound as they got off of Faith and Truth, leaving them on the path by the last Lighted Pearl. They followed Purpose through the thicket off the path. Purpose had gone ahead so as to be aware of any turns along the way. He walked with such certainty that what was with the three of them in the beginning of this part of the journey, was slowly becoming an increasingly doubtful and dubious detour. Gigot had come to realize that they were no longer on the Lighted Pearl Path at all and perceived that Purpose had gotten confused in the thicket that he was so accustomed to. Purpose had gotten so far out front guiding them through and out of the thicket that his determination to deliver the three of them had taken them onto a sided patch of chiseled rocks that happened to be quite pointed when stepped on.

Will yelled out to Purpose, "Where are you taking us, are you certain where you're going?"

Purpose retorted smartly, "Certain? The only certainty is that if you don't follow me, you'll be poised for pain!"

"Pain," Gigot sounded off. "I think we've reached that destination! These rocks are killing my feet and my ankles are getting sore from trying to avoid the unavoidable points."

Finally, in exasperation, Will demanded, "Purpose, stop! You can't possibly be going in the right direction. Come back here and let's figure this thing out together on how to get back to the Lighted Pearl Pathway."

"No, I know what I'm doing and I know where I'm going, and you two need to stop complaining about the pain, if anybody should know pain, it's me! I know pain intimately!" said Purpose sharply, resenting them questioning his certainty. "There's a clearing up ahead, there always is with thickets and sharp pointy rocks."

"Who told you that?" Gigot asked.

Will looked at Gigot with a raised brow, tilted his head and said to Gigot, "I'm not going any further. Something's not right about this direction. Are you certain that following Purpose is the right thing to do? What are you sensing?"

Gigot glanced over to Will and said, "I figured Purpose knew what he was doing but now I'm not so sure. I sense we're going in the right direction, but I'm not so certain that this is the particular way to get to the final destination. It's as though the ultimate direction is forward, but somehow we missed a turn, or two. We're going straight to the mark and yet we both know that roads are not always straight. They take their turns to the right and the left…possibly to make it more bearable, I'm not sure, but that's what I've always seen."

"I agree," Will breathed in and exhaled a sigh of relief just to stop for a moment from the pain of the pointed rocks.

Purpose had ceased his forward progress as well wincing secretly from the jagged rocks into the soles of his boots. He looked back at Gigot and Will sitting on a boulder to get away from the harsh points of the stones beneath. It wasn't until then that Purpose realized where he was standing as everything was pointed stone all around with no thicket to cause a trip upon a deadly point. Etched in the wall of stone to his right were these words, "The Altar of Isaac," and as he looked to the bend around his left, he saw stone steps that led upward and so he followed them to a flat hewn stone large enough to lie down on.

Purpose was baffled. In his mind, he knew for certain that he had been leading Gigot and Will in the right direction. Even Gigot knew they were heading in the ultimate direction, though the pain of it from the thicket and the pointy stones made the traverse quite unbearable.

In the same moment that Purpose realized where he was, Gigot sensed a dagger go through his own heart where he was standing. His breath was momentarily taken away and as he sat upon the rock, his breath became shallow and his life became cold. Will did not know what Gigot was sensing and Gigot was too frightened at the sensation that he could not speak. Neither of them could see Purpose anymore for he was out of sight around the altar mount up ahead.

"Help me up, Will," Gigot reached for Will and gave him his arm to pull him up.

"What's wrong with you?" Will inquired.

"We need to get up to where Purpose is, let's go," Gigot stammered, uncertain of what was happening in his spirit. He knew that following Purpose to this point was necessary if they were going to walk their road together.

Will moved forward over the pointy stones as the last thicket tugged its final pull and there he saw a snake in the crevice of the rocks, hissing, with his fangs prepared to pounce.

"No, not now, I'm not dealing with you now! Scoot!" Will demanded and raised his shoulders high thrusting his torso forward unafraid of the hissing viper. The snake recoiled and sat back abit.

"Where are you, Purpose?" Will yelled out to make certain he was headed in the right direction. He didn't want to take any more steps to the right, or to the left, as a result of the pain the pointy stones made on their feet.

"I'm up here," Purpose shouted in the distance. "Get to the wall of rock and go left, and follow the steps upward," he told them as they could hear his voice in a windy distance.

Gigot and Will got to the wall of stone and read the inscription chiseled into the stone and wondered exactly where they were and how they got there. There wasn't really any other way to go, but the way Purpose had told them. At this point, they couldn't go any further to the right or to the left because the wall of stone seemed to go on forever. They tripped over the pointy stones that led to the stone stairwell and pushed themselves upward following Purpose's voice.

"Up here, come up here!"

"We're coming, we're coming," Will and Gigot shouted as they tip-toed and side-stepped and inward-stepped, to do just about any kind of weird movement on top of the painfully pointed jagged edges of the rocks. Both Gigot and Will were quite confused as to where they might be and its historical significance. Their feet were in the extreme of soreness from the pointed rocks and the stony steps were quite steep and narrow through the upward ascent. They heard a silent groan as they approached the top of the steps that led to a surfaced opening. They could see what Purpose had seen just moments before. It was a flat hewn stone made out to be an altar of sorts built out of the top of the mount and there lay Purpose on the flat hewn stone.

"What are you doing?" Will yelled at Purpose, but Purpose didn't respond. In the twinkling of a moment, Gigot and Will both lunged forward running to the altar of hewn stone from the mount and there lay Purpose with no breath to his being.

"Purpose, Purpose, wake up, wake up! What has happened Gigot?" Will screamed, "How did this happen?" Both Will and Gigot looked upon Purpose while Despair arrived with Panic hiding behind the rock.

"How could this be?" Will again questioned, "Who is here? Is someone else here?"

Will grabbed the heel of his sword and started his search for whoever might have had a hand in this.

Gigot stood over the lifeless body of Purpose and was dazed and confused. He thought that they were to walk this journey together. He thought that now that he had found Purpose, that that was a part of the whole plan to show them the way to Crested Hill.

"What is going on here?" Gigot questioned in his mind. "How can this be?" "Who did this? Did he just die?"

Will had gone around every corner of the top of the mount as the center was the altar and the smooth stone formed a short wall around the entire top of the mount with the exception of an opening exactly opposite of the way they had ascended. No one was down those steps, at least as far as they could see. Will walked right through Panic as Panic's apparition he could not see, but feel. Will was taken aback from the invisible foe and stumbled for a moment feeling as though he had just been run through by a sharply pointed sword through his chest.

Despair, equally invisible, covered the area with a thick mist that made it unbelievably difficult to breathe. With bated breath and stricken with slowness, Will and Gigot trudged on the mount for moments that felt like a lifetime. After their quick search for an assailant, they both walked back to Purpose's side and they each stood on opposite sides of the altar, not knowing that Panic and Despair had overtaken them on the Mount of the

Altar of Isaac.

"What is He telling us, Gigot? You know I'll do whatever I'm supposed to do, but what just happened here? I thought that Purpose was a part of the plan to take back Crested Hill?" Will held back his emotion and yet he couldn't. Panic had him in his clutches by the chest and the throat and refused to let him go. Gigot didn't try to hold back the tears. Yet, both of them sensed together that there was some strange and disparagingly wonderful occurrence going on here.

"What are You saying?" Gigot asked aloud to the Great One and yet there was no answer.

"What is He saying here, Gigot?" Will demanded an answer as well.

"I don't know. Purpose seemed to definitely be a part of this plan. He sure acted like he knew where he was going. But why Purpose had to die, I don't know…this doesn't make any sense. Why here? Why here, at the Altar of Isaac, what's the significance in that? Even Abraham didn't have to kill his own son, Isaac. Isaac lived because a sacrificial ram was provided."

At that moment, they both looked intently at each other and stopped their breathing as if to listen to hear some ram in the bush that the Great One would have provided so that Purpose might live to show them the way. Alas, there was no sound of any ram; only the wind rushing through the entrance, the one from which they came and to the other entrance that obviously was an exit. They presumed this would be their way of escape from the mount…but to where, they did not know. The pressure that Panic and Despair had on them was taking its toll as each breath seemed like their last.

"What are we going to do now, Will?" Gigot asked.

"I still don't know, I guess we move on, we still have to move towards Crested Hill. At least from here, there is a clear and definitive direction to go…see there!" Will pointed off to his right with his right hand and Gigot looked off into the distance and clearly saw the top of Crested Hill. There was their destiny, to take the Hill, with, or without Purpose.

But even in that thought, as they both trudged with all of their might towards the second entrance on the other side, they looked back one last time at Purpose and he had disappeared. They climbed back through the thickness to the altar where Purpose had lain and on the altar they read these words.

"You shall have no other before Me."

Panic and Despair came along side them and they wept. Yet, the Truth they received in the words written on the Altar began their release from the clutches that Despair and Panic had on their being.

IX

Seeing What You're Shown

As they both wept together on the mount, a freezing cold wind blew from the one entrance over the top of the mount and out the other entrance that led to where they did not know and had not been. Panic called for Fear and the mist had turned to frozen fog. Will and Gigot both knew that there was a plan in Purpose and the confidence they all had together was more than extraordinary and yet…they knew they were being told otherwise. Could it be that their certainty had been entrusted to Purpose when in reality their trust should have been solely in listening to the Great One? But what's the use of Purpose if that is the case and as that thought crossed their minds, they realized the Truth in the purpose of the words upon the altar, "You shall have no other before Me."

"Gigot, we know we have to follow the Great One, He is the only One for certain that is going to conquer Crested Hill and yet we have to show up for Him to do it. He gave Purpose his name and gave Purpose to us as a friend. We were made complete with him, weren't we?" Will implored.

As the thickening and unrelenting wind turned the frozen fog into a blazing blizzard, Gigot yelled out, "Will, no, our completeness is found only in the Great One. And even though I know that, I followed Purpose like he was the Great One Himself. Obviously, the Great One sees that and in our selfishness, we followed Purpose because he was so much like us and made us feel…well, he made us feel together and I guess the real problem is that it's easier to follow what you can see and do rather than listen to what you can't see or try to see what you can't hear. I don't know what to do."

Gigot sighed as he sat by the altar shivering from the freezing wind passing through the top of the mount. He shivered and wiped the tears from his eyes as he pondered their future and Purpose in all that had just occurred. Even in his tears, he pondered at exactly what he was crying about. Was he grieving over a new found friend that he'd not even known but for a few days or was it the depth of who he believed Purpose was. This Purpose had died and Gigot was at a total loss.

He thought, "Why did Purpose have to die? And why are we being told, again, to basically listen to the Great One?"

As he thought his thoughts, even with the rustling and howling of the wind passing over the mount, he could hear, beyond the shadows of Doubt, a voice within saying, "Go this way."

He looked over at Will shivering as he was and said, "Get up. Let's get out of here! Purpose is with us in Him. Let's go! But we're only listening to the Great One from here on out, Ok?"

"That's fine with me, Gigot. I'm willing, besides there isn't anyone else to listen to now!" Will stated the obvious.

As they approached the edge of the mount and started through the other entrance with the freezing wind at their backs, they stepped down an even steeper descent than when they had ascended for this side of the mount had a much steeper decline. At this point, there was no turning back for the wind was driving them downward away from the rush of its strength and the further they progressed down the steep, the milder the wind became until they could feel it no more.

The steps wound to the right along the side of the mount and got wider the more they descended until there were no more steps to step upon and the ground was ground and not stone. Just then, they heard a voice in the distance calling out to them, saying, "Gigot, Will, where have you been? I've been calling out to you all to follow me here for some time now."

It was Purpose, the same Purpose that they had just walked with the past few days and had seen his death…and here he was, yet dressed profoundly in very different clothes.

"Purpose, it's you, it's you!" Will exclaimed, running towards him and Purpose wondered at the excitement that Will was exuding.

"It's you, it's you! You're alive! Gigot, look here, Purpose is with us!" Will shouted.

"I see, I see," Gigot responded. "Purpose, you're, you're…different!"

Purpose just stood there in wonderment. "Where have you been?"

Gigot and Will gave him a bear hug and Gigot scratched his own head and said, "Well, Purpose, it's great to see you," and Gigot looked over at Will sensing the Great One's power at hand. "Purpose, you're very important to Will and I and I personally want you to know that. But! You're not leading us, ok? We're in this together and we're going to walk this road together, even though you believe and we believe you know what you're doing. We were just given a little lesson up on the mount and we realized that we need to be following the Great One and not you."

"I know what I'm doing. Me and the Great One are like this," as Purpose showed them both two twisted fingers and his arms twisted about himself in order to get the message of oneness across to the two of them.

"Yes, I agree that you are, Purpose, but we can't be placing our trust in you, we have to trust in the Great One, not you. Nothing can be greater than the Great One, right, Purpose?" Gigot asked.

"Of course, Gigot," Purpose responded as he scrunched his eyebrows at the two of them in amazement. "I'm not the one with that problem… not following the Great One…that is. That might be your problem, but not mine."

Will looked at Gigot and Gigot looked at Will and they both looked at Purpose with his big bulging eyes and Will questioned, "What does that mean? You led us off the Lighted Pearl Path!"

Purpose's brand new clothes revealed that there was more to Purpose than they had imagined. He was different and even sounded different.

"Where did you get those clothes, Purpose?" Will inquired wincing at himself as soon as he asked the question for he might already know the answer to his question.

"You tell me, Will. Where do *you* think I got these clothes?" Purpose chuckled knowing they both knew the answer to the question. "Where is Faith and Truth?"

Will smirked out of the corner of his mouth and Gigot did the same, just out of the opposite corner of his.

Gigot spoke, "We left them by the Lighted Pearl Path to follow you."

Purpose raised his brow and asked, "Well, are we on the right road or are we someplace else?"

X

An Interlude

The moon set and the three of them rested by the way pausing to think through the moments before re-living the humiliation of Panic's failed attempt to crush their spirit. Breathing, simply breathing, encouraged them together to share what they had just escaped and what they had just discovered.

Epaga appeared and said, "Purpose is who he is…a gift from the Great One and is the way in which you will eventually win the battle for Crested Hill. Purpose will enable you, but Purpose is his Purpose and not yours. At no time should you seek to glorify Purpose as something as your own. Purpose is to be found in Him, His way. Most men look to a purpose for their work and their destiny and eventually their purpose becomes their guide and their god, so they fall away chasing after the idea of what they perceive their purpose is to them. This chasing reveals your inward desires to constantly seek direction from something tangible and identifiable. Oftentimes, walking with Obedience to the Great One seems to be too difficult because walking by sight seems to be far more illuminating than traveling with Faith."

Will and Gigot were discovering that their moments revealed their inward parts, what they're made of and the root to their fruit. They had not exemplified the truth of the matter and to their concern, they are correct in being concerned when they do not see what is supposed to be there, a fruit of the Great One. In some moments, they see a sprig from a fig of another tree unlike the Great One's Desire. The testing of their faith through opportunity allowed Panic to have his way and opened the door to Despair and his wares.

"How can this be, this way in us?" Gigot pondered and asked Epaga. Purpose remained silent as Gigot and Will pondered their failing on the Mount of the Altar of Isaac.

Epaga continued, "Unbelief comes cloaked in disobedience and will refute faith if it is willed to be. The voice of Unbelief comes as a thief in the night, blinding, cloaked in invisible ways. He is subtle as he distorts towards disobedience. Unbelief sneers in arrogant stay and if allowed will have his way in secret, or in the moments that arise before the eyes and the ayes with his conquering friends by his side, Panic, Despair, Lie and Deceit. They work in tandem and friends they are, to cheat and to steal life and love and to separate Faith from Truth. Weaker foes they are, but unbeknownst to most, they are seen and heard as the strong and the brave. They come in as quick as breath to take that which is not theirs to take, including the breath they ride in on."

Epaga continued, "Death guides their passage with reigns of fire brandishing their secrets kept in store, hiding and cloaking in invisibility worn. Leeches they are, all sucking the life and the breath from life itself. Clucking and poking and choking with all things seen and all things temporal, they seek to devour and destroy the ones who believe in unbelief. For even that is that an unequivocal thing, this believing unbelief, the destroyer of souls and the thief in the night. To catch a tail with a tale, a false one at that, a simple tune, an abbreviated lie meant to steal the word so aptly planted. Mere birds of prey they are as is told of old, to take what is not theirs so that what is not theirs cannot become what is His, but powerless souls in the way. Here lies the battle for men's souls in the way on the road, where the seed is sown in precarious ways. But as men think in precarious ways, the seed that is sown is not, but is very specific and not precarious at all. The seed of the Great One goes to all who will to receive and to those who will to believe. But know this…simply believing is not believing, but, believing is believing with all that is within you, leaving nothing to chance and leaving all to follow Him."

"Receive that which Will can believe or he can choose to allow the cares of what he thinks he sees to determine his fate; but fate is not fate at all, any more than seeing is believing. For how many are those who have seen what they've seen and heard what they've heard…discovering at the end, it was not what they thought they saw or what they thought they heard? Things are hardly what they seem."

"The will to receive and the will to believe excoriates the Panic in the way for Panic came this way by Unbelief, even to the ones who believe they believe. There is no Confusion now, nor Despair or Deceit in the will to believe in the Way. Gigot and Will, your eyes are focused. Discover, by the moonlight's beam, that the Great One is here and among you, with you and in you. It is what you will to believe with all that is within you and in that…the Great One's Purpose can work with you to get you on your way to where you should be in the each and every moment that you join as one."

And with that, Epaga concluded his being with them to allow them to to rest and see the words spoken in their spirit and he was no more.

XI

Humility's Song

Gigot, Will and Purpose rested by the way and woke to the most glorious song in the distance. The voice was the voice of one crying in the morning a song of gladness and joy, of adoration and praise. Refreshed, they sat up, hearing the music and as they looked at each other, a glib smile was on each of their faces. The smiles they bore were the smiles you would see on someone who is apprehended by what they do not know, but it's a good thing and their backs sat straight up and erect as if that would cause them to hear the melody better.

Jumping to their feet, they gathered their belongings as quickly as they could and scampered down the hillside through a trail that led them through tall maples and a grove of a variety of magnolias and myrtles all abloom. Azaleas covered the ground in swirls and the colors of fuchsia, bright and bold in their purplish regalia decorating the trunks of the maples. White azaleas appointed just so, so that the ground would not seem so bloody. White magnolia blossoms were blossoming, too, and the aroma of the blossoms filled the hillside with its own song of praise. The hill leveled off as the trail led them directly to the morning song that they all had awakened to.

There he was, singing, with a few others singing with him, joining in as one, none too loud and none too soft. The three were singing with one voice and yet from the distance they all thought it was only one voice. As they approached the three singing, they surmised that they might be interrupting the singers, but soon realized they had not…and stood amazed among them that they could not interrupt them. The three singers were focused, more focused than imaginable in their song as a warrior would be on the battlefield. They sang the song that had been given them. It was a song of praise and adoration to the Great One:

BLESSED BE TO THE GREAT ONE, THE LORD MOST HIGH AND TO THE LAMB THAT WAS SLAIN.
BLESSED BE TO THE GREAT ONE, THE LORD ON HIGH WHO REIGNS FOREVER AND EVER.
BLESSED BE TO THE GREAT ONE, THE LORD MOST HIGH WHO CONQUERS ALL WITHIN,
BLESSED BE TO THE GREAT ONE, THE LORD MOST HIGH WHO REIGNS FOREVER AND EVER!

With one voice they sang the melody and with one focus the three breathed together to sing the song once more. Gigot, Will and Purpose sat upon the nearby rocks and listened until they joined in one with the three singers. As they sang together, all six voices got louder in unison and they came together to form a sort of circle with arms over each other's shoulders. The three did not know the other three, but the other three knew the three as their voices sang above the trees the glad song of praise and adoration to the Great One.

All at once, they ceased to sing for each one knew it was time to cease. Smiles were on each face as they greeted one another and introduced themselves with arm shakes and the clasping of shoulders to and fro. They were six soldiers of sorts with very different looks and temperaments, but they perceived their unity as one. Humility was the first to speak to introduce Obedience to his left and Suffering to his right.

"Greetings, this is Obedience," as Humility spoke, he offered his hand to his left and then his hand to his right, "and this is Suffering. We know you three, Gigot, Will and Purpose. I am Humility."

He smiled his smile with a wincing face as though he were about to say something else, but did not. He breathed deeply and with an erect back, corrected his neck with a grin and said, "What say you, this day of reckoning?"

Gigot looked straight forward into his grinning face and said, "This day of reckoning?"

Will and Purpose straightened their backs as well as Humility had as though they were braced for the unknown and they stood there in their moments realizing that in all that they had gone through, it seemed that Humility, Obedience and Suffering had been there with them the entire journey.

"You were with us?" Will inquired of Humility as he perused the three.

"We are as we have always been," Obedience stated.

A tad bit confused, Gigot spoke in his honesty and said, "So, you three have been with us the entire journey?"

"Even as the Great One insists as He is as well, we are here as we have always been," Suffering conceded what he knew to be right and true.

Gigot breathed heavily as he was realizing exactly what 'this day of reckoning' might be and then he thought back to a time when he was visiting his mother and afterwards he would go to the open meadow where the others would come and rest and eat a meal. It was a time when he believed he had done what he could and could do no more and then he would buy his lunch and eat in the meadow with the others as they ate theirs not knowing them and them not knowing him or what he had been doing and feeling as he thought about the time with his mother and then she was no more.

He looked around himself and realized he was standing in the meadow in the moment, yet this time there were no others to eat his lunch with and the azaleas were here, but not there, and they were all in bloom as blood on the ground.

Humility spoke, "You remember?"

"Yes…yes, I do. Are we here? Or, there? Is this the place?" Gigot inquired.

Obedience placed his hand on his shoulder and Gigot shuttered in the lost memory of a time long ago when there was still a chance to see and hear his mother's voice and then she would drift away in sleep. Gigot could see that there was nothing truer than true than what lie within the memory of a love gone by and a desire for the more once again. He breathed as tears came to his eyes and Suffering, who was standing on his left, placed his hand on his shoulder in comfort and with the same tears as Gigot, he wept with him on his day of reckoning.

Gigot could not stand for Will had succumbed as well. He fell to the ground on his knees as Obedience and Suffering took their charge over him.

Humility looked at Purpose and said, "You are beginning to understand, aren't you? You have to do what you were told to do."

"I know, I understand now, I agree," Purpose said intently understanding now what it was he had to do and could no longer be the ambivalent spirit that he had been before.

"Your agreement must be enacted continually now, Purpose, for you are not your own, you and the Great One must walk together." Humility continued.

As Gigot and Will kneeled together, they looked up at Purpose and Humility with a gaze of comprehension that they had not had before. They realized that they could not follow Purpose, but follow the Great One with Purpose by their side. The Great One was real and true and no thing and no one could ever take the place of the Great One in their lives. Purpose was a way for the Great One to be exemplified and glorified, but they would never find any Glory in Purpose for that always leads to Significance's rise. All Glory belongs to the Great One.

Humility spoke tenderly and said, "Now you are beginning to see why Purpose had to be sacrificed in order to live. Purpose has to dwell with Obedience and Suffering for they are one. You do not have the one without the other. The Great One has chosen it to be this way and we all agree. There are those who elevate the Purpose that they know as their god and they believe that the Purpose that they know to reign supremely in their lives, but not you and not here. There is only one Great One and He is the Most High. It is He who will direct your paths, not Purpose. Purpose is your friend and a great friend, indeed, even as we are."

"We have much to learn," Will spoke up, gathering himself with Gigot and straightening themselves and their swords.

"Do you remember Humility's song that you heard in the distance as you awoke from your rest?" Suffering asked. "Blessed be to the Lord Most High and to the Lamb that was slain…" he repeated in their ears so that it stuck this time in remembrance.

"I have it and agree," Purpose said, "All Honor and Glory belong to Him, the Lord Most High and to the Lamb that was slain. There is One God. The Lord, our God is One and we shall have no other gods before us."

"We all agree," Will and Obedience said together and smiled their smiles of concurrence.

"Gigot, you lead onward, we are by your side the rest of the way," Humility said. They all reassured one another walking through the azaleas in bloom and with the fragrance and magnificence of magnolia in the air. The air was full of His Glory.

XII

Listening to the Right Voice

Gigot led on in the bright sunshine as they could all see Crested Hill in the not so distant distance. The mountain was clearer to see as in their approach they recognized that the closer they got to Crested Hill, the more it lost its foreboding cloudiness. Seemingly, they were figuring out that with each setting of the moon, they found themselves getting ever closer to the mountain and the mountain appeared to be getting clearer in height as well. At this point in the journey, it was as though they were going down a slowly decreasing and declining plateau for their struggle was lighter and the distractions fewer.

It is not to say that the mountain did not have its darkness surrounding parts of it, for it did, but what they could make of it was that things were getting easier and freer. But, was the reasoning for that rationale partially because there were six of them now walking together as one? There is hardly a much more enjoyable thing than agreeable friendship, particularly when the friendship has such overwhelming commonality.

There were two friends missing, however, and those being their highly favored horses of Truth and Faith. Gigot and Will had left Truth and Faith behind when they had gotten off of their horses and followed Purpose through the thicket. They had so lost their focus in following Purpose, they had actually forgotten about Truth and Faith left by the edge of the thicket. As the six of them were journeying along on foot in the bright sunshine, the thought occurred to Gigot and Will at the same time and they stopped, looked at each other, turned around with a gasp of their mistake and saw Humility, Suffering and Obedience standing there behind them with the most sly of faces not really desiring to say, "We know what you've done." So, the three of them remained quiet and allowed the revelation to sink into Gigot and Will as even the two of them were becoming more in tune with one another.

Purpose had taken a few more steps forward, stopped abruptly, and when he noticed that no one was with him, he turned around at the five and said, "What?"

All at once, four of the five sighed, folded their arms, tilted their heads in a maturing fashion and started shaking their heads back and forth as if to say, "Here you go again, Purpose, leading the way without knowing the way to begin with." This was with the exception of Humility who had a look of disappointment and really stood out among the rest for when Purpose looked into Humility's eyes, he saw his undoing once again, dropped his head and trudged back to the pack behind Gigot and Will.

"What are you all thinking about? You all know something that I don't, what is it?" Purpose inquired rather humiliated in his ignorance.

"Purpose, you simply cannot get ahead of us, particularly Gigot. Gigot has to listen to the Great One and he is the only one who can. We have been made in the Great One's image, but the Great One has chosen it to be this way. Yes, we all have our traits and jobs to do, but we have chosen to submit to the Great One by submitting to Gigot." Humility calmly spoke to Purpose to get the attention placed into the right place.

"But I can hear the Voice of the Great One as well. He tells me what to do and I do it. He has made me more than capable and I know beyond the shadow of a doubt that I am made in His image and He tells me what to do and I obey." Purpose implored, defending his position and perceived ranking within the group.

"We all have our parts to play Purpose," Suffering interjected, "but when anyone of us gets out of line, I am called to the forefront and I don't think you realize that just yet."

Obedience stood there with his arms crossed and an intimidating demeanor and Purpose wasn't going to get any agreement out of him. Purpose shrugged and said disparagingly, "Then, what am I good for? I know that I've been doubtful and dubious at times, but I've also been enlightening and have earned my keep by going out and making something out of nothing!"

"Purpose, you are important to all of us, but have you stopped to think about how you came to be Purpose out of Ambivalence?" Will asked.

"Stop to think!? That's what I do, that's a big part of my responsibility, why that's why we're here right now…in this place…because of me!" Purpose retorted getting loud.

"Stop and think, Purpose," Gigot said, "listen to Will's question again, how did you come to be Purpose out of Ambivalence?"

At that moment, Purpose paused and thought back to his moment of transformation and realized that Truth and Faith were there speaking to him of who he was and who he was to become and without them, he would still be Ambivalent living in Middletown without a right to do or say anything. The light came on and Purpose exclaimed, "Truth and Faith, where are they? Where are Truth and Faith?"

"We had to leave them behind just outside the thicket you led us into just off the trail of the Lighted Pearls," Gigot responded.

Purpose breathed a deep sigh and with saddening eyes, he looked at each of the men in the eyes and said, "What have I done?" Ashamed of his new found revelation, Purpose looked to his left and saw Pride leaving in the wind along with his closest ally, Significance.

"So I'm the reason why we are where we are…right now…in this place," Purpose said again, but this time, he said it with the revelation of the meaning of it and the ultimate responsibility for his own actions apart from it. Purpose was evidently becoming aware of his role and responsibility on this road to the Crested Hill and he wasn't what he thought himself to be.

"Gigot, do you see that Purpose cannot be your guide and he cannot be controlling you?" Humility asked quietly before them all. "A man without purpose is a lost man, but a man's purpose is no more to be his guide than his god. Will, you have to see that. You're partially responsible here for allowing this to happen. The Spirit speaks to Gigot and Gigot speaks to Will and Will tells Purpose what to do and Purpose does his thing according to his gifting. Purpose is a gift, yes, we all agree, but he is not THE gift, is he?" Humility spoke, teaching well the ways of the Great One.

"I agree," Obedience concurred in his deep voice in a rather matter of fact kind of way.

"Purpose cannot direct and lead because ultimately what you allow to direct and lead you becomes your controller and whatever a man allows to control him, he then becomes the servant to. It has been evidenced that although Purpose has been given power in what he does, he does not dwell within that power as if he is the creator of it. The source of Purpose is the Great One, even he knows that and has told you that himself, but it is too easy for you to allow that which works well to do the work itself and that

96

was never its intention. Unguided purpose leads to an alternative; it may be good, but not the best or the right and it will never be the set intention. Men dwell on their gifts and talents to see them through and then depend on the gifts and the talents as a part of themselves setting themselves up as the alternative to the Great One Himself. It is not to be," Humility spoke finishing his teaching on the matter.

As they had been walking along, they came to a deep crevice where the depth was deep and the across was wide. In the far off distance beyond the great divide, they saw two horses grazing in the green...Faith and Truth. They had managed to stay on the right trail to where everyone was supposed to be going.

"We have reached the Crevice of Mum's Deep," Obedience stated with gloom. "We're not going to be able to cross here at all and it's impossible to climb down into the Deep and too dangerous at that. We'll have to go to the edge of the Carb to the left and cross over from there."

The Carb was far off and many miles to travel. There was talk of a natural bridge one could work towards to get over the Crevice where the Crevice was not as deep and the land was green. The Crevice was hewn from a quake many moons ago and therein lie the waste of what was "not meant to be" and the "should not's" and the "better not be's". It seemed as though these creatures of the Crevice had been around for generations for they had inhabited other Crevices of moons gone by. These were the Dark Ones serving the Darkness that draw a man under into the wasteful devices. Why these Dark Ones in the Crevices of Mum's Deep were here, only the Great One knew for certain. They had been allowed to go in and out of the Hallowed Places and until Gigot, Will and the rest of them retook the Crested Hill and determined them to be gone, they all would remain to spread their Dark cancer for many days to come.

THE CREVICE OF DARKNESS
CREVICE OF MUM'S DEEP
TAVERN IN THE MOUNTAINS
THE LAND OF I DON'T KNOW
MOUNTAIN STREAM
JUNGLE OF OPHIS
BATTLING TREES
VILLAGE OF GRUDGEON
VILLAGE OF GUINEA
VILLAGE OF INHIBITION
TUNNELS OF DARKNESS
WHITE CHAPEL
VILLAGE OF GOING THROUGH
SPECTO'S CABIN
FRYING PAN
CALUMNIA'S CALL
PLAIN OF SPRING
CREEPHOLE FOREST
HEDGELING VILLAGE
ALTER OF ISAAC
LIGHTED PEARL PATH
MOUNT BEREFT
TRAIL OF LIGHTED PEARLS
BANKER'S TOWN
HALFWAY BLVD
MIDDLE TOWN
THICKET OF BEREFT
THICKET OF AMBIVALENCE
LAKE OF SINKING SAND

Section Two – The Villages by The Crevice of Mum's Deep

XIII

The Village of Going Through

There was nothing easy about this journey and the rest of the way the Crevice of Mum's Deep was to their right and a rising plateau to their left. They believed that as long as they walked along the craggy rock trail, they would eventually get to the Carb where there was no crevice. It was appearing to Gigot and Will that the detour of following Purpose off of the Lighted Pearl Path was indeed a regretful one. They apparently had gone too far right out of the Way towards the Crevice unnecessarily. Now the journey was to go too far left along the Crevice Highway, otherwise known as the Darkend Road, through the Crevice Villages in order to get back to where they should have been able to cross over in the first place.

Suffering spoke up and said, "I've been through these Villages by the Crevice many moons ago and it's disappointing that we have to make this journey all over again."

Gigot and Will were learning to listen well to Suffering and realized that if Suffering had been through these Villages, then it could be possible they had as well and did not necessarily desire to go where Suffering had been. Gigot and Will listened intently to Suffering as he spoke about the differences in the Villages, but they also had a few things in common as all of the villages were fed by the same water that was drawn from the Crevice of Mum's Deep. The water was quite toxic and Suffering told them all not to drink any of the water along the way because it would take them to a sickness that would cloud the Crested Hill even further.

"The water is one of the key common denominators in all these differing Villages that we'll have to pass through. Don't drink any of it," Suffering demanded.

The Darkend Road was filled with craggy rock, mixed with patches of soft grass worn with time and energy of travelers attempting to keep away from the debilitating pain that walking on craggy rock can do to the feet and ankles. As they made their way along the trail, they seemed to be dancing in a way as the patches of soft grass apparently was placed there by jig to give the slightest bit of comfort along the undesirable path.

It was not long that they entered the first of the Villages by the Crevice of Mum's Deep; it was the Village of Going Through. No one seemed to be on the streets paved with smooth brick and there was no bustling along the thoroughfares, all lined with brick and stone houses and shops with colorful signs signifying the types of shops and how these villagers kept their living. There was quite the commotion and cheering that was coming from what seemed to be the town square.

"Are you here for the concert?" one pretty maiden asked excitedly. "If you're here for the concert, where's your satchel? I have my satchel. Everyone's supposed to bring their satchel. I have mine, where's yours? Are you going to the concert?" She said excitedly, repeating herself over and over again.

She didn't wait for an answer; she was too excited to get to the concert.

She was a very cute girl, but with strong muscular arms and the closer the group got to the center of town, the more they saw that the rest of the town were dressed much the same. The maidens dressed in their dresses that were of varied, bright colors, long and flowing with long sleeves whose cuffs seem to be able to fit a horse leg. The men dressed in semi-formal regalia with frocks and frills made to impress. The whole village was of old brick and thatch roofs, of sorts, and everyone was carrying a very heavy satchel filled with whatever it was filled with and they all had very strong and muscular arms…some more than others, as a result of carrying these satchels everywhere they went. The thick, musty smell of all things old permeated the town. Gigot and his men began to think it must be them in close quarters among the buildings, but the closer they got to the rest of the villagers, the more they realized that the villagers' clothes didn't just look old, they smelled old, too. It was as though no one had taken a bath in some time and they had never washed their clothes.

The villagers were all too excited to recognize the visitors as Gigot, Will and the others waded their way through towards the front of the vaporous crowd to see exactly what all the excitement was about. Everyone was bubbling with cheer and talking wildly in their anticipation of the guest singer that was to arrive at just any moment. Curious looks were sent by the ones who did notice Gigot and his cohorts for three simple reasons. They were not dressed as the others, they did not have huge muscular arms as the others and they carried swords and backpacks and not side satchels as all of the villagers did in solidarity.

In no time, did the band begin to play the entrance tune and the singer ran onto the stage, dressed to the hilt in a formal tuxedo, of sorts, for it was of a vintage from many moons gone by. He was smiling from ear to ear and everyone cheered for the guest singer as the band played on their favorite tune. The singer surprised Gigot and Will, for before he grabbed a hollow log to amplify his voice, he placed two satchels by his side. Both satchels were filled to the brim as he could not even buckle the satchels notches to clamp them shut. All of the people cheered and were enamored with this guy as he proudly flexed his gargantuan arms as though he were a contender in a muscle contest. He posed and posed, flexing his muscular torso and the buttons on his tuxedo jacket burst from the exhilaration and the odor that exhumed from his body was beyond incredible. The crowd was in a frenzy, yet he had not even sang a note. The band played louder than before and he picked up his two satchels and held them up high for all to see. That was too much for the crowd as the females swooned and the men, energized from his seemingly heroic deed, began picking up their own satchels in unison along with him.

He placed the two satchels down again and with one hand grabbed the megaphone and with the other hand, he shushed the crowd to silence.

"Now, now I know that you have come here to hear me sing, but you got ta' know what I do when I sing. You jus' got ta' know what I do when I sing," he said with a cry in his voice.

The women were continuing to swoon and fall around where they stood, but none of them passed out, it just seemed that that was what they did, in a very pretentious sort of way.

The singer had a very dark complexion as his skin was rough and worn from age and all the things he had gone through in his life. His face looked burnt, like the color of burnt toast…almost black. As he spoke, he spoke with an overwhelming sense of authority and as he was speaking, the band's playing was down to a whimper and the band members were pulling out dirty white cloths from their pockets, preparing for what was coming next. Gigot, Will and the rest did not have the faintest clue what was about to happen…except for Suffering, he had seen all of this before.

Obedience believed he had as well as his eyebrows began to scrunch in with a tad bit of trepidation of what was about to occur.

"You all know why I'm here, don' cha'?" the singer said. So far, he had not sung, but flexed and flexed his arms and torso and now that he was speaking, it seemed that his speaking was what they had come to hear as they leaned towards him with every word he spoke.

"I tell ya', I've been through! And I'm here to tell ya', I'm still going through!" he shouted, shaking his head back and forth and smiling as if he had not exactly said all that he was going to say.

All of the villagers erupted and raised their satchels in adoration of the singer who was going through. Gigot and Will just chuckled at each other because this guy was very much the entertainer and even he had not said much, he held the villagers in the palm of his hand.

"You know what I've gone through because I've been here before," he said, as he was interrupted with cheers and shouts of agreement and "Amen!" throughout the vibrant crowd.

One of the villagers shouted, "Tell iiit! Tell iiiit!" as he raised his strong arms in glee and the under arm odor made Will sneeze and his eyes water.

"Now, now, now, I am going to tell it, but I'm not just going to tell it… I've brought sometin' to show you all today that's gonna blow yo minds away!" he tailed off with a cry in his voice.

"Bring dat udder satchel out 'chere!" he exclaimed, as the Mayor of the village managed to make his way towards the front. The Mayor was sliding and pulling and pushing this huge satchel that was so filled with whatever it was filled with, he couldn't manage to pick it up. Mind you, the Mayor was no soft villager, for his muscles were the biggest in the village and yet, he could not lift this satchel an inch off of the platform.

The crowd was mesmerized by the size of the satchel for it dwarfed the two satchels he brought on stage. He slowly glided towards the heavy satchel that lie upon the platform and he teased the crowd with leaning towards the satchel over and over again, then quickly standing erect each time he leaned towards the satchel. The satchel was twice the size of any satchel seen in the land and no man in the village could imagine picking it up. It was a veritable treasure chest of weight beyond their comprehension.

By this time, Gigot and Will were mesmerized themselves as to how this so called singer, was going to pick up this huge satchel, which was actually his third…most of the villagers only had one.

Someone in the crowd yelled, "Pick it up, pick it uuup!" He looked around at his fellow villagers wanting them to chime in along with him encouraging the singer to pick up the tremendously laden satchel.

The singer just winced and smiled his big smile and said, "I done told ya' that I've been through, right?" he asked.

The crowd responded in respect nodding their heads up and down in agreement.

"And I done told ya' that I'm still going through, didn't I?" he said.

"Yes!" "Yes, yes, yes!" they all responded in unison, still nodding their heads up and down in agreement. Anticipating his next words, they all leaned forward in anticipation of what he was about to do.

"Well, now's the time," he said as a quiet stir came over the crowd. Only a soft drum roll was playing by now, preparing the crowd for the next exciting feat.

He walked over to the tremendous satchel, all filled and heavy laden with whatever he had put in it and he squatted before the satchel and placed both hands on the handles. With a hush and an ooh from the crowd, he slowly and surely picked the satchel up with both of this mighty, strong arms. He lifted the satchel to his thighs and then he lifted it to this waist and then he lifted it to his chest and then with one swift jerk, he threw the heavy satchel into the air and caught it from beneath lifting the heavy satchel above his head. The crowd went beserk! They were furiously out of control and in a frenzy that the likes Gigot and Will had only seen in a few places. Everyone was dancing and shouting and picking up their satchels and throwing them in the air. The men were dancing with the women in jigs and jaunts in circles and cheers.

The singer shoved the huge satchel to his left shoulder and let it rest there as he asked for the head servant of the village to bring him the megaphone. When the villager complied and gave him the megaphone, the singer sang these words, "I'mma goin' through, yes, I'mma goin' through. I's got my journey and I'mma goin' through. I'mma goin' through, yes I'mma goin' through. I's got my journey and I'mma goin' through."

He said, "You all know what I've been through all my life, 'cause its right here before ya'. But I's wants ya' to know! I sa-id, I's wants ye to know…that I'm still goin' through. No, no, I ain't overcome nuttin'. I'mma still goin' through!"

The crowd was spell bound by his words and fell down and worshipped him. They knew they were still going through, too, as they carried their satchels of everything they'd ever done in their lives in their worn out satchels. They carried what they carried everywhere they went.

Someone from the crowd shouted, "We're still goin' through, too." Another one chimed in with a cry in her voice, "Yes, yes, I am, too."

Other villagers from the crowd shook and nodded their heads together in agreement that they all, for certain, as one, were all going through something and were glad for it.

The singer, glancing over the cheering crowd, noticed Gigot, Will and the others and that they were quite different from the villagers who had strong arms and carried their own satchels of all that they had gone through all of their lives.

"Hey, hey, hey…I notice that you have some strangers here among you," the singer spoke of Gigot, Will and the others. He pointed his fingers at them and shook his head in disgust, saying,

"Dey act like dey ain't got no past, don't dey?" he inquired of the crowd. The crowd looked fearful and dismayed and sullen all at the same time looking intently at Gigot's group with pierced eyes of disgust and shame.

"I see dat dey don't gots dey's satchels of da' past wid dem, yet all my peoples got dey's satchel of de past wid dem, don't dey?" he inquired again of the crowd desiring agreement. "Why, I bet if ye askt dem if dey gots any past at all, deyed say dey ain't got none, no, none, at all. But, I'm here to tell ya', I do! Dat's right! I gots a past in my present. Why, I'm still going through!" he screamed, raising his muscle bound arms into the air and bringing the attention back to himself and away from the visitors.

The crowd broke out in cheers once again and the band started playing a rousing number that stirred the crowd to higher heights. Humility and Suffering grabbed Gigot and Will and said, "Follow Obedience, we need to get out of here…now!"

Obedience took the lead as Gigot, Will and the others followed him through the roaring crowd who had become quite warlike in their spirit.

The group sensed that if they didn't get out of there quick, it might be the end of them. The crowd was pressing forward towards the platform as the singer rushed off the back of the stage with his three satchels. He didn't want anyone touching his stuff because it was his and he was proud of it. He rather enjoyed showing off his past and relished in the thought of collecting more mess so that he could profess at every concert how just how much mess he had and continued to go through.

Gigot, Will and the others pressed through the crowd as openings would allow and by the time they had gotten to the center of town square, they came to a tall statue of a woman that had the look and smell of…salt. The statue itself was a tremendous one at that, more than three times the size of any human and it was all made of the most hardened grains of salt known in those parts. The inscription that described the village heroin read as such:

Here stands the heroin of all heroins. She is the one woman who refused to give up and never forget where she came from. Her Majesty…Lot's Wife! The testimony of her life and death remains with us today that we should never forget where we have been, never forget all that we have done and to always wear it well!

The tops of her feet were worn smooth from the villagers running their hands over her salty feet in honor of her being their standard of always looking back and never being completely delivered from anything.

Beside the statue was an open grave-pit whose tombstone read:

Never bury what you can carry

Never let anything die

Never forgive and never, ever forget!

XIV

The Village of Inhibition

Obedience led them through the opposite alleyway of the platform and in no time they were out of sight of the villagers. They continued running as fast as they could through the alleyway as it quickly came to an abrupt end. There, they found themselves on the outskirts of the town, back on the craggy Darkend Road leading to another village off in the distance. Not much was said in their escape from Going Through. The trail leading from Going Through to the next village had tall grass as though there hadn't been much traffic on this road for some time.

The sensation of being stuck in Going Through was very much like the idea of their clothes that seemed to have the fragrance, or odor of an old, musty smell of the kind of things that had been lying around way too long and needed to be burned. They all had brushed against so many of the villagers that they smelled the village on their clothing. Purpose began to sneeze from the odor of the village as though he were allergic to the smell of stagnant musk. Each time he sneezed, he held his arm to his nose and face and each time he held his arm to his nose and face, he sneezed from the musk on his arm. His sneezing became quite uncontrolled and he fell to the roadside in a fit of sneezing and getting red-faced in the process.

The group stopped as Suffering pulled out a white handkerchief from his pack, handing it to Purpose and said, "Hold this to your face and you should be all right."

Purpose took the handkerchief and did as Suffering said and held the handkerchief to his face and his sneezing abruptly stopped. He breathed in deeply, thinking he was about to sneeze again, but didn't.

"Thank you," Purpose said to Suffering. "I guess I just couldn't quite handle the odor of the village. Why do they do as they do, not washing their clothes and all? They were kind of stuck in who they were, weren't they? I can't do that…I have to keep moving."

"We all do," Obedience said, "Now, get up, we need to keep going and moving forward. These villages don't have anything we need, do not touch what touches you, nor embrace the thought, learn to say, 'No'."

After managing to get everyone together going in the same direction, Gigot, Suffering and Will continued on up ahead to the entrance of the Village of Inhibition. The three stood before the huge cast iron gates. The name of the village was in iron draped atop the gates that were locked with a gargantuan iron lock that had rusted over the thought of anyone passing through the gates would have been quite ludicrous. The gates were twenty feet tall and each gate, the left and the right, was ten feet wide as they met in the middle. Brilliant limestone columns bolstered the entrance and held up the gates with a sense of elegance and power. A very strange thing about this entrance, though, was even though there was this most elegant and powerful rod iron gated entrance, there were no fences attached to the gated entrance. As they stood before the gate, they observed a foreboding darkness hovering over the village up ahead.

There were limestone columns on each side of the gates and each side, the left and the right, had stone walls that went out ten feet with a tall wooden door in the middle. Each side, the left and the right looked the same.

As Gigot, Suffering and Will stood at the iron gates, Will tugged on the lock and chain that guarded the gates and as he tugged on the lock, a voice from the right, over behind the wooden door, shouted,

"Who goes there, speak your name and your business and be gone!"

The gate guard was standing behind the wooden door to the right as another guard was standing behind the wooden door to the left. Will let go of the lock and it clanged on the gate of iron and at the sound of the clang, the guard on the left stated the same thing, "Who goes there? Speak your name and your business and be gone!"

At this point, the rest of the group had arrived as they all could hear the two guards behind the doors. Being that there was an end to each of the stone walls, Purpose walked around the right wall and saw the guard standing behind the closed door, frightened at the prospect of who might be standing at the locked gate.

The right guard shouted once again with his face firmly planted into the door-jam opening, "I demand you tell us, who goes there? State your name and your business and be gone with you!"

By this time, only Gigot and Suffering stood before the locked gate and the rest of the group divided and some went to the left of the stone wall and the others followed Purpose around the right side of the wall. Purpose placed his forefinger to his mouth to tell the others to remain quiet and they were standing there on the other side of the wall unbeknownst to the two guards who, at by this time were not only frightened at who might be on the other side of the gate, but were getting frustrated that no one had said anything.

Gigot shouted, "I am Gigot and this is Suffering. We come in peace. We mean you no harm!"

Purpose and the others observed the uneasiness of the guards from where they stood as each of the guards stepped back from facing the back of the doors and leaned around to look at each other on how to proceed. The moment they stepped back to look at each other, they each saw the visitors standing behind the other. Purpose and Obedience on the one side and Will and Humility were on the other. The two teams of visitors more than startled the two guards as the guards each grasped the shaft of the their spears and, in fear, fell back towards their respective doors and shouted in unison,

"How did you get here? The gates are locked!"

Will and Purpose both raised their hands in peace and surrender as they were equally startled by the guards' lack of common sense in that all they had to do was walk around the wall to get to where they were, but the guards repeated themselves saying,

"How did you get here, the gates are locked and we did not give you permission to enter!"

Suffering had walked around the one side and Gigot had walked around to the other and as the each side of the visitors went from two three, the guards became increasingly frightened and the one on the right cringed in fright and begged for his life from the visitors.

"Do not harm us, we mean you no harm, please leave! We give up, please do not harm us," and they each began to cry on their knees in fear.

Suffering lent his hand to the one guard and said, "You know me, we mean you no harm. Look at me."

The frightened guard wiped the tears from his face and with a great amount of trepidation, lifted his eyes to the visitor who spoke and with tears in his eyes said, "It's you, it's you, Suffering! Look General, it's Suffering!" He composed himself and stood up to hug Suffering.

"I remember you, look General," he spoke and got out of the way so that the General could welcome Suffering once again to his village.

"Welcome, Suffering," the General gladly spoke welcoming Suffering with a hearty clasp of his arm and then a manly embrace. "Welcome, indeed! Tell me, how did you get here? It's been so long since you've been here, it seems like yesterday."

Suffering breathed in and held back a response, but opened his arms to the showing of his friends and said, "General, we mean you no harm, we only mean to travel through your village in order to get to the Carb to cross over to the other side to Crested Hill."

"Crested Hill! Why, Crested Hill! My, my my!" he smiled and looked at his lieutenant, "They're going to Crested Hill, but why? Nothing can be done about Crested Hill. It's been taken over and nothing, not a thing can done about it," he said over and over again.

"Why, it's so good to see you, Suffering, isn't it, Lieutenant?" he said as he grasped Suffering's arm once again in joy. "We have always welcomed Suffering here in Inhibition, we just love us some Suffering, don't we Lieutenant?" as he hugged Suffering tightly to his chest.

"We sure do, General! But who do we have here? Who are all your friends, Suffering, are they just like you?" the lieutenant had let go of his spear and placed his hands on his belt and was twisting about with even more joy than the General. The lieutenant began to shake each arm of the visitors and had obviously let go of his fear and his questioning of how they had gotten to that point on his side of the gate.

Purpose piped up, "Uh, Suffering, don't we need to be going?"

Obedience stepped on Purpose's boot with a grimace and Suffering said, "Now, Purpose we don't want to be rude to the General, this is his town and we are always guests passing through."

"Oh, you could never be rude to me, Suffering, you're always welcome here in Inhibition. Just keep walking down the trail and you'll get there soon enough," the General kindly spoke in grace and said, "Now you boys keep on going down that road and say hello to everybody you meet. We're going to stay right here and guard this gate. Lieutenant, we need to figure out how they got around to our side of the gate, ya hear? I'll let you figure that one out for us both."

The General just smiled his smile and beckoned the visitors along their way towards the Village of Inhibition.

"Bye, bye, now!" the General said as he turned to see his lieutenant with his hand to his chin, looking at the gate, pondering how those visitors got to the other side with the gate locked and the doors shut tight.

It took no time to enter into the Village of Inhibition. All of the town's people were much ado about everything. Everyone had something to do, but most were cleaning. People were cleaning the windows, the door fronts, the shutters on the shops and the homes. There were those who were sweeping the streets with wide brooms and no one spoke to the visitors. One by one, one person would stop and lean over to whisper to another and then that person would stop what they were doing to go and whisper to another.

"Failures they are, all failures as one," each one would say as Gigot and his group of visitors walked by. More whispering began to occur as it seemed that the first one who said what he said was, "Failures they are, all failures as one." This was being repeated over and over as each person who looked at the visitors would share the same mantra. What was even stranger about the village was the way they communicated and that was when they would speak, their tongues would protrude from the mouths and their tongues would wag in their neighbor's ear.

"Failures they are, all failures as one!" they continued to wag into their neighbors' ears. "They must be from the other village," one would say and still another would say, "They're from Grudge. Oh, no, they're from Going Through!" and the one would laugh as his tongue would way in the wind.

Still others would wag their tongues and whisper, "They're not from here, no, they're not us, they're failures they are, all failures as one."

Gigot and Will continued to follow Suffering and Obedience through the town as more of the villagers would lean on their brooms and whisper and gawk, not speaking a word to the visitors as they walked. The town was bustling and they brustled as they bristled at the visitors walking through their town. They wondered in wonder for what reason these visitors were visiting their fare village. Cleaning and more cleaning they all seemed to do, but as the visitors walked by, they'd stop and waggle a whisper, not knowing who they were.

By the time, Gigot, Will and all got to the center of town, they were stopped by an entourage of more than a few. These were well spoken, the only well-spoken few…or so they believed. The leader confronted the crew and stopped them in their tracks, "It's us against you and what shall you do? Will you stop and gander or are you just passing through?"

"We're going through, but we're not from Going Through. We've just been there and we just went through," said Purpose with quite an inquisitive look on his face as he didn't really know where that came from.

"People from Going Through do not do what you do, if what you say is true," said the Leader who was choking to say what he said. The rest of his squad just stood behind him, as a group, all fearful of confronting the visitors.

Will placed his hand on the shaft of his sword and someone in the crowd said, "Oh, my, what shall we do?" and then ran back to his broom and briskly brushed the street clean as fast as he could move.

Suffering spoke and the others listened, "Please let us pass, we mean you no harm. It is true we are just passing through and at that, it will be soon. There's no need to be afraid, for we mean you no harm, just let us go and we'll return no more to you."

The leader turned to his flock with rags in their hands, all busy they were, a tight cleaning band. Their busyness pleased his eyes and he turned to Gigot and gave him this reply, "All failures you are, all failures as one, we've been told what you are and it can't be undone. We're clean you can see, all clean as can be. Leave our town for we're troubled that you're here. We'll look the other way as you bring us no cheer."

The villagers had surrounded them with their brooms and their rags. With whispers, they spoke with their tongues all a-wag. Inhibited they were 'til they had something to say, something like gossip or something to sway. In their whispers, they whispered and whispered all day, afraid to speak up, afraid of the day. They parted as one and let them go through, but whispered and wagged, their tongues all a brew.

Humility stopped in the middle of the crowd for he had something to say. It was his peace to give them that day. He waved his arm high and to silence they went. The cleaning all ceased and the whispers were spent. The whispers ceased as Humility spoke, in tenderness he said and said with a choke, "Dear people you need an encouraging word, a word of truth and a word of faith. Don't be alarmed, we mean you no harm. This day you can cease from your endless way. It's your endless talk and the wagging of tongues; this gossip of others and the mean spirited throng. You don't have to be so into yourselves, let go and let live the Truth is the way."

The crowd was silent, as silent as could be. Not a drop of a whisper, it was a though they could see. All at once they turned to the other's close ear. They whispered and whispered and wagged with their fear.

Humility shrugged and said, "What's the use? It's the clamor, the toil, the state of abuse. Let's take our leave of this inhibited place, a moment of silence, without any grace. The inhibited heart all a feared and a flutter, their refusal to change in grief they do shutter. The gossip and whispers take the place of the truth; where if they would see, they'd be delivered from gloom."

The villagers were so busy tending to their whispers and wagging their tongues that the visitors made their way out of town without any fanfare or good-byes.

XV

The Village of Guinea

The team of six, learning to move as a team of one, escaped as a vapor from the Village of Inhibition. The villagers had become even more preoccupied with their whispers. Their whispers were strong in the gloomy town, but as they walked further away, the whispers drew to a faint sound and eventually to no noise at all.

"How much more of this nonsense?" Will questioned in frustration as he looked over to Suffering.

"This nonsense has been around as long as I have. Why do you think I am here? I'm not here only in the present, but am sent as one who has reckoned with these things as they have been allowed." Suffering responded.

"You may not have been aware of Suffering's presence, Will, but he is here as he has been and only now you see through eyes that reveal what has been for a very long time," Obedience commented. "You have seen me come and you have seen me go, but that is not as it should have been."

Will huffed and realized that he was hearing the truth as it had been with him and Gigot all along and what they were seeing and going through was what they had seen and gone through, but now with the eyes that truly see. They were not as they had been, but were being shown those things nonetheless.

"How many times do you believe that I have been present and it was as a result of my own doing?" Obedience queried.

"What do you mean?" Gigot asked as they continued walking the craggy trail to the Village of Guinea.

"I am a choice on whether or not I am employed," Obedience commanded, "I cannot make my own self useful if I am rent useless. If I am not employed to do as I am purposed, it has not been up to me, it has been up to you two."

Gigot and Will turned their heads in wonder, tilting towards each other as they walked.

Will said, "I'm sorry I said anything. It seems as though that all of this nonsense is the product of our own doing and as you travelers who travel with us have a purpose in being here, it is as it has been and what we are seeing and going through, it is as things were and not as they are. Obedience, it is not a sign that you are here, it is imperative that you are here."

"It seems that our traveling days are being more consistent now in this time out of time. But we still have to see what is to be shown for we will not pass these ways again," Humility stated as he followed behind everyone.

"Here, here," Will shouted.

"I agree," Gigot affirmed.

"What we have here together, we have what has been proven to be necessary. You have not always listened to the voice of the Great One, but have lent your ear to what has been you and others and as you now know the voice of the Great One, you have the opportunity to walk with Obedience in a greater strength now than as before. Choosing to walk with Humility and Obedience is a choice to walk with Suffering, but at times, you have walked with me alone as a result of not walking with Humility and Obedience," Suffering added, "Wouldn't you agree?"

"We both agree," Gigot and Will stated together.

As the six were becoming one, walking along the craggy trail, they saw the Village of Guinea on the horizon. The dark shadow over Inhibition was nothing compared to the dark cloud that hovered over the Village of Guinea.

"It is becoming evident that we speak with the voice of the Great One and as you hear his voice, your walk with Obedience becomes clearer and strengthened, does it not?" Humility asked.

"We do not lead astray, even when it seems that we do," Obedience said as he shuffled his way in between Gigot and Will. "What is and what you see is not always the same, that's why listening and moving with me is imperative and as you have seen, my sword is far superior in strength to yours, but my sword is never alone. It is always as a result of the three of us joining as one and the all of us being as one. You see now, don't you?"

"Seeing, yes, doing, no. I doubt too much." Gigot said. "The distractions, the detours, the doubts, and the debilitating division have been a course meant for destruction and as we see what we are seeing, we see what we have seen, but this time from the eyes of a far higher sight than we've ever seen on our own."

"Being out of time is real and I thank the Great One for that!" Will said expectantly, "Now what do we have here?"

A villager from the Village of Guinea approached the group and said with a cry in her voice, "You're here, you're here! Somebody is here, oh, wonderful day! Somebody is here!"

With that, she turned joyfully back towards the Village of Guinea and ran as fast as she could to the town square, shouting, "They're here, they're here, they're all here together!"

"Who is here, who? Who is here?" another lady asked, "You don't mean the one who has come for me, do you?" she said in fright and fear.

"Oh, no, no, no," she said gleefully, "Somebody is here, SOMEBODY is here!"

"SOMEBODY IS HERE!" Someone said.

"Oh, my gosh!" another person piped up, "You mean to tell me that our deliverer has come!"

As they all walked into town, the townspeople were all in an uproar as they approached the town square. Gigot, Will and the others continued to walk towards the center of town with some folk flowering them with rose petals, others running in fear and still others doing what they did best and that was watching from afar and scratching and eyeing and doubting and raising their noses far above the others as if to say, "If SOMEBODY is here, then it certainly can't be these!"

A few of the villagers stood with their arms folded at the town fountain and spoke to one another, "That is not SOMEBODY! When will the foolish ever learn that I AM SOMEBODY?"

"I AM SOMEBODY!" a different one screamed at the others.

Gigot and Will stopped before the townspeople and Gigot said, "Who is your leader?"

"Why, that's the Mayor, the Mayor of Guinea, someone go fetch the Mayor," one spoke with authority.

In no time at all, the Mayor and his entourage appeared, seemingly from out of nowhere and the Mayor and his Strongmen parted the bewildered crowd as the Mayor approached each of the six and shook each of their hands, moving them away from each other as he saw fit. The crowd had parted into six portions, as well, as they each relied upon their clan and their tribe in no uncertain terms.

"Ahem!" the Mayor clearing his throat, "On behalf of the Village of Guinea, we welcome you to our beloved township! I am Mayor Kavalus. And who, might I ask, are you?"

"Gigot spoke with authority, "We are travelers traveling through and on our way to Crested Hill. My name is Gigot and this is…"

Before Gigot could utter another word, the Mayor said, "You go here, and you go there." The Mayor began appointing the team of six to each of the portion of the townspeople according to their beliefs.

Gigot and Will, bewildered, did as they were told; as did the others, though, quite reluctantly. The Mayor's Strongmen placed each of the six one by one in view of each of the portions of the townspeople according to their beliefs. Some of the villagers believed they were SOMEBODY and Will was sent to them. Some believed they were Persecuted by SOMEBODY and Humility was sent to them. Still others believed they had Some Thing crawling on their skin and were constantly checking their clothing for bugs and creepy crawly things and Purpose was sent to them.

Some of the villagers believed that Gigot was the most important of all and yet they sensed they all had known him all of their lives. Somehow they were convinced that Gigot was their very best friend and even some of the female folk believed that Gigot was in love with them and fluttered their eyes and waved their fans fanning the flames of whatever was in their minds.

Still others believed they were sick and dying and each one of them had varied types of sickness and ailments that required the Mayors constant care because he was a doctor of the mind and body, so he sent Suffering to them to make them feel more comfortable in their beliefs.

Lastly, the Mayor, not knowing exactly what to do with Obedience, sent him to the village group that didn't trust anyone, especially Obedience.

"We don't want him; he's the last to be picked!" they murmured and complained. "We don't need him and don't trust him. He's not like us at all!" Obedience stood there straight and tall and took the abuse like a strong tree.

"Why did we have to get him?" another said as they were jealous of one another and one by one, turned their backs on Obedience and on each other. Nothing ever satisfied them as they all thought they'd do better in SOMEBODY'S group.

Mayor Kavalus was helped to the village monument platform by his Strongmen. He said, "People, don your face!"

At all once, every one of the villagers, in each and every group, pulled a mask of pig snout from their back pockets and fastened them to their faces with different colored strings tied around the back of their heads.

"Stop it!" one of the women shouted at another as she pushed the other woman in her group.

"You can't push me!" she responded.

"You're always complaining about something, aren't you?" she retorted.

"Mayor, did you see what she did?" the persecuted woman shouted.

"I think I love you!" another woman whispered into Gigot's ear, "Do you love me?"

Gigot stepped back away from her and ended up bumping into another lady who said, "He's mine, he's always been mine, back off, Jezebel!"

It was like the first of a stack of dominoes had been pushed over because this ruckus by the two women got the entire Village in an uproar, but in each of their respective groups according to how they believed.

"Get off of me! Stop touching me!" a man shouted as Purpose jumped away from the man who was flicking invisible bugs from his arms and shoulders and dancing a jig started jumping a bit, flailing his jacket to remove the unwanted and invisible creatures from his clothing.

"Stop throwing them on me, you crazy loon!" another one screamed aloud shielding his body from the onslaught of invisible rodents while others in his group were scratching their heads, their arms, pulling their pants legs up and scratching their legs…movement was everywhere and each crowd got in on it.

"Listen to the Mayor, people!" a man shouted at the top of his lungs from the SOMEBODY group.

"You can't tell them what to do, that's MY responsibility, I'm in charge of this group!" said another SOMEBODY.

The Mayor lifted his arms and raising his hands and turning them to soften and control the crowd, "My people, my people," he winced. "Now,

now, you're embarrassing me in front of our guests."

He motioned to the Strongmen to each of the groups and each Strongman picked a person out of each of their groups grabbing by their arm and dragging them to the front of the monument platform where the Mayor could reach them. The Strongmen threw each of their respective villagers to the feet of the Mayor as the Mayor pulled out his stethoscope and placed it around his neck. The moment he did that, he winced again and shook his head back and forth in disappointment and said,

"Now you know what's going to happen now, don't you?" he asked the entire crowd.

A deafening hush fell over the villagers with "ooh's" and "hums" and "no's" and gasps. Some of the more frightened villagers placed their heads and arms over their faces so they could not see what was about to happen.

The six stood in their respective groups bewildered at the behavior of the town as the Mayor spoke once again, "Now, now you guests," he spoke with bated breath and a wincing smile, "I apologize on behalf of the town, our lovely town at that. It seems that we have a case of unruliness today."

The villagers shuttered and bowed to their knees joining the six villagers who had already been strong armed at the front of the crowd. The six remained standing as they were unaware of the custom in the town that when the Mayor Doctor of Guinea had the villagers don their masks of pig, a representative was chosen from each group to be therapized by the Mayor Doctor. The Strongmen took great pleasure in administering the Strongholds as the Mayor Doctor would perform his Doctoring in private and he took leave of the platform with the Strongmen following with their captives in hand. The rest of the village merely bowed the knee in fear being thankful that it was not their time to be therapized in the Mayor Doctor's office.

The captured villagers were screaming as they were being dragged through the street to the Mayor Doctor's office and by this time, the rest of the villagers were lying on the ground crying in fear of their captors.

Will shouldered his sword and went after one of the Strongmen and yelled, "Stop this! Stop where you are!"

The Strongman turned and with one arm holding his captive, raised his other arm against the sword of Will and Will remained frozen stiff from the obvious power of the Strongman's invisible strength.

Gigot pulled his sword from its sheath and before he could raise his sword, another Strongman turned and flew his arm at Gigot and Gigot was flung backward to his backside.

Suffering knelt with Humility and Obedience and they prayed as the Mayor turned to observe what was happening, he said, "You all know for certain these who live here, live here by choice. Don't try me, for I have been given authority here by these wonderful town folk and they submit to me of their own free will. Why, they've even signed the papers over giving me the right to their minds and their bodies. I AM the Mayor of Guinea and no one who comes to this town stays who they are, for they are mine and I make them what I want to make of them."

"It is by Mum's Deep that you have come and it is by Mum's Deep that you will go," Obedience stood and said.

"You have no power here over me, not now, for you have come too late!" the Mayor Doctor replied.

He added, "I'll go when it's time for me to go, but these, these are mine for they have given themselves to me as the Mayor of Guinea. They are my pigs and they belong here with me."

The Mayor Doctor raised his outstretched hand at Obedience's throat and began to close his hand. Obedience began to choke from the invisible power of the Mayor Doctor and brought Obedience to his knees beside Suffering and Humility. Purpose merely stood there realizing that this power that had enveloped the village was far too strong for anything they could muster so he remained quiet and still with his hand on the heel of his sword.

Suffering stood and said, "It is true that these you have in your grasp have given themselves over to you and indeed they have signed a pledge to you giving you full permission over their minds and their bodies. But," he breathed a breath, "You have no power over their souls and as it is, that is what you desire most, is it not?"

The Mayor Doctor released his power over Obedience and allowed him to fall to the ground as he heaved and heaved trying to catch a breath of air to breathe.

"Go on, I'm listening," the Mayor Doctor responded.

Suffering remained quiet for he had nothing else to say for what he had just said was the Truth as it was and as it should be.

The Mayor Doctor walked towards Suffering, closing his cloak tight to his chest and raised his right hand pointing his right index finger into Suffering's face and said,

"You bring a strange fire here, Suffering, I know you all too well. I thrive on your kind and there is none better than you to bring me pleasure."

He put his hand to his chin and rubbed his chin grabbing at his whisker, shirking a smile and said, "You know me all too well, don't you, Suffering. Why you and me are two peas in a pod. I use you and you use me, that's how we like to do things here, isn't it…Suffering?"

He smirked and whispered into Suffering's face, "It's too late here, they're mine to use and abuse as I see fit. They gave me that right and I own them!"

"My life and my task, as it has been given to me has been given to me by the Great One. What I do I do as unto the Lord that I might bring others to Him for His Glory. My hand is not your hand, it has never been, and your hand has never been mine for your hand is of the Deep and to the Deep you shall go!" Suffering spoke with the authority of the Great One.

"My suffering that I give and your Suffering is the same!" the Mayor Doctor screamed. "I won't go anywhere! Not before I have my way with…" the Mayor Doctor screamed again and as Suffering breathed out, he blew his breath with the force of Light.

The Mayor Doctor breathed in his last and was thrust back first into the Deep along with his Strongmen. All at once, they were thrust with the power of the Great One into the Crevice of Mum's Deep and as they flew backwards, the Mayor Doctor threw shards of Darkness towards Gigot, Will and Purpose. The three stood with their shields to withstand the Power of the Darkness and the other three, Suffering, Humility and Obedience stood with them as six and stood with them as one and as one they Dispelled the Darkness into the Crevice along with the Mayor Doctor of Guinea and his Strongmen.

Gigot and Will turned back to the town's people and they had vanished and all that remained were the ashes of their bodies.

Gigot fell to his knees in remorse as it was too late. The Darkness had taken their bodies and their minds and all that was left was the memory of the last remaining moments of their spirits.

"Where did their spirits go?" Gigot asked Suffering.

"I will not say," Suffering responded, "It's not for me to say."

Will knelt beside Gigot as they wept together with Purpose of the lives lost to Guinea and the suffering that was caused from the free will offering of all the things that were too good to be true and the delusion of lives spent believing things that never were and never were to be.

XVI

The Village of Grudgeon

No sooner had they all gotten up off of their knees, but a villager from nearby town ran over to them and said, "What have you done? Are you crazy? Why did you destroy the Village of Guinea? Why would you do such a thing? Our village relies on this town and others like it to survive! Some of us had family there. What have you done?"

"We have done no such thing," Suffering said.

"Ooh, wait until I tell my village what you've done," the villager said contemptuously. "There'll be hell to pay for this! We needed this village for the good they shared with us and the family we shared with them."

"What good could this village possibly share with yours?" Will asked.

"Good? Did I say good? I'm going back to my village and report this, there's gonna be a rude day awakening, I tell ya, a rude day awakening!" he said walking backwards to his village pointing his spiny finger at them. And then he turned about and ran away as fast as he could.

"What does that mean?" Gigot asked. "Wait! What are you talking about?"

"Let him go," Obedience said, "We'll be there soon enough to hear what they all have to say, let's go!"

The other villager ran quickly ahead as his village was just around the bend. As he ran out of sight, they heard him yelling, "It's a rude day, indeed, a very rude awakening day, indeed!"

As the group traveled forward around the bend, their certain confidence was found in their oneness and agreement and as they were all discovering, it was going to be their oneness and agreement that was going to continue to get them through each of the villages to come until they crossed the Crevice and then on to Crested Hill.

As they continued around the bend, the trail seemed to fall out of sight because of a severe drop down the hill and it continued down a gradual decline in altitude. The air was getting thick and the noise coming from the not so distant village was getting louder so that they could make out that there was quite a ruckus going on in town. They were all fairly certain that they were the ones responsible for what had just occurred in Guinea.

As they entered into the Village of Grudgeon, there were signs posted of "Do Not Do This" and "Do Not Do That". There were signs posted of "You're Not Welcome Here" and "Do Not Enter". Other signs said, "Don't Tell, Don't Listen" and "Do Not Do Anything Without the Curmudgeon's Permission".

There were a few stragglers looking out for the visitors and when they spotted them, they yelled up ahead, "Here they come, here they come!"

The group kept moving and walking at a steady pace towards the village center where the town's people awaited them with closed arms. As the visitors walked through the seemingly resentful crowd, they kept their hands on the heel of their swords just in case something vile occurred. The angry crowd, spewing their venom and cursing the air that the visitor's breathed parted so that they could reach the town's center where the Mayor stood with his very dark brown suit that had a tinge of something dripping from his arm sleeves. As the visitors approached the Mayor, he said these words,

"What do we have here this rude day of awakening? I'm Mayor Curmudgeon the Mayor of the Village of Grudgeon."

The six stopped before the Mayor as one and stood at attention as the crowd anticipated their response. Gigot spoke up and said, "We are mere travelers traveling through. We are on our way to cross over the Crevice and on to Crested Hill. We're simply passing through and we mean you no harm."

"No harm you say," the Mayor responded. "Well, we'll be the determiners of that!" The Mayor looked out to the other town's folk that he was encouraging to follow his lead.

"Why have you come here?" the Mayor asked as the town's people gathered around and said, "Here, here!' and "Tell us what you want!" while some said, "Take what they have, they'll take none of ours!"

Humility, noting that the Mayor must have been preoccupied in his mind when Gigot told them why they were there simply repeated what Gigot said, "Sir, Mr. Mayor Curmudgeon, if I may, we are mere travelers traveling through. We are on our way to cross over the Crevice and on to Crested Hill. We're simply passing through and we mean you no harm."

Mayor Curmudgeon looked intently at Humility and said, "You sound like other visitors we've had here today, are you them?"

"Are we them?" Humility asked inquisitively tilting his head slightly not thoroughly understanding the question.

"He mocks the Mayor, take what they have!" one villager shouted raising his fist in the air.

"Take what they have, they'll not take what we have!" said another in fear.

The Mayor spoke up and shouted to the crowd, "You see what you've done here in our quaint little town. Why, you've disrupted us and I've heard of a rude awakening that you are responsible for destroying the Village of Guinea. Those people were very dear to our hearts," he said as he held his clasped hands to his chest as the villagers "oohed" and "ahhed" at his words.

"We mean you no harm, we simply want to pass through and we certainly don't want anything you have," Will added.

The village was meager in its demeanor and Gigot, Will and the others could not figure out what the villagers must be treasuring that they would be so concerned about losing. And, to ask would be presumptuous and lead the villagers to believe their beliefs of harm and not good.

"We'll let you through, but you'll be watched every step of the way," Mayor Curmudgeon begrudgingly said.

"Hide!" he yelled to the villagers and all at once, they ran to their quarters and their businesses, slamming their doors and the locking of the locks and the chains on the doors one could hear in unison. The villagers went inside their tiny rooms and found their treasure chests still locked and then ran back to their windows to peak through the curtains waiting for the visitors to leave.

"You have permission to leave," the Mayor said and as the visitors slowly moved around the center of the town monument, which happened to be a very large treasure chest, the Mayor stammered, "Stop right there, I suspect one of you has stolen something from here!"

The Mayor motioned to one of his underlings and said, "Bring him here!" pointing his finger at Will.

Two of the underlings took Will on each side by his arms and when they touched him, the slick oily sludge that was dripping from their arm sleeves dripped onto Will's arms. They shoved Will over to the feet of the Mayor, who by this time, had gone to sit on the Mayor's throne directly in front of the very large treasure chest.

The Mayor shouted down at Will, "I see you're bearing a grudge! Where did you get that? Did you steal that here, or did you steal it from another village? What say you, you thieving grudge bearer?"

Will looked around for his friends while the underlings held his arms with their dripping sludge continued to drip from the end of their sleeves. His hands were becoming severely soiled by the oily sludge that emanated from the underlings and then the Mayor questioned him again.

"Where did you get that grudge, you lying sludge?" Mayor Curmudgeon angrily winced his eyes as he spoke. "Let me see his hands!"

The two underlings with sludge dripping from their sleeves turned Will's hands over so that the angry Mayor Curmudgeon could see what he was looking for. The Mayor arose from his throne and stepped down towards Will and took both of his sludgy hands into his. As the slick, thick sludge dripped from the arm sleeves of the Mayor, the Mayor accosted him one more time, "I'll ask you one more time, where did you get this grudge?"

By this time, the villagers had come out of their homes and their businesses and had wondered back towards the town's center where the Mayor's throne stood and for the first time they were able to see what the Mayor saw and that was Will, the visitor with his hands full of sludge and they all at once pointed their spiny fingers towards him and said, "There stands the man with the heart of a grudge for his hands are a slick and filled with sludge. To the earth you shall go with your heart filled with pain for the one who has hurt you has nothing to gain. Your heart bears a grudge and this is no lie, the grudge is in the sludge and you wear it with pride!"

All at once, Mayor Curmudgeon and the entire town's people threw up their arms and cheered and oily slick sludge went flying everywhere. People were shouting and cheering from as far as they could hear for to them a child had come home and that they held dear.

Mayor Curmudgeon grabbed Will and said, "Welcome home, son, welcome home!"

In the Mayor's embrace, Will turned around searching for his friends as he stood there embarrassed and in wonder at what was happening to him.

A band began to play from around the other side of the town center as the Mayor took out a huge key from his chest coat pocket all dripping with sludge. He brought Will over to the town treasure chest and opened the chest with the key from his chest. At once, the top of the chest popped open and an odor that would turn death sour rose from the chest.

"Come here, my son, let's take a look at the grudge you have here. I have the right place to put it." Mayor Curmudgeon explained. "You see, this is where we keep our prized grudges, the ones we've held onto for a long, long time. I see that yours is quite sludgy indeed. We have had a rude awakening day, this day of your return. Now give me that grudge and let's place it here among the treasured grudges of old so that it will be kept safe distilled by the sludge and the thick black drudge."

About the time the Mayor reached out to Will to accept his grudge, he noticed the blackened sludge beginning to drip down Gigot's face. The Mayor, with his left eyebrow raised and a rather uncomely smile, he motioned with his head for the others to direct their attention to the other visitor.

"What is your name, young man?" Mayor Curmudgeon asked.

"My name is Gigot, why do you ask?" Gigot responded as he felt the sludge across his cheek and wiped his face rubbing the blackened sludge all over his face and onto his hands. He touched the other side of his face with his left hand and the same thing occurred. Unbeknownst to Gigot, the black sludge was dripping from both eyes and down his cheeks and as it was that the black sludge was so oily and sticky and slimy, he couldn't get it off of his hands or his face and he didn't know exactly what to do.

Purpose was becoming rather uneasy because now both of his companions, as he knew them, were no better than some of these town folk…he just didn't know why.

"It looks like it's time for the Judge," said Mayor Curmudgeon. "The Judge will see fit with what to do with you two."

Will and Gigot stood there amazed at what was happening to the both of them as Suffering, Humility and Obedience stood behind with nothing to do but wait until the right time to escape. They had to see this thing through, no matter how Dark it may seem to be.

A villager in the crowd exclaimed, "He who thinks he sees and he who thinks he knows doesn't really see because he doesn't really know…does he?" he said with a most terrifying curdle pointing and twisting his finger at the black sludge emanating from Gigot's eyes.

"He sees with his memory, this one, he does, of what was…or was it?" he came around from behind Gigot's back and swirled around to Gigot's right.

"This one believes his memories…whether they be true, or false… doesn't he?" he said as he stepped around to Gigot's face glaring him in the eyes. "Doesn't he?" he hissed.

Gigot's head fell back as he continued to wipe the sludge from his eyes and face as the sludge was taking its toll on his eyesight, he couldn't see very well through the darkened sludge.

About that time, the crowd shushed and parted on the right in order to make way for the Authority in the village. It was the Judge, the Judge of Grudgeon, none other than the main Authority, Judge Grudge. He was the one who decided which grudges warranted being placed in the Chest of Grudgeon. These grudges that went into the Chest were the grudges of all things remembered and all things kept so that none would ever pass away and anyone's grudges that were kept in the Chest of Grudgeon were charged to remember their grudges all the days of their lives.

Judge Grudge, dressed in a flowing black robe with sludge dripping from the train of his robe and with old, tired eyes filled with sludge used a cane to make his way to the front of the center of town. He was blind, you see, blind from the sludge, but not blind enough to know what the sludge of a grudge smelled like. It was by the smell and the taste of another's grudge that he could determine just how deep their grudge came from within. "The deeper, the darker, the darker, the better," Judge Grudge would always say as he approached his bench by the throne of the Mayor.

"Help me up here, young man," he speared Will in the stomach with his dark wooden cane.

Will felt the pain of the cane in his middle as his shield wouldn't move to protect him. It was stuck to the ground by the sludge. The Judge reached his arm out to Will and Will knew nothing else to do but help the old, blind Judge to his bench. Will simply did not know the consequence of his memory unforgiven.

Old Judge Grudge approached his bench, placing his cane in his right hand and sat down easy, making himself comfortable on the flat granite bench that had the shape of a tombstone. He sat on his robe as the sludge made the seat of the granite bench a bit more comfortable to his backside. Sludge oozed from beneath him as the odor of death was stronger than any other sludge in the village. The vapor seemed to attract the miniscule vapor of the rest of the sludge of the town and once the villagers smelled the odor of their own sludge, their grudges began to come back to their memories.

The villagers began to bite the insides of their mouths and some foamed with anger. Others gritted their teeth so hard that you could hear their teeth cracking and grinding. Soon, the sludge was coming from their mouths as well as all the other orifices of their bodies. The grudges of the town, it seemed, were being exhumed through their bodies by the odor of the Judge. Judge Grudge began waffling his hands to his face as he breathed in the dark vapor with his wicked smile, inhaling every dark odor of grudge known in the village. His teeth were black from sludge and rotting with decay.

"Yes, yes, my people, remember what they did to you, remember and regret that you didn't get them back for the pain they caused you. It was they, the ones who caused you so much pain…yes, yes, remember!" he hissed and slathered the sludge upon his breast and wiped the odors of enjoyment across his nose and face and licked the back of his hands as the vapor of the sludge landed on his body as thick, molten tar.

The Judge was in a trance by the odor of the grudge's sludge as the town's people were becoming increasingly dark by the vapor of the sludge. The villagers were lifting their arms and hands in the air as though they were worshiping the Judge which allowed their sludge to emanate the vapor flowing to the Judge. They were oohing and hissing and seething in darkened anger; heaving in agony worshipping the Judge of the grudges as their anger increased into a bitter rage as they pressed against Suffering, Humility and Obedience.

Gigot and Will had fallen to the ground in shame as their sludge seeped from them becoming a vapor before the Judge.

"Receive it, yessss, receive it!" Judge Grudge pined for Gigot and Will to become darkened by these hidden grudges that they bore and that for some time. "Let them come to me," he hissed, as the town hissed with him in an injurious gore flailing their sludge at the backs of Suffering, Humility and Obedience. Their white garments were being lathered in dark, molten sludge.

"Stop protecting them, you have no power here," Mayor Curmudgeon cried out to the three who were covering Will and Gigot as they knew how.

"Ha! Ha! Ha!" Judge Grudge chuckled with scorn at the weighted heaviness that Will and Gigot were suffering at the hands of the sludge.

"It's only a matter of time. You thought you would take Crested Hill, but your little mind game ends here. You were never meant to take Crested Hill for Crested Hill belongs to my father," Judge Grudge professed.

"You lie, you deceiver from hell," Obedience shouted. "You have no power here," he continued.

"Look at them whimpering and suffering; soon they'll be all mine, just as the other two captives and I'm well rewarded for all that I do," Judge Grudge said with a wry smile. "I'm very accepting of these sorts, those who think they've gone through and overcome, when all the while, what lies hidden beneath, I know all about it and they do, too. Why, let them lie in their shame and wallow in their sludge, it's good for them…isn't it?" he hissed and wrangled his twisted finger smudging the sludge on their heads.

As Gigot and Will lie on the ground motionless, choking on sludge, all at once, Suffering, Humility and Obedience raised their arms and hands to the sky.

Suffering shouted in a clear lighted mist that broke the spell of the vapor between Gigot and Will and the Judge's Chest, "You have no power here, let them go. Whatever is inside of them will not remain here in your Chest of Grudgeon for anyone to remember. They release it to be remembered no more!"

The villagers hissed and clawed at Suffering, but had no power to touch his person. Judge Grudge stood with Mayor Curmudgeon and as they stood, they joined in allegiance to fight the Light that Suffering displayed.

"Darkness overtake you and Darkness to dwell, Darkness is mine and mine to give…" Judge Grudge began his spell over Gigot and Will as the Light of Suffering, Humility and Obedience flared towards the Dark Vapor.

"From the Darkness you came and to the Darkness you shall go, you have no place here!" Suffering shouted with a thunderous voice as he thrust his sword forward and cut the Vapor away from the two and towards the Judge and the Mayor. At once, the Darkness swirled out of control of the Judge and swirled around him and the Mayor driving the two of them into the Chest of Grudgeon, With a darkened flap at that, they soared into the chest as fast as the Light could take them. Immediately, the Chest shut tight with the Judge and the Mayor sealed away. Obedience touched the Chest with his sword and the Chest went into flames as white smoke billowed in the midst and the villagers fled.

Humility had flung himself over Gigot and Will and as the white smoke billowed, Suffering and Obedience touched the sides of Gigot and Will as Suffering said,

"It's time we made our escape! Let's go!"

Thunder was in the sky as red clouds quickly formed. As they ran away from the Village of Grudgeon, fire fell from the sky and began to burn everything in sight. Billows of flames soon became ashes, as the heat from the fire was all that was felt as they ran and ran as fast as they could. Nothing in the town survived, no, nothing at all. All of the villagers were gone as well as the Mayor and the Judge. All of the darkened sludge of the grudges was burned along with them. There was nothing to remember and nothing to forget.

XVII

The Village Tavern

They ran as fast their legs could carry them and they dared not look back at the fire raining from the red clouds in the sky. All was burning in the village down to the very last grudge and the sludge that they emanated from lie smoking hot in flames of tar with the billows of smoke billowing high into invisible vapor without any power.

The trail led up a gradual, but steep incline that seemed to never end. They had not realized how gradual the decline was into the Village of Grudgeon, so making their way up and out was becoming a bit of a chore. They were out of harm's way from the fire in the sky and the incline was proving to slow them down, so they stopped to catch their breath before moving further towards the Carb to cross the Crevice and on to take the Crested Hill.

"It seems it's constant, finding the within of a thing. I had not realized the grudges I had been holding onto for so long. I feel lighter now," Gigot said to Suffering.

"And I do as well," said Will. "The fact that he called me 'son' was a bit too much to absorb…frightening!" Will said as he looked over to Obedience.

"You are beginning to realize all that has been and in the middle of all that is now that we are here. It's not that you do not fight, for you are here, that means everything. But, the power belongs to the Great One, you see," Obedience said.

"There is no power greater than the Great One," Humility added as he placed his hand on Gigot's shoulder. "Trust in Him, He's here working through us all, even you Will."

Will was looking rather despondent as he was trying to remember what just happened and how easily he was overtaken by Judge Grudge. Gigot pulled Will up to his feet with a mighty tug and said to him,

"You see and know what is on my face; it's fear and failure and fear of failure. Let's agree Will, let's agree together and let's agree with them, they're here for us and they're here with us. We can't do this alone and we won't."

They circled together, the six into one and bowed their heads in the circle joining their heads together in solidarity and their arms wrapped around the one on the left and the one on the right forming a bond that they prayed would not be broken. From this moment on, they referred to themselves and their group as the one unified in purpose and plan, the Echad.

It's was time to get a move on, though, so they gathered their things and moved on up the steep incline along the craggy trail…that much had not changed. The trail was still full of rocks with patches of grass, but this time it was leading to what seemed to be a mountain side filled with pine trees and poplars of all types and thicknesses. The trail winded right and then it winded left, but continued ever onward, upward and their lungs and legs were wearing from the climb.

Just about the time they felt like they could go no more, the steep incline leveled off into a casual plateau that made the journey smooth. Two females, robed in white, stood on each side of the path. They each had striking features with piercing eyes and long, flowing hair, identical in every way, but one. The difference in the two was that one had hair of blackish brown and the other had hair of glistening blonde. As the Echad approached them, the shimmering spirits tilted their heads toward the middle of the path and the blonde one on the right spoke aloud,

"I am Innocence and this, my sister, is Purity. Although we look the similar, we are not at all," said Innocence.

Purity spoke, "You travel long and you travel hard on the Darkend Road leading to continued Darkness. What you have seen and what you will see is not who we are. I am the one who was willing to pay the price and she, my sister, is from above. You have not seen us in this realm for you did not look for us. You chose the Darkend Road yourself. You know this and you know it to be true."

As they spoke, a glistening vapor emanated from their lips.

"You left me long ago, Will," said Innocence. "I breathed deeply that you would stay with me and yet your choices left me alone. Even still, you left my sister from your own wantonness and yet, here we are. Once again, we meet on the Darkend Road leading on."

Gigot, humbled by their presence, bowed on one knee and Will did the same.

Gigot spoke, "A time in the past and my heart fills with wonder at the beauty of your smiles. We did choose, we cannot deny, forgive us, I pray."

Will could not look up, but knew by remembrance the things he had done.

"Grace Walker is a good man, isn't he, Will?" Innocence asked Will.

Will mustered the strength to think through what she had just said and looked up from his past shame, smiled and said, "Yes, Innocence, he is."

"Remember Grace Walker, Will," Purity whispered.

"Remember, Gigot," Innocence spoke louder. "Grace is greater and where you go, we cannot, but the grace of the Great One walks with you with Humility, Suffering and Obedience."

And with that, they were no more.

Far off in the distance, music was coming from a faraway building that sat nestled on the side of the mountain. It was surrounded by green after green of rolling hills of fresh cut grass. Odd people dressed in strange clothes were whisking by hitting round balls with clubs in some sort of game. The players that played were focused, all dressed in their gaming garb, colorful and stout. The players were happy as they pounded the balls as hard as they could and the Echad stood in amazement at how energized each of the players were as they pounded their little balls with the ferocity of a lion.

"We'll meet you in the tavern, the drinks are on me," one of the players said to the group. A couple stopped behind him, smiled their cheerful smiles and hit their balls together as the balls went sailing high and over the field of play. Back and forth the players played as Gigot counted there were nine holes in all along this mountainous terrain of rolling hills.

"Looks like you need a drink," another man said to his wife about the group observing his shot. "Ah, let's forget this and go to the tavern, you guys wanna join in the fun?" he asked waving his arm along to the others encouraging them to join them all at the tavern. The tavern was just up the hill and was an old rustic building with swinging doors and quite a bit of ruckus going on in and around the building. Men with women drinking and dancing, partying and playing cards and a piano player was banging hard on the old out of tune piano. Every time someone walked out of the tavern, they were carrying a drink of some sort in their hand and walking sideways to get out the door. It was a strange setting. The tavern looked tattered with beaten gray wood on the outside. The rolling hills of green looked new and green as ever there was and the players looked to be wearing the garments of a gilded age in another realm. The servants were all out on the huge front porch playing games and drinking just like the players, both men and women.

Gigot, Will and the others trudged up the hill to the entrance of the tavern as the music was getting louder and louder. The patrons were getting quite smashed inside and were bringing it all outside to get a breath of fresh air. The air here was crisp and clean and cool as it has the feel of cool mountain breeze blowing about the entire area.

They looked at each other with hesitating grins, knowing that if they stepped inside, they would see what they would see, but not partake. They were all easily in agreement on this one. So, they each stepped up the steps leading to the swinging doors and entered the raucous arena. Once inside, it was exactly like being in an old hall with small tables everywhere, with at least four or five patrons at each table. Everyone was giddy, happy, singing, drinking, carousing, playing games, gambling and having the time of their lives having a good, ole time.

There was an enormous mirror on the wall behind the even more enormous bar counter. All of the stools were filled and each time someone would leave the bar, someone else would take their seat. All of the bartenders had their nametags on. Names like Jacob, Adolphus and

August, Frederick, William and Adolph rounded out the draft ale tenders and over at the short side of the bar there were Jack, and Jim, Evan and Blanton serving up the short shots of a much stronger brew to anyone who had the hankering of a sniff of a brewer's brew. Every seat had a patron and an excited one at that and those who drank the brewer's brew didn't have their socks on.

Not all of the patrons were walking tall, though, inebriated and doused by their wares, some of the folk couldn't walk, some couldn't stand and some of them were by the walls slumped over and anesthetized by their over indulgence.

Will looked over to the right as the tavern had a split level with just a few steps to go up and there was a little more breathing space there. He saw someone he thought he knew. The boy looked like his own son looking down into a hole in the floor. Light was coming up from what seemed to be a basement, of sorts, as the youth was staring down and the light reflected off of the boy's face. All of a sudden, the boy jumped up and ran out the side door. Strangely, the side door disappeared as he rushed out the door.

There was light coming from the hole in the floor and Will's curiosity got the best of him as he walked up the steps to see what was emanating from the floor. He walked over the cracking wooden planks of floor and looked over into the hole in the floor. This was actually no hole, but a doorway opened with the door lying flat on the floor. The doorway led to the underneath. It wasn't a basement. No, it was the underneath of the tavern that had been dug out and the tavern had been built over it. As Will walked over and approached the open door in the floor to see what he could see, the room faded to gray and the sound of the piano slowed to a whispering faint of a noise. It was as though he had walked into a different realm far away from the wide open sound of the raucous party. Yet, he was still there.

He looked back at his friends as they looked over at him. They were distorted…or was he distorted, he couldn't tell. All he was drawn to do was to look through that door in the floor, it was overwhelming in its drawing and wooing and singing began to play in his mind.

He fell to his knees and placed his hands on the floor to get a good place to stick his head down through the open door in the floor. As he looked down, he saw the vibrant red clay beneath the tavern and he noticed that some people were down below over to the right gathered in the darkness, carousing just as they were in the main room. He felt a pull and thrust of his body of some sort of sucking sensation pulling his body down into the open pit of clay. Over to the left, the earth began to move and it was a large earthen mound stuck solid and moving upwards towards him. The bottom of the red clay floor was at least twenty-five foot deep, or more and so the square mound of earth had room to move upward.

Emerald green ethereal illuminations were coming up from the opening in the clay floor below and the moving earth was actually the top of a space, a roof to what was coming up from below the earth. Below the moving earth roof were four columns holding up the roof and in the middle of the rising platform was an emerald woman dressed in the fashion of a long, cloistered dress that held something within her bosom. Dramatically, the music from the piano was getting louder and the higher she rose from the beneath the earth and the louder the music became the stronger the pull was on Will to fall through the door in the floor into the embrace of her power..

The higher she rose, the more she turned. Her back had been to Will as he peered down below drawn to her intoxicating charm. She was turning to her right as her platform rose ever closer to Will. At the right moment, with the right amount of space to go, the music at the piano pounded its same sound. The enchanting woman dressed in a gown of green turned her face towards Will opening the sharp slits of her eyes and her bright emerald green eyes pierced through the darkness of the dungeon spewing her green, entrancing gaze upon Will.

Will gasped at her sight. He had seen this beast before and felt the urgent and dreadful draw upon his breast. She was pulling him into to her domain, the domain of the fallen; the domain of the dead. Her brilliant emerald green eyes were as bright as the sun and shone through the horizontal slits in her face. It was this power that he had seen before, a power that he knew he had given into, a power like none upon the earth, but under the earth it was. Her platform was the door to her dungeon and Will was the chosen one…this time. Of all the men in the room, she had chosen Will to be her next victim.

She raised her right arm to welcome him down. Her face was motionless and body was covered in the beautiful gown. She stood there, still rising closer to Will and his head was through the door in the floor wanting more and more of whatever it was she had to offer. She was relentless and compelling, magnetic and powerful.

As Will was entranced and could resist no more, he released his right hand from the floor to take hers lowering himself beneath. In the blink of an eye, Purpose and Obedience flew across the opening in the floor and grabbed Will as he began to fall into the beam of her trance. The three of them rolled on the floor away from the door as Humility's sword whipped the door shut and threw a lock on its handle to lock it down tight.

All the room went quiet at the slamming of the door to a resounding silence, but once the lock was on tight, the place went back to its rocking and carousing and laughing and drinking. There was a knocking from under the door in the floor and a pounding at that. The door was shaking and rattling as the pounding got harder and stronger and louder and just about lifted the door from the hard wooden floor.

"It's time to go!" Suffering exclaimed as the patrons from the bar were coming over. This time they weren't happy for they had a grimace on their faces. They didn't like party poopers and the still, rested life to destroy the good times they were having. No, they didn't like people like that at all. It seemed that as long as Gigot, Will and the others didn't do, or say anything about what they were doing, they could stay as long as they wanted.

Not now. Now it was time for these visitors to go. They had tainted their atmosphere.

"Nobody ruins our party," one of the player's said, as he became an enraged wild boar and his clothing changed to suit his demeanor. Others' clothes were changing in the midst, as their faces and mouths reflected their anger and hostility towards the party disrupters. Scowls and moans came from all over the building as the force of the underneath continued its knocking, attempting to burst through the door. The players were becoming wild animals of the Dark and the wood.

"Open that door, you little specks," a man yelled as he quickly became a beast from his brew. "Open that bleaking door," he scowled, enraged and running towards the Echad.

"This way," Suffering sparked as he pointed to a door to the right, the only door, for that matter…as the angry, drunken crowd rushed towards them. The door to their right had a sign upon it that said, "I Don't Know" and as the power of Light that Suffering possessed was expelled, the door of the "I Don't Know" was opened to them and at once they all rushed through the door with Obedience pulling it shut behind them.

The angry mob in the tavern had all become animals and had rushed towards them with all of their might. Suffering enveloped a power over them as though they were moving in slow motion as they were filled from their wares. The mob, in slowed existence, screeched for them to the open door, but once it was shut they flailed against the closed door and rammed one another with their monstrous bodies of furious rage tumbling on top of one another filling the floor. This raucous crowd did not know all things, nor did they know the consequence of all things, but one thing they all knew and that was this: no one goes through the Door of "I Don't Know" and ever comes back to that place. So, they all just started laughing and shouted to one another, "The next drink's on me!"

Laughing and chaotic they all went back to their usual selves in their gaming clothes, dressed to have fun and having fun they did, not really caring to know what lies beyond the Door of the "I Don't Know".

They all went back to themselves as they trosseled back towards the bar and the tables and down the few small steps to what they knew best. The thumping and knocking from beneath the door in the floor ceased to be. The piano played its sour tune and the lock on the door in the floor was popped from beneath as a spiny hand with long, black bones reached through the crack in the opening of the door and pulled the lock to see it no more.

Green illuminations and vapor came from the cracks in the door in the floor and a young man walked over to see what lie beneath opening the door mesmerized by the ethereal green vapor as it reflected in his eyes. The young man's gaze into the vaporous green light softened his strength and he melted with delight and despair at the same time. He looked towards the men at the bar, but the vapor was far too strong for this one. He smiled with fear and loss of breath as his strength failed him. As he fell down into the decadent and treacherous gaze of the emerald green eyed woman of death, the vapor rose and the people were full of cheer. They did not care of the fate of the youth. They relished in their joy, in their glasses of cheer. Somehow they all knew and held it dear. For fun they sought and fun once again, pure entertainment was theirs to begin. No cares in the world with their mugs of delight, no knowledge of consequence, no room for the Light.

"Who cares?" says the one.

"Who cares?" says them all.

"Who cares, I've got mine," as a man bounced a ball.

XVIII

The Land of "I Don't Know"

Apparently, the laughter and raucous noise from within the tavern let the Echad know a few things. One, they were no longer being pursued and two, it was obvious from the lack of a path or trail out the door that the pathway had not been visited in a very long time.

"Where are we now?" Gigot pondered at the sight of where they perceived themselves to be.

The last they had seen of the outside was the beautiful rolling hills of green, but now on the other side of the tavern, the side door exit of "I Don't Know" looked more like a thick amazon jungle than any mountain scene. The air was cool and crisp, but if there ever was a trail out the side door, it was so grown over they had to use their swords to plow a pathway through it. The poplar trees were enormous and the thick brush and undergrown trees proved to be a challenge to wade through.

Suffering and Humility knew for a fact they were heading in the right direction as Gigot was now sensing the exact same direction as they were. Gigot led the way with assurance as his sword proved worthy of the task of cutting through the brush and down the ever sloping side of the mountain. Gigot was becoming confident in listening within to the Great One and he affirmed was he was thinking with Suffering, Humility and Obedience.

"Why would a door exit be labeled 'I Don't Know'?" Purpose asked as he followed behind.

Suffering, walking and cutting the opening pathway with Gigot, looked over to Gigot and smiled. Humility asked Purpose, "Why do you think, Purpose?"

"Other than the obvious 'I don't know', I don't know," Purpose exhaled as he continued to cut the remaining brush away. "Oh…I get it…'I don't know!'" he laughed to himself and Obedience stopped on the slope, scratched his chin, wiping away the sweat from the chopping and said,

"You don't get it, you're still wondering as you wander, just like you're doing right now!"

"I do, too, get it, it's not that difficult," Purpose stated sarcastically.

"Oh, ok, Mr. Purpose, I can know what I don't know means, tell me, exactly what does I don't know mean?"

Purpose smirked as the others had stopped as well and turned to hear his answer.

"Well," Will said, 'tell us what it means."

Purpose shrugged and bit his bottom lip a bit on the inside as he was thinking and conjuring a response and then he started laughing, "You all don't really know what it means? I may not know all that I don't know, but I do know what I don't know and I can freely admit that."

Gigot shrugged and sighed and as he was thinking through himself what a door exit labeled as "I Don't Know" would mean and then it hit him and the others at the same time and they all started laughing together.

Will was about to say it, as was Purpose. Suffering just looked at the two of them and shook his head in a humorous shake. They all went back to work chopping and heaving their swords back and forth clearing their pathway down the hill. As they worked their way down the slope, Purpose started laughing out loud at Will and Will's eyes scrunched a bit as he didn't see the humor of it all according to Purpose,

"I know something you don't know," Purpose sang to Will.

"Well, why don't you write about it one day, Purpose?" Will retorted, "I'm willing to follow now and that's good enough for me. I no longer desire to do my own thing, isn't that right, Obedience?"

Obedience lifted his left eye-brow as he listened and begrudgingly nodded in agreement. The slight grin on Suffering's face was the same slight grin on Gigot's as they continued on as one through the brush until they had to sit and rest where the ground had leveled off. They could hear a stream of water through the brush and it was a calm scene sitting down to rest on the brush they had just cut, listening to the stream trickle its own path over the rocks. They couldn't see the stream, but they could hear it. They laid back on their packs and rested from their work.

Gigot wasn't quite ready to sit down and rest as something beyond the brush seemed to be beckoning him to peer through the brush. As the thick bushes and growing trees supplied work for them to wade through, it also provided quite a bit of foliage in the form of camouflage. Gigot had to move a few branches down with his right hand to get a view of the stream a little ways away from the group. Will and Purpose got up as well and moved to either side of him in order to see exactly what it was that they were supposed to be looking at.

"Do you see that?" Gigot whispered.

"I see it," Will said, "It appears to be two eyes."

"Should we run?" Purpose asked inquisitively, "I think we should go."

"It looks like a very large animal. Can you tell what it is, Gigot?" Will asked.

"It's a large…cat, of some sort, on the prowl, I suppose, but with only seeing it's eyes, it's hard to make out just how large it is," Gigot said, "It doesn't seem to be looking at us, but at something in the stream."

"What is it doing? What's it waiting for?" Purpose whispered.

"Now, how am I supposed to know that, Purpose, I don't know," Gigot gumpft and then trickled his eyebrows and said with a wry smile, "Don't breathe…"

Purpose looked at Gigot with a snarl and they both looked back through the brush as they could sense the eyes of the animal move just a hair. All they could see was his eyes through the brush, but he had shifted for some reason because his eyes shifted a bit. Just then, a monstrously large snake came around the bend of the stream. It was minding its own business and slithering along the stream side. This snake was no mere snake. It was larger than anything imaginable with a pointed viperous head and a shiny silvery coat of thick scaly skin. This snake did not belong here and in the ensuing moments they all wondered where it had come from as it moved slowly, yet precisely, upon its wet belly.

A spirit in the wind breathed and hissed, "Ophissss," as the serpent slithered purposely all full to the brim with whatever it had just eaten. His eyes moved to and fro, with one eye looking forward and the other searching the rear. His skin, changed from light to dark and dark to light.

Then, all of sudden and quicker than a flash, the eyes that they had peered to see moments ago through the brush, became a lurching, ferocious, orange and black tiger to pounce upon his prey.

The violent tiger, with its front teeth, long, sharp and pointed, roared as it lunged for its prey and pounced upon the viperous snake in less than the blink of an eye. The snake did not flinch, nor did it look back as the sabre teeth of the tiger, with his mouth open wide, landed a terrific punch upon the back of the snake. The tiger had not taken into account the quick forward motion of the snake as the tiger's sabre teeth landed on the snake's back, too far from the neck.

All of this was happening so quickly, yet, seemingly, in slow motion. Gigot and the others could see that the pointed tiger's fangs could not penetrate the scaly mail of the snake. The snake's skin was of kusarii mail, impenetrable, leaving the sabre tooth tiger bewildered and the back of the snake unaffected.

Quickly, the tiger surmised his prey was protected and undistracted, but how, he did not know. Gigot and the others were amazed at the slithering beast as they hunched dumbfounded at its covering and the long protruding teeth of the sabre tooth tiger not making even the slightest hint of a mark through the mail-like skin of the snake. The tiger still had grabbed the snake, but the tiger's eyes moved to the neck of the snake and you could see his thinking towards that mark on the snake, to sink his teeth for the kill.

Without another moment's blink, the giant tiger with orange fur and black stripes let go of the snake and lunged his teeth towards the neck of the snake, but again, did not take into account the continued quickness of the snake in motion. In the flash of an eye and faster than that, the tiger made his release to move to the neck of the slithering beast. As the tiger let go of the snake and moved his head left towards the neck, just below the head, simultaneously the snake moved forward with its back and the tiger landed his blow even further down the back of the snake than the first. The surprised and distraught look in the tiger's eyes told it all in how he had made yet another mistake. He was too far down the back of the snake to prevent the snake's counter attack and he could not penetrate the skin of the back.

With a counter blow, the snake had whipped his enormous head around the back of the giant tiger with the swiftness of light and at once opened its monstrous mouth with its own long fangs and clamped down on the back of the head of the tiger. The viper's fangs sunk deep into the tiger's brow just above his eyes as the snake pushed downward with the strength of its body, with its fangs ripping deep into the head of the tiger. Nothing like it had ever been seen as the tiger's look of despairing surprise with his own fangs exposed on the viper's skin and the head of the snake above his brow.

The sabre tooth tiger sighed a deafening whimper, closing his eyes shut and falling into the stream to the right of the snake out of the clutches of the viperous fangs. The snake made no sound, brushed the enormous tiger to out o fhis way and proceeded without cause or care out of sight to the right following the trail of the stream. He glided undaunted to the Darkness below.

Something inside Gigot and the rest went thump in their hearts as the tiger fell to his death beside the quiet stream of flowing water. What seemed to have only taken seconds, this wonderful beast was alive and then he wasn't. Gigot and Will had a sense of connection with the tiger, but did not know the why or the how. They had never seen the tremendous beast and as he lie there with his blood filling the stream, they parted the brush they were hiding behind and brought themselves to the tiger's side.

"What is this, this beast, is it you, or me?" said Will. "Is this to be our demise?" he said as he had knelt by the beleaguered and dying beast panting fiercely, breathing his final breaths.

"Why would you say that, Will?" Purpose asked. "That doesn't make any sense. What does this tiger have anything to do with you or Gigot?"

"You don't know?" Gigot said to Purpose with tears in his eyes as he fell down in front of the tiger onto his knees.

Purpose was kneeling at the back of the tiger looking over its body and actually had nothing to respond with to Gigot. He didn't know and it was on his face. Purpose pondered these things in his heart with wonder trying to make sense of all they had been through until these moments and what Gigot was thinking and what he had in his own mind were not the same thing. This, he knew for certain. There were things he knew that Gigot couldn't explain and there were things Gigot knew that Purpose couldn't explain and the disparity of the divide, in that moment, was greater than the Crevice.

"Tell me what you're thinking," Purpose insisted.

"I can't, not right now," Gigot hesitated. "I'm trying to figure out what has just happened and why it is that we had to see this on our way to cross the Crevice. That slithering beast is from beneath, just like every other Darkend creature from the Crevice. What it is or represents, I do not know…the wind called it Ophis."

Just then, the tiger blinked his eyes, shaking his head back and forth of the blood pouring from above his eyes. He had blood flowing from his mouth and he moved to get up and then quickly back down again. The blood could not be stopped. All of a sudden, the tiger leapt to his feet, moving away from the three and into the water of the stream. He was dazed and imbalanced with weak legs, unsure of his survival. His head fell forward into the stream to use the water to wash his eyes swishing back and forth as quickly as he could and he fell to his front knees whimpering and yowled. His yowl was that of a cry and a moan, an unfortunate one. He was dying, suffering in agony from the pain of the fangs deep into his head. On his knees he yowled once more and fell to his defeat in the blood flowing stream.

The hunter now hunted and conquered lay dying in the mist.

"Help us!" Will demanded. He and Gigot were pulling him out of the stream and onto the brush that he had crushed just moments before.

"Help him," Will cried out, "He's dying; he can't die!"

Gigot and the rest tugged and pulled the enormous beast from the water as Will fell on the beast's side crying from the experience and the loss of so magnificent a beast that only he could identify with.

"He needs to live, why can't he live?" Will cried out, as he looked up to Suffering from his laying on the beast.

As the rest surrounded the tiger, his spirit departed to be with them no more.

"Some things that seem to be great in us need to be surrendered, Will. If we don't surrender them ourselves outright, something of a far greater power will kill that which we will to not let go." Suffering said as he looked down upon the distraught Will.

It was in this moment that they all caught a glimpse of what lie beyond the door of the "I Don't Know". Purpose took note of it as he was discovering himself what he should have been doing all along.

XIX

The Fettered Souls

They got up and away and traveled a bit further as the annoying thicket bore way to a clearing. A time of rest had come for the moon was setting and they all took leave immediately to their sacks to lie in rest as long as the moon was set. They all pondered the villages they had gone through and the meaning of them all. Gigot and Will were seeing themselves in the faces, the mirrors, of what had been treasured for so long and all that needed to be given up in order to take the Crested Hill and deliver it to its rightful owner. Yes, the price had to be paid, every price at any cost.

A calm peace moved over the earth where they rested and the chance to fully relax was theirs for the taking. It had been too long since they were able to simply relax each muscle and be free from any anxiety of some alarming and outrageous attack. Obedience kept watch as they slept for he had been given a special gift that they all desired and that was this… he was able to maintain and keep going in the face of every and any thing.

The exhaustion had built up within each of them with physical depletion wearing at their bodies and their minds. Gigot could feel his body relax, muscle by muscle, tendon by tendon, bone by bone as he lay there on the ground in the mist. Gigot fell asleep and as he slept, he was brought to a dream of old. In this dream, Gigot saw a Woman of Vanity, fair and beautiful was she in her house of dreams living out her life waiting for another to come and take her away from her miserable life of leisure. As the Woman of the Vanity lay sleeping, another woman sat beside her. This sitting woman was the Woman of Thorns and Thistles. She sat and watched others waiting in blaming regard for her torment that had caused her so much pain. Gigot walked by them both and went through the Glass of Fantasy down into the Darkness where Darkness dwells in caves and tunnels Darkened with Darkness where no Light exists save from the Fire below. Here, in this dream of endless Darkened tunnels of earthen ware, a familiar voice spoke within.

"Walk with me and do not fear," Suffering whispered.

Gigot walked fearless, with Suffering as his guide, breathing in the cold Dark air through the ancient tunnels that had led so many to demise.

He continued on following a path for him to see that not too many see in their dreams. The flickers of light up ahead were just around the curve of the wall and there he stood amazed. He saw an Old One, a worker of the lord of the Dark he was, at work in his laborious task. This worker of the lord of the Dark was what men think him to be. He wore no clothes and bore no meat, nor hair. He was Dark and spiny; burnt was he. He was strong enough for his task without any meat, but darkened skin and bones was sufficient for his time out of time. The tone of his shovel was as he was and there was no difference between him and his shovel. They were one and the same as though he had been born with it.

There he shoveled the Fettered Souls, stuck in the Walls of Darkness. The Fettered Souls were bound and sealed like a babe in swaddling clothes with only their faces to show. The light from the Fire was to the right and there the worker of the lord of the Dark shoveled to and fro and to and fro. He would use his shovel to shove it through the Wall of Souls shoveling out as Gigot could hear the shovel push through the Dark earth and bring out a soul ready for eternal Torment.

The Fettered Souls all bound in woven Fear lay sleeping in the Wall. The Wall was endless, as endless as could be.

"Are they sleeping?" he asked Suffering, "Or, are they dead?"

Suffering continued his drawn down gaze upon the worker and said not a word.

The worker of the lord of the Dark would take his shovel and fill it with a soul and take it to beyond the wall and toss it into the Fire. Then, he would come back and shovel another. There was no Shame and no Remorse, just work and work enough to share. The Demon turned to see Gigot and looked right through him and Suffering and offered no respite from his labor, nor did he care that his visitors were there. He merely went about his work of to and fro, shoveling the Fettered Souls into the Fire of Old, all blazing hot beyond the wall.

As Gigot stood in wonder and awe at the prize that awaited these, there was one soul in the Wall of the Fettered Souls awakened with eyes of yearning and eyes of Fear, saying, "Help us, help us, please."

Gigot could not cross the boundary to the Fettered Souls. It was too late for these. He stood there for what amounted to for days and days on end, but in a moment he came to himself in wonder if he simply Did Not Know and wondered most if even he really cared.

In his moment of curiosity at the lack of compassion he had for these in the Wall of Fettered Souls, he became embarrassed at the thought of being found out at his lack of compassion and wondered within himself. In that moment, he sensed Suffering and he looked to his left and Suffering was there...staring through him…knowing his thoughts.

Gigot was undone and found out.

Oh, he cared as he tried to convince his thoughts.

Suffering winced at Gigot's thoughts for his thoughts were not as the Great One in His loving compassion.

"I must, I must," he said to Suffering. "I must care and I must obey! But it's too late for these. What have I done with the time that I've been given? Are these I've known or these unknown?"

"To someone they are known…of this, I am quite certain," Suffering responded.

"What shall I do with time again to do what I am told? I must care and I will obey, for Souls…for Souls…for Souls…" Gigot thought within.

Suffering led Gigot forward through the ancient Tunnels of Darkness rambling, following the Darkened Walls with his hands, leading up to Death's Darkened Door. As he travailed upwards through the tunnel, he passed upward through the Darkened Walls that grew tighter and tighter and upward to a Door that sat above. He pushed and pushed with all his might with his back and the Door opened to the grass clothed earth above.

He found himself in a graveyard, an old country church graveyard. He pondered, "Was this a church building of his future or of his past?"

It was a pristine place, all clean and pretty, well-kept and secure. The outside yard had flowers of beauty of all types and kinds, tulips and daffodils, gladiolas and red roses, too. All was maintained to perfection, yet no one was there, there was no one there to care.

The lawn was mowed all lush and green and trimmed to a tee. The old country chapel was mesmerizing, sparkling white, shimmering in the sunshine. The pure white chapel sitting on the old, country road glowed and glistened with a flickering halo. Gigot was overwhelmed at the glow of the building and the aura it presented.

"Perchance, there must be someone inside, someone who cares, someone who has the taken the time to take care of this place must surely be inside," he thought to himself. So, he walked up the brief wooden steps to the front of the chapel of old, all glistening white in appearance.

The door was not locked and it easily opened with a creak and to his amazement, the inside of this chapel of old was as white as could be. Inside, there displayed the brightest of lights. Everything shimmered inside…glistened and glowed, just like a halo of old.

No one was inside or out, yet he continued towards the front of the chapel, the Altar, they used to call it. There was the table, the one that said, "In Remembrance of Me". On the table of Remembrance sat the bronze offering plates, all empty as before. He walked the red carpet around the table to the side steps and walked up to the platform where the preacher used to preach his preach. There, on the bright wooden pulpit of oak and slick varnish were the notes of the preacher. The holy writ was open, on the table of Remembrance and its pages were clean, having never been touched or read, yet aged, from the show of appearances on the table of Remembrance.

Gigot walked up to the sturdy, wooden pulpit made of oak and slick varnish and touched the notes of the preacher who had preached his last preach. There were three pages of notes, but none to delight, on each were these words, these words brought him fright.

"All you have to do is Believe!" that's all they said. Three pages of notes and that's all they read. "All you have to do is Believe," they said once again. "The devils believe and tremble, and all God's people said, 'Amen!'"

He heard a whisper, a faint voice coming from outside the front door. He looked up through the empty chapel and out the front door to see no one, but he heard the voice again. It was the voice of the one crying from the wall,

"Help us, help us, please!"

XX

The Darkness of Mum's Deep

As Gigot and the others slept, not too far away, the darkened clouds of the Mendacium slithered up from the Crevice of Mum's Deep. The Mendacium was attempting to cover the land in its rich tales of whatever was, was not and whatever was not, was. The tales it shed in its thick, darkened clouds came in the dark and stayed in the slightest of crevices wherever it was received. The Mendacium is the breath of the Crevice and all that dwell there. It is the breath that created the tales of the Singer and the Mayors and even Judge Grudge. Not only does it tell its tales of what was, was not, but it also told and tells the tale that whatever was meant to be, could not and would not and never would…that the Truth that beheld Glory never was and never would be for it never was in the first place. The Mendacium told the old, old tale over and over again, that Truth never even existed except in some old tale made up by some old tail. "Truth is not and does not exist," is just one of their messages of old. "Imaginary," they said.

The Mendacium is not of its own, it was sent as the breath of the anointed one, at least, he said he was. This one, the anointed one, had taken that which was not his to take, but said it was and covered himself with it in what he said was the message of the kings of old. He said that it was forever and ever the way it was to be.

This anointed one they called Ementior, the one they believed was sent from heaven. In lightning, he fell in a flash from above to rule and reign and say what was to be and say what is forever. In him, there is a spell of his is and was and only he knew for certain, so he said. In a matter of speaking, it is his to say and the Mendacium repeat it over and over so that it covers all the land in what he said for what he says is Dark, but what he says, he says, is Light.

As the darkened clouds of the Mendacium came up from the Crevice, they brought with them what they had been born of…the Creepholes, the Ambush and the Gaze Ats. These were not their names. These were what they were and learned to be. They had been created by the Creator, the True One, the Great One, but they fell as their leader and with him they fell as stars from the sky. As all True Light comes from Light, these are they who left their former Glory to follow the Ementior as he duped and bedazzled and deceived and distorted all that ever was in their ears and in their eyes. They cried for what he cried for and that was power, real power of the kind of their choosing as they chose what he chose as he said it was to be.

The Creepholes followed their Master Calumnia. With cunning hiss and trickery, Calumnia led his merry Creepholes with delusion, illusion and false accusation. These dark ones were wordsmiths and tore the mightiest down to their knees with the swoop of a word, or two, or three. They had been taught well and taught well indeed that it is what you believe is what you will deed. They've learned their craft well, to dupe and deceive to make what you believe unbelievable.

They had also been taught that the word was more powerful than a sword, so they exchanged their weapons of warfare, their swords for some words and their darts for some more. Their words so dark and refined were whistled and tooted and grinned about. They slather their swords of words with the blood of lives past and present. They only take by what they give and life is always for the taking.

Crested Hill is theirs they say in tales up from the Deep. The Darkened lore of tales they creep up from their holes beneath; they say, "from above." At times, who knows for certain where they lie or lie in wait or just plain lie. Exasperated they wait in frustration, all filled to the brim with guile. Their mouths, they wipe the slather away with their arms as there's so much to say, so much to harm.

The Ambush lie in wait as well for a fair one to pass by with, or without their cares. For if the fair ones have no cares, the Ambush give them some to share. It's funny, a very Dark kind of funny when a fair one has no cares and then they do. For the fair ones share their cares as all men do and then the cares are shone about and dreaded with regret and anxiety and wonder; the kind of wonder that maybe others will share the cares and catch the cares, the dreaded cares to weigh and wait and lie in care.

Insidior has taught his company well. Insidious desire and thoughts run rampant on his tongue and he whips them out as well as Ementior as he is so proud of his slave. With plots he plots his time and out of time is he. He works his words with shock and awe, attempting to deceive. Deceive he does and that he does, all perfect rolls of yarn. He wipes his mouth with dripping lies, intended to do harm.

"Suffer by my words, you will," he says, "Suffer, suffer, please!"

"You will believe my shock and awe, your health, your mind diseased."

Insidior's relentless Darkness breathes from Ementior's veins. They say that life is in the blood and so it is with words. Some choose life and some choose death, all with the words in the mind. Others believe it to be a sword that kills, but Insidior's plots are far better than any single sword of gore. A plot with a plan made up of words can take down an entire army or even a nation if given enough time. But here, for Crested Hill, it's just one plot, a very Dark plot at that. It is the sinister kind, the one easily believed that works its best, intended to deceive. Insidior, though is just a tad bit different than some and that with his followers who lie in Ambush. Deceit is not enough, for defeat and destruction are where they lie, it is their true abode.

The Gaze Ats are those who bring the Dark to the forefront and call it Light. They whisper and say, "This is true, it's what I say, for what I say is truth. My words are mine and mine is true even though there is no truth." The sharpness in their tongues create a bolt of light from sparks in ambiguity. They say that iron sharpens iron and with tongues of iron, they flip and flop with waving bands of steel that become a sight to behold.

Specto is their guide in all things spoken. For what is real is not so real at all, but conjured from the Deep. With spells of Fear and Fright and Death awaiting, Specto bedazzles his group with his forked tongue of old saying this and saying that, they move to their right and then move to their left, not knowing why or where or what to believe if they believe anything at all.

"Watch me! Watch me!" Specto says with his desire to aim another's focus at his words. "Did you know?" he asks with questions to question to lead astray the lonely and the gullible and the wanting to believe. "Are you sure?" he asks again and teaches to deceive. "It's plain right here, you're wrong again," he says with perfect ease. He leaves the mind with despairing thoughts and battles he does win. It's with a tip, a nod, a wince of the eye, a doubt he places within.

"Watch me! Watch me!" he says with illusions he tempts to allude. He tricks, he trades the real for the naught, never was and he makes sure.

Specto is the smiling one, the salesman of the tales. "Measure what you're told," he says, "Test and prove and strike the teller, the teller of the Truth, for Truth is not, there is no Truth! Believe ME!" he says with a glistening tongue of gold.

As each of these companies of armies breathe their breath and speak their speak, the darkened clouds of Mendacium rise from beneath the shadows of the Crevice of Mum's Deep directly to the Carb. The Carb is the bridge that bridges that which has been to the final mountain, the mountain of the Crested Hill. All that lies within the Crevice desires the Crested Hill and its Mendacium has said, "We own it!" But that is only breath from words untrue. So, it is to the Carb that the Echad must go to reach the Crested Hill. There is no other way and all meets all on the day of meeting, the day of meeting at the Carb. For whoever and whatever takes the Carb, takes the Hill. The final battle awaits, while Gigot and the Echad lie sleeping.

XXI

The Lady in Waiting

Gigot, Will and Purpose lie in a semi-conscious sleep to almost awake. They all smelled the incredible aroma of frying ham and bacon drifting through the wind and it carried through their noses into their subconscious. They were all smiling in their sleep when all of a sudden Gigot was rudely awakened by Obedience standing over him saying,

"Wake up, you're drooling…wake up!" he said shaking Gigot and jerking Will's cover away from him.

"Wake up, it's past time to go, we're wasting time here," he said again impatiently.

"Don't you smell that?" Will asked. "Where is it coming from?"

"It's time to go," uttered Suffering. "I know you're distracted, but whatever you're smelling, it's not real!"

"Not real, how can that smell not be real? Fried ham and bacon! Let's go find it!" Will said gathering his things quickly, folding them up in his sack and throwing it over his shoulder.

They quickly got their things together motivated by the drifting wind down the craggy Darkend Road. There was smoke billowing not too far off and was blowing right in their direction.

"This is too good to be true," Gigot said, laughing.

"I don't care," Purpose laughed back as he was falling forward down the mountain side. The brush had cleared way and they were just down to the bottom of the mountain as the trail led to what seemed to be a fork in the road, but the road hooked to the left as a small wooden cabin was just to the right. The billowing smoke was coming from inside the cabin and the rest of them walked up to the door encouraged by the pleasant surroundings.

Everything seemed like spring was in the air. The air was crisp, yet filled with the aroma of bacon. Birds were chirping, flying and hopping around. A great sense of relief was there in those moments as Will walked up and knocked on the hard wooden door.

"Hello, anyone there?" Will asked. The knock on the jarred the door open a bit, so Will stepped back so as not to frighten the owner.

The rest stood further back.

"There's something about this that isn't right," Humility said.

"Not right? How could anyone that could create that aroma not be right?" Will said. It was quite obvious that Will and Purpose had given into the impulse of the fried ham and bacon aroma as it was proving irresistible to the senses.

Will pounded on the right door post, stepped back and said, "Hello, anyone there? We mean you no harm."

About that time, Suffering, Humility and Obedience turned around knowing they were being watched.

"Come out from there, we see you in the bushes," Suffering admitted.

"We mean you no harm," he said. "Come out at once!"

A hooded soul came out from behind the bush and held her bow close to her side.

"What is your name?" Humility stepped forward as the hooded soul stepped back.

"What is your name?" he asked again.

She pushed back her hood and let it fall to her back. She raised her bow with her right hand and held it to her chest, whispering she said, "I am Lady in Waiting. I've been here so long waiting for my man to come and deliver me."

"Who is your man?" Gigot inquired.

Suffering turned around and looked back at Gigot and Will raising his left brow as if to say, "I'll ask the pertinent questions here."

Suffering knew all that lie in waiting for the Echad, but the form of their appearance would be another matter.

"Your man, is he here someplace?" Suffering asked.

"Oh, he's here, he just arrived. I've been here waiting for him to be his guide to the Carb," she said confidently, but whispering, speaking through her teeth keeping her mouth as closed as she was able so as not to reveal her what's inside.

The three looked at each other in amazement and smiled. Will asked her, "You say he's here, but where is he?"

"You are he," she said. "I've been waiting for you to take you all to the Carb. You are on your way to the Carb, aren't you? I have been sent to be your guide and I prepared a meal for you before we go. Would you like to go in?" She asked, pointing towards the door.

Purpose turned about face and began walking towards the door, as did Will.

"Ahem!" Humility said.

Will grabbed Purpose's arm and said, "Purpose, what are you doing? This is her house, lady's first!"

"That's not what I was saying," Humility spoke further. "Do not go in there!" he commanded.

"I mean you no harm, gentlemen. It's only a meal before we go on our way," she said welcoming them into her cabin by the way.

"Where does this road take us?" Suffering asked her pointing to the trail leading to the left.

"This road widens and I can easily see that not too far up ahead that it's a very wide road," Obedience said questioning her motive.

"The road is wide so that all may pass, even you and your friends," she said and continued, "the Carb is not too far this way. There may be other ways, but this, by far is the easiest way to travel, I know, I've lived here for some time."

Suffering and Humility had had enough of her and her talk and tightened their grip on their staffs.

"Please allow me to go inside and retrieve the food that I've prepared for you. I know you're needy."

Obedience said, "Needy?"

She smiled her smile and Will was entranced. She was beautiful, yet extremely rugged and tanned. She had long, flowing hair that glistened just right in the sunlight. He skin was taut as her muscles were even more. Rugged she was, but beautiful in a very rustic sort of way. Her look appealed to Will and Purpose was siding with him.

"I please you?" she asked Will.

Will took a breath, sighing and realizing that whatever she was, she was probably too unreal to be True.

"I've displeased you, then," she said seemingly reading his mind, but watching his disposition according to what she was saying.

"Where does this road lead, then?" Suffering interjecting himself into her trance of Will breaking the charm she held on him.

Will shook his head back and forth.

"What road…in this direction. There is only one road here and it is the wide road that leads…"

"Leads to where?" Suffering said interrupting her. "This road leads away from the Carb, does it not?"

She moved herself over in front of Will, turned her back to him, separating Will from the rest of the group and then spoke to Suffering, "I am Lady in Waiting and I am to be your guide."

She pressed her back to the front of Will and turned to her left to catch Will's breath over her left shoulder.

"I've found my man," she said wryly smiling pressing further back against Will, "haven't I?"

The rest of the company were shocked at Will as he became entranced with her again and stood there motionless hardly being able to breathe. She had relaxed her bow on her right shoulder and had placed her hand on the shaft of her dagger on the right of her waist. Will could not see what she was doing, but Humility got Will's attention and caught his eye and expressed with a nod of his head to move left away from the oncoming point of the dagger.

Will conceded to Humility as Obedience stepped forward quickly to grab her right arm. Simultaneously Gigot pulled Will away from her as Obedience attempted, but failed to grab her right arm holding the dagger.

Quicker than light, she pulled the dagger out and flipped it backward pointing the sharp point towards Obedience's face and held it tightly just under his chin.

"You're disappointing me, Will, come back here and I'll take you where you need to go," she said through her gritted teeth. She was seething by this time with anger, but she took a breath, composed herself and said again, "Will come here, darling, I've been waiting for you."

She used her left hand and pointed her forefinger downward to her left foot implying that Will should leave where he was and stand beside her.

"Let him go," Gigot said, speaking of Obedience.

Her grievance came back and she shoved the tip of the dagger under Obedience's chin just enough to cause a drip of blood.

Her eyes glanced at Gigot as Gigot had moved forward shielding her sight of Suffering.

"I'll kill him, move!" she yelled at Gigot and at the same time, Suffering thrust his staff into her top teeth shoving the shaft of it up through her nose and her head flew back as she lunged backwards releasing the grip she had on Obedience's chin. As she stumbled back in pain, Humility stabbed her foot with his staff and although her backward motion was to fall back completely, Humility's staff and the pain on her left foot was too excruciating to move either way, so she corrected herself as quickly as she could and screamed revealing her tongue of gold,

"I'll kill you all!" she screamed as she stepped back and attempted to grab her arrows behind her head. Suffering hit her hard again with his staff in the midsection. She bent over in pain and when she came up, she was not who she was, but had become what she was and that was a Spectre. He grew three feet in height and his muscular arms became monstrous as did his face and head. He was growling with golden drool and clinching his fists ready to pummel Will who had fallen to the ground. Everything about him had enlarged to monstrous proportions and he was enraged with hate ready to kill.

He raised his left leg to strike Will lying on the ground, yet Humility used his staff once again to whip his right leg from out beneath him and he fell back with a hard thunderous sound against the small cabin. His body crushed through the front wall of the wooden cabin and his long hair fell back into the fire where the pig was smoking on the pit. The back of his head bounced again against the fire pit enraging the flames and exploding the fire brands around his head and hair.

The Spectre jumped from the fire as his head became engulfed in flames with the ash and the grease from the pig making his head as a torch and he ran through the back of the small cabin and fell down an embankment to the right of the cabin, rolling down the hill in flames falling fast into the Crevice. Harsh yowls came from the monster with the sound of something far more sinister than any human on fire. It was the sound of a demonic force on fire being burned until there was nothing left to burn. The torn down cabin with flames and embers still rising from the pit gave way to the other side of the cabin and that was the other side of the fork in the road. It was the narrow trail that led to the Carb.

Gigot and Purpose picked Will up from the ground as Suffering and Humility brushed him off making sure he was travel worthy. Obedience kept watch of the bottom of the hill that led to the forest of the Dark side of the Crevice. The body of the monster burned its last flicker and there was no movement in the Darkness.

XXII

Calumnia's Call

The Echad took off running down the narrow trail leading to the Carb as Suffering seemed distressed by the revelation of the Dark forces gathering there. They still had some land to cover and as they ran, the trail became more narrow as it led through a rocky divide that had been cut through a small mountain of rock. On the other side of the rock, they proceeded into a forest with high trees. Once into the forest, the narrow, rocky trail split into six trails of equal width. Once there, they could hear voices, whispers in the forest among the trees saying, "Go this way." While other whispers retorted, "No, no, no, go this way…"

No one was seen as they came to an abrupt halt and waited for Suffering to speak.

"What are we to do?" Gigot asked.

"The trails lead to Division and there are six of them. We seek the trail to the Carb," Suffering said loudly as though someone in the forest would be listening and tell them which trail to take. It seemed as though they had been guided to some sort of enchanted, wooded labyrinth that lay before them in forest trees and unclear pathways.

At that moment, the two outside trails that led to the far right and the far left disappeared leaving four trails that went in varying directions.

The rest of the Echad was dumbfounded at this strange occurrence, yet, Gigot mustered enough gumption to say the same thing loudly so that the whoever was in the forest would hear.

"We seek the trail to the Carb!" Gigot shouted.

Again, in the moment, one more trail disappeared, but the three remaining trails moved their directions as sunlight shone above through the forest below onto one particular trail in the middle. Once again the invisible whispers started back up again saying, "Go this way." And others said, "No, no, no, go this way." "No, absolutely not, go this way!"

A warm breeze blew from the back of them and blew down the trail with the sunlight on it brimming through the tall, dark forest.

"This must be the way," Will opined moving towards the trail that led to the light.

Humility moved his staff in front of Will blocking his way of moving forward and said, "Are you leading again dear man?"

Will erected himself and stiffened his back, raising his arms and hands in surrender, while Purpose chuckled behind him.

"What are you laughing at, bacon lover?" Will admonished Purpose.

"Bacon lover? Oh mighty man of love of the Lady in Waiting who had the GOLDEN TONGUE!!" Purposed shouted sarcastically.

"You two be quiet!" Gigot said adamantly.

Obedience, who had stepped forward himself to get in between Will and Purpose, smiled a sided grin being glad that Gigot had finally taken charge over the two so that he didn't have to force the issue.

"What are you thinking?" Gigot asked Suffering.

"What do you think?" Suffering replied.

"There are three roads and the one has the light and the wind. I would say go there, but I'm learning that things are hardly ever what they seem and deception also seems to rule the day."

"Deception may rule the day, but deception does not have to rule here and here," Suffering replied pointing to Gigot's head and his heart.

"We need the trail to the Carb!" Gigot exclaimed loudly.

Immediately, the trail with the sunlight and wind upon it disappeared and the remaining two trails moved once again and crossed into the darkened forest.

"And then there were two," Purpose said.

Suffering and Humility turned and looked at Purpose with sarcastic faces and didn't say a word.

"Allow us to go to the Carb," Suffering said with authority.

Immediately, an enormous tree fell on one of the trails blocking the way of the sight of the rest of the trail.

"Go that way," Suffering pointed with his staff in the direction of the fallen tree.

"No, no, no, follow me," whispers appeared once again in their hearing.

They did as Suffering spoke as Obedience led the way climbing on top of the tree to get a better look at where that trail led.

"There, go there," Obedience pointed with his sword. He pointed to the far right and sure enough, there was the rest of the trail that lie hidden by brush and other fallen trees. If the one tree had not fallen, then they would not have had the sight from a higher view to see the hidden trail further into the forest.

Here, the trail was not so rocky anymore, but plush with moss and as green as ever. The soft moss, appearing to move in places, cushioned their walk and certainly made their way easier to maneuver through the shadowy forest. There were no birds and no other 'forest' sounds to speak of and silence became the moment. They had confidence they were going in the right direction on the right trail, however, the silence of the forest was deafening and there was very little light from above. All of this created a tad bit of doubt in Will and Purpose.

"Are you sure we're on the right trail?" Purpose questioned Gigot and Suffering.

"We've been wrong before, haven't we?" Will said, remembering his failures and how often he had taken the wrong roads and their consequences. Will had looked away to his left and saw Doubt peering through the trees. Will, shuttered, took in a deep breath and Doubt vanished before him.

"This reminds me of who I was," Purpose said remembering the days of his former self, Ambivalence. He stopped and said, "I don't want to go any further, this is definitely not the right trail."

Obedience, who was leading on the mushy, mossy trail stopped abruptly and shrugged. He stiffened his back and then rested with his face looking forward further down the trail.

About that time, blood started to flow from Will's nose and he was wiping and blowing his nose and the more he blew, the more the blood flowed.

"What is wrong with you?" Purpose asked. "It's something about this trail. We're on the wrong trail, I tell you! Will, you don't look so good, I doubt Will is gonna make it through this forest. We need to stop and think this through."

Humility walked up to Will and shoved his head back to help stop the bleeding. He held a cloth up to his nose and pressed his fingers clinching off Will's nostrils.

About that time, the mushy, mossy trail that they were walking on seemed to be moving more than mushy as though they were being conveyed backwards. The moving halted abruptly and out from under the moss began to crawl, long, thick, black worms that seemed to grow the more they moved.

Suffering looked at Obedience and as they quickly looked at each other, they both yelled at the same time, "RUN!"

Obedience led the way as the rest of them ran as fast as they could, staying on the moss trail in the forest. With each step they ran, the moss erupted beneath their feet with hundreds of worms crawling from beneath the moss. The worms moved quickly out from under the moss and were slithering towards them chasing them through the forest. The worms grew into hundreds of tiny snakes and were snapping at Purposes' heels.

"RUN, RUN FASTER!" Purpose screamed as they all ran as fast as they could.

As the moss ran out into a clearing, Suffering turned about face and allowed the rest to pass him. He stood firm where he was and made a stand stretching his arms open wide and with his staff he pointed towards the oncoming snakes.

As in an apparition, the snakes became one and monstrous and raised its head up and forward to swallow Suffering with its viperous fangs.

With outstretched arms, Suffering pointed his staff at the snake and shouted, "NO! You Creephole!"

The snake immediately stopped slithering as the rest of the group abruptly stopped running forward. They turned about face, running back to the rear of Suffering.

"You have no place here," the Creephole Snake hissed, shifting to and fro with his neck and head preparing to strike Suffering at any moment. The Creephole Snake's tongue was flat coming from his mouth and appeared as a sword rather than a tongue.

"You have no place here," Suffering said mocking the Snake telling him the truth of the matter.

Hissing and laughing, the Creephole Snake mocked them, "Fear! Look at you, the glorious Echad, running from ME."

He hissed all the more and his tongue erupted as a sword as he waved his tongue of sword in front of Suffering and said, "Bow before me, or die."

"You have no place here," Suffering repeated.

In the moment, Gigot and Will realized that the repeated phrase had definite meaning as Purpose didn't quite get the fact that the Creephole Snake had no place there.

Gigot and Will went to each side of Suffering and repeated together what Suffering had uttered, "You have no place here, Creephole Snake.

Be gone!"

Immediately, two other Creephole Snakes crawled quickly from the forest and joined their wicked brother.

"The forest is filled with us. We are many and we are undefeated!" one of the Creephole Snakes hissed his saying slithering a bit more to the left in order to flank the Echad on their right.

Obedience moved immediately as the others formed a circle with their backs towards one another.

Suffering was facing the first Creephole Snake and said once again, "You have no place here. Disappear!"

Laughing, the Creephole Snake replied, "He does not care for you, He never did," he said looking at Gigot.

He had Gigot's attention as they each prepared for the onslaught of what they did not know.

"Who? Who doesn't care?" Gigot responded taking a breath tightening his grip on his sword.

"The Almighty, the Great One, as you believe you know him," the Creephole Snake chuckled, "But you know that…don't you?" He hissed, "You'll never win. You'll always fail like all the other times before."

Gigot wiped his mouth as he was panting and drooling profusely as his mouth was full of spit.

Will's nose began to bleed again with huge drops of blood dropping down upon the clearing. Will wiped his face with his arm as the blood continued to flow from his nose. He stood ready even though he was becoming light headed from the loss of blood and the unknown as to why it was happening to him. Each time he swallowed, more blood was flowing down the back of his throat and he began to spit out the blood instead of swallowing it.

Unbeknownst to Will, Doubt had cloaked himself to minutia and had crawled up into Will's sinus cavity and had Will by the throat with one hand and had two spiny fingers pressed through his eyes just above his nose.

Each of the Creephole Snakes continued to maneuver separating themselves from each other until they formed a triangle against the Echad. Each of them stood fast as Obedience demanded, "Hold true."

Suddenly, with all of the prospective violence that was about to occur, out of the forest there came walking a small man, a very small man. He had a white handkerchief waving it with his right hand. In a very peaceful way, he walked towards Will, who was standing in his own blood, becoming pale and faint.

Doubt sneered at the small man as if to say, "I have this."

The Creephole Snakes, more larger than life, had grown thirty feet long, hissed more powerfully and slithered back and forth continuing their movements pretending to strike with their tongues of sword and fangs of white.

The small one, walked as an innocent child towards Will with his white handkerchief and as he approached Will, he stopped within a few feet of him and said, "My name is Columnia. You need to realize that we care for you, Will. Although, the Great One does not care for you and probably never did, we do. Please take this cloth as it will sooth the pain of it all and we'll leave you alone. Suffering is right about this, we have no place here, do we?" as he smiled, winked and offered his cloth to Will.

As soon as Columnia spoke, he reached out to Will with his handkerchief and smiled a wry and deprecating look at Suffering. Doubt released some of the pressure from his spiny fingers in Will's eyes at the same time that Calumnia had offered Will the handkerchief.

"He's the one whose caused this, you know…or, maybe you did?" Calumnia said of Suffering.

"Suffering," Columnia said with a sarcastic gumpft.

"Why do you think they call him that?" Calumnia uttered as he stood there with his small arm outstretched for Will to take his cloth. At this point, Calumnia believed that he had transfixed his power over the mind of Will and waved Doubt away. Calumnia sought, with all his darkened spiritual might, to persuade Will to surrender. "All you have to do is take this cloth and all of this will be over. Then, we'll leave you alone. Your blood shouldn't be spilt here. Take it and be healed."

The Echad readied themselves back to back for it was evident that a very dark trick was being played out on Will who was becoming more and more weakened by the moment. Their backs were full to each other as the Creephole Snakes hissed and agreed with the small one, "Take the cloth and we'll leave. No more blood needs to be shed and we'll leave just as he said."

Will was about to fall as Calumnia's reach of the cloth became closer with the Creephole Snakes approach.

All of a sudden, Suffering shouted, "Will!"

Will shook at the call and came to himself. With a guttural burst of strength, he shouted, "NOOO!" and raised his sword high towards Calumnia, heaving it downwards cutting off the arm of the small one.

The moment the cloth touched the ground, Calumnia disappeared in black vapor.

Simultaneously, the Creephole Snakes each lunged towards their two enemies as they had divided them in their minds. The Echad had learned from the fallen Tiger to get the neck just below the jawline and as each team of two drew the ire of their respective Creephole Snake, one of them battled the swords coming from the snakes mouths and held steady while the other sliced through the throats of the snakes slicing their necks partially away from their heads.

With a thunderous thump, each Creephole Snake fell to their deaths gasping for air and slithering and sliding and jumping as all snakes do when they've been partially separated from their head.

As the snakes bodies and tails jumped, hopped and wiggled aimlessly about, Gigot, Will and Purpose lunged and lurched towards each of the heads of the respective Creephole Snakes avoiding the whipping tails and thrust their swords through their heads striking the final blow to their death.

XXIII

Lying in Wait

Will collapsed to the ground as blood continued to run from his nose. He was drooling blood as his head was bleeding internally and he coughed up the blood that flowed down his throat. Gigot and Purpose shouldered their swords and ran over to Will. In the fight, they presumed that Will had been struck in the head, before the final blow to the head of the snake. Will coughed up blood that was beginning to slow a bit, but he was so exhausted from the fight that all he could do was lie there. Gigot and Purpose pulled him over and drug him away from the dead creatures. Humility, Suffering and Obedience came to their side and managed to prayerfully tend to Will unlike anything Gigot or Purpose seemed to be able to do. They laid their hands on him and as he drank water, he was slowly reviving from the fatigue.

"We've not much further to go to get to the Carb and I fear that this type is only the beginning of our troubles," Suffering said.

"Well, tell us what we're up against, then, before we run into it. I knew that this trail wasn't right and look what happened," Purposed stammered, as his demeanor had changed to angst.

Obedience, kneeling beside Will, looked up at Purpose and said, "We can't tell you all that we're up against because we don't know all things. What we do know is that we have a common enemy set to take the life away from you and it's not going to stop until it's defeated."

"I've had enough of this place, I need air," Purpose said begrudgingly.

Purpose, tired, exhausted and fearful huffed away on the open trail that led towards the Great Mount. As he walked, he was intent on simply getting away from the miry death scene of the snakes.

"What's gotten into him?" Gigot asked, looking to Suffering and Humility for an answer.

"It hardly ever ends, Gigot," Humility responded. "There's always something else to learn, the Great One calls it 'being perfected' and when one is 'being perfected' the crucible is met with all sorts of internal dealings that always fail. Few learn that submission to Him is the key. Fewer still learn to operate within submission in the each and every moment. It seems that reversion back to the former state is always available for the one who simply doesn't get it figured out. That's how Doubt and Ambivalence work."

"So, Purpose needs to 'get it figured out'? Gigot asked.

Obedience and Suffering were helping Will up from his weakness to see if he could stand on his own two legs. His legs were shaking from the weakness, but in the ensuing moments, the healing from the laying on of hands mixed with the water seemed to be working. Will began walking with his head fell back so as to alleviate the bleeding, taking in deep breaths dizzying himself and then looking forward with blurred vision. He held his hands out to touch the trees that seemed to be right in front of his face, but they were far away. He bent over forward and rested his hands on his knees, spat on the ground, looked up and all of a sudden, began to feel better. With a shrug and a sigh, he walked forward on his own to let his friends know that he was going to be able to make it.

"Let's go!" Will said, as he turned back to look at his friends. "Purpose has gone up ahead, hasn't he?"

"Let's go, then," Obedience said, agreeing with Will. "We need to catch up to Purpose before trouble catches up to him."

Purpose had, for certain, gone ahead and was out of sight. He was wondering in the right direction, alone with his thoughts thinking he was not alone. Thoughts are that way, they are almost always around. They can be as a brother or a sister, a mentor or a counselor, or they can be a blind guide leading the blind into all sorts of trouble. Thoughts can be friends or they can be enemies and if the one doesn't know the difference, then being alone with them can be frustratingly unkind and demonstratively destructive. Thoughts can lead the one to the right road or they can lead the one to be confident in self-assurance having thought through a thing until even the thinking becomes tiring and then another thought comes to the mind that says, "I'll take it from here, you, follow me."

That's where Purpose was unwittingly allowing himself to be. He was doing what he was thinking and that was wandering aimlessly in the right direction, but not realizing that what lie beyond the next tree or mound or under the ground might not be to his liking. He didn't know where his thoughts were coming from, whether they were coming from within or without. And, as it is with most confused folk who have made their beds with the attitudes of the ambivalent, he walked away from his friends far enough to not realize whether he was walking towards the Great Mount or away from it.

Inadvertently lost in his thoughts, he had walked up and down, mound after mound and then down into a valley. When he came to himself, he didn't know if he was to proceed forward or turn around or if he'd already turned around. He was lost, as all of the mounds, hills and valleys all looked the same.

"I do believe I'm lost," he said as he was turning around to see if he could remember from whence he came or if he'd know if he hadn't seen what he was looking at before.

"I'm confused," he said to himself. So, he sat down on a rock believing he had not walked too far away from the Echad and that they would catch up to him soon enough.

As he sat upon the rock, a Hedgeling, short and stout fellow, with a very wide nose, walked up to him, as meek and mild mannered as a Hedgeling can be. The Hedgeling said to him, "Good man, can you tell me how to get to the Great Mount? I have some wares to sell to the one they call the Echad that others say is headed there. Are you the one in whom I seek?"

Not knowing who this Hedgeling was and what he was about, Purpose was not purposed to tell him anything, yet the Hedgeling asked him a question, "From where have you come?"

Purpose knew there was an up to the mound and a down to the mound and that in one direction there was the Great Mount and from the other direction his friends would come from whence he came.

"I've come from there," Purpose said as he pointed to furthest extent of the valley.

Purpose, still in his confusion, hadn't thought about that particular direction, but was still alert enough to try to get to why the Hedgeling was trying to find out about the Echad.

"Who is this Echad that you are talking about and how do you know about them?" Purpose asked.

"Them, did I say 'them'? Oh, I'm sorry, I thought I asked you about your friends, are they a 'them'?" the Hedgeling inquired. He was short and unbecoming, a rather daft looking soul who seemed to be the epitome of harmlessness. He had short cropped bangs, puffy cheeks, an even puffier nose and the only thing he carried was a sack on his back.

"You said, 'they', you didn't answer my question," he said again.

Purpose stood up at attention as the Hedgeling seemed to be getting the better of the conversation. He was already a bit agitated at the rest of his group not catching up to him and now he was getting a tab bit more agitated at this Hedgeling who was asking too many questions.

"How do you know about the Echad?" Purpose demanded.

"So, there is an Echad, and the one is a them, indeed…" the Hedgeling retorted.

"You just asked about them, didn't you, why did you just say that?" Purposed responded realizing that he had just confirmed the Hedgeling's question.

"You said that there is a one, I just need to know where they are so that I can sell him, or them, what I have to sell him, or them. I have what he needs," the Hedgeling stated.

"How do *you* know what *we* need?" Purposed asked sarcastically.

"So, you are him, or, no, no, no, you are a part of them?" the Hedgeling smiled. "So, where are they?"

"I don't know," Purpose bit his lip curious as to why this creature wanted to know the whereabouts of his friends.

"Where are they?" Purpose pondered in his mind, yet staring down the Hedgeling begrudgingly.

"So, you don't know where they are, it seems, is that what you're saying?" the Hedgeling inquired again. The Hedgeling smiled and said, "Do you know where *you* are?" chuckling at Purpose getting the best of him…it seemed.

The two stood at a stalemate with neither of them saying another word. Each time Purpose took a breath to say something, the Hedgeling would mimic him and get ready to say something himself. The Hegeling decided to break the silence with this query,

"You said…"

"Stop this, I didn't say anything," Purpose stammered.

"But, you asked me 'how do you know what we need?' didn't you, you said that yourself. Don't you remember what *you* said? So, tell me, where are they so that I may meet them? Oh, and, yes, why are you out here all alone away from them?"

Purpose didn't respond.

"I've heard of your Great One, you know, 'the one who cares', they say. Tell me, does he care about you?"

Again, Purpose did not respond, but he was beginning to look a little disheveled from the conversation and he was all the more confused by it as well. His confusion was blaring on his face.

"You know," the Hedgeling pondered, "if I was working for someone who said he cared for me, I think I would need to see a little proof of that. Otherwise, what he said wouldn't be true." The Hedgeling took in a deep breath, smiled a big smile and shook his finger in Purpose's face and said, "That's it, isn't it? That's why you're out here all alone, isn't it? He doesn't care for you and you know it," he said laughing, pulling a soiled, white cloth from his pocket.

"Do you need this, you poor schlup? You're lost and you don't know where you are," the Hedgeling laughed as he waved his version of a handkerchief in front of Purpose's face.

Purpose sat back down again on the rock bewildered as to why his friends were taking so long to catch up to him. He thought to himself that maybe he had veered off the trail too far and that he really didn't know where he was or where they were for that matter.

"I'm not a schlup, you Hedgeling," Purpose retorted as his bewilderment was turning to anger, but his defeat was, again, on his face.

"You said that they were coming this way, did you not? That's why you're waiting here, isn't it? So, if we wait together right here, they're bound to find you here all alone with me, what will they say to you then, 'What are you doing with this Hedgeling?' Why don't' we go down the Valley and rest? That would be helpful to you, wouldn't it? Don't you need some rest? You look awfully tired, you do. The Valley is THE place of rest and I know you need some rest and some…"

"Stop it, stop saying what I said," Purpose screamed.

"Now, you're angry, do you always get this way, when you don't get your way, or…" laughing the Hedgeling added, "lost your way, ha, ha, ha,"

Exasperated, Purpose tucked his head down in between his legs waiting for the Hedgeling to simply leave him alone.

"Look, you said, you knew what you were doing, didn't you? You said that you could lead and that you could win this thing if they'd all just listen to you. You said that, didn't you?"

Purpose jumped up and screamed, "Stop it, I said, did you hear that? I said. I said to stop it, you don't know me and you certainly don't know what I think!" Purpose placed his hand on the heel of his sword threatening to use the sword on the Hedgeling, but the water welling up in his eyes shared a different sight from that of the grip of his hand.

The insidious Hedgeling wryly smiled and cocked his head to the side. He began shaking his head back and forth and said, "You thought, you thought, you said, you said. Don't you get it by now? The Great One does not care for you, never did! Why are you defending Him? Can't you see how defeated you are, how defeated all of you are? The one, the glorious Echad, the savior Echad, indeed! These are they, the one in spirit and truth, who fought together and fell in defeat! There's just always some thing or some one around the bend, isn't there…to lead you astray? You always, somehow, manage to go astray, fail and lead others to follow your path of doom. That's why you finally decided to go nowhere and…you should have stayed there in nowhere, in Middletown, where you belong!"

Purpose thrust himself back down again on the rock and tucked his head in between his legs once again to hide from his own shame of ambivalence and all that he once was and all that he'd hoped he'd ever be.

"And one last thing, Purpose," the Hedgeling said as he stood breathing his venom over the backside of Purpose's head. "All men get what they deserve."

Purpose pondered the Hedgeling's musings, but it was the last statement that struck Purpose through the back of his mind all the way to the bottom of his heart.

"All men get what they deserve," Purpose posed within, whispering the line to himself knowing how great a failure he truly was and how, at last, he was getting what he deserved from all of his failures.

Purpose wept.

The Hedgeling, knowing he had defeated Purpose with a few simple, yet heart-destroying words, patted him on the back and said, "Now, now, there, there. All of this will be over soon, won't it? It will all be over soon."

The Hedgeling, glorying in his victory over the mind of Purpose, soothed the back of Purpose with one hand while he pulled a dagger out of his shirt with the other.

"Now, now, now, just rely on me, I'll take care of you," the Hedgeling said as he continued to sooth Purpose's back with the one hand and raising his dagger high in the air to thrust it down into Purpose's spine.

Purpose had relaxed, folded his head over on his own knees and got lost in his bewilderment and confusion. He stared down at the ground and the feet of the Hedgeling before him. Purpose repeated what the Hedgeling said, but in his own words, "I get what I deserve…I get what I deserve…"

The Hedgeling, dropped the soiled, white cloth down at Purpose's feet and lifted both of his hands high with the dagger placed to go into Purpose's spine into the backside of his heart.

With his hands raised high, the Hedgeling shouted, "From the Valley of the Thicket you came, to the Valley of Hell you shall go…"

At the pinnacle of the height of his hands and his shout, the Hedgeling, just as he was about to thrust the dagger downward, fell back and staggered, with a dagger in his forehead and a most bewildered look on his face. His own dagger fell to the ground as his outstretched hands could no longer grasp the blade intended for Purpose, but felt his hands go upward to make a grave attempt at grabbing this dismal dagger from his forehead. Obedience had suddenly arrived and flung his dagger pinpoint into the forehead of the Hedgeling at just the right moment. The rest of the group ran down the mound into the part of the Valley where Purpose sat upon the rock. Obedience drove his dagger deeper through the Hedgeling's head to make certain of his death.

"Purpose! Purpose! Wake up! Wake up from this trance!" Humility shook Purpose out of defeat. Purpose breathed a heavy breath and a sigh, raised his body up from his position on his legs and looked up and about at his friends.

"You came, you didn't leave me! You do care!" Purpose shouted in joy.

Suffering looked at Gigot as they all looked at one another and Gigot said, "Of course, we care!"

Purpose looked on the ground at the Hedgeling who had a surprised and tortured look on his dead face as the blood ran out of his head onto the ground. His blood was dark, as black as the snakes.

"We know," Suffering said as he comforted Purpose with a hug.

"But, how do you know, do you know, really?" Purpose asked embarrassed at what Suffering might know and if he knew all.

"Suffice it to say that we know…Humility, Obedience and I," Suffering responded. "It is enough to know that we know and that we care. It is how He loves, Purpose."

"Let's stick together," Obedience chided Purpose. Purpose, humiliated, looked to Obedience and said, "I will."

XXIV

Obedience Calls

There comes a time when a demand is given and you're told what to do and if you don't do it, then the demand sits waiting out the window for you to decide to obey and until you do, you'll have to do something else in the meantime. Saying, "I will obey and I will go," and then not doing it is basically lying to the one who has given you the command, but it is also lying to yourself in the words that you speak don't match your within or your walk. The within has to be activated to submit and follow the demand first, otherwise, words will flow like streams in a desert. You don't know where they come from and they're basically useless because they lack meaning. They soon dry up from not having a constant flow in the midst of the heat. Do what you've been told to do by the Great One and stick to it until the task is completed. No one likes to be called a schlup… particularly when you think it's true. Do all men get what they deserve? It is the fear of the fallen and the failed. It is also the mantra of those who hate the others in whom they disagree.

But, is it true? Or, is it false? Could it be either, neither or both? It is true to the mind that hates and desires the worst upon his enemy. To that mind, his enemy should get more than what he deserves, punishment, eternal… even to be sent to the depths of hell for what they did to me or mine or what they said to me or about me.

It is also false to the same mind when it is said of oneself.

All men get what they deserve. "I hope not, that judgement cannot be for me," says the one who seeks pardon and mercy for himself, but not the other. "No, no, no, no judgement meant for me," we say and think within. But…what if?

"What if we really do get what we deserve as we wish it upon our enemies?" Purpose pondered the paradox as he pitied himself and the paths he had taken. "Perhaps, selfish pity desires its own punishment," he opined. "Do I, have I, wished for my own punishment?" he questioned himself.

The time was far past for Gigot to get his friends in order. Wavering, doubting, waiting and disbelieving had taken its toll on himself, Will and Purpose. The depths of the Crevice of Mum's Deep were deeper than he could ever imagine and their playing with his thoughts and imagination was proving to be his undoing. He had to get Will and Purpose believing and working together with him and with the Great One. Suffering had too much work to do and the less work Obedience accomplished, the more Suffering became activated into constant and unabated activity of various sorts and design.

Humility simply sighed most of the time in wonderment at what was going to transpire next in their journey. He knew for certain what awaited them at the Carb, yet Gigot had floundered at just about every scheme thrown at him and the worst was yet to come. He also knew that all of them had heard the Hedgeling's final words. Words spoken, heard in the ear have a way with a man, particularly with a fallen man. At times, all he needs is the tip-end of the breath from an errant spirit to precipitate his own demise. It is, after all, that last thought that comes from the spirit of Darkness that drives the man to total submission and surrender to the depths with Depression and at a man's worst, suicide.

"Purpose," Humility gently whispered, "The Great One is full of mercy and loving kindness, isn't He?"

Purpose wryly smiled in response, thought about it for less than a moment and said, "The Great One is merciful and kind. He is, indeed." Purpose gave Humility an upside down smile, perked one side of his mouth up and then the other and smiled to his self a merciful smile. It seemed that the spirit of Grace Walker had appeared and Purpose smiled all the more.

Humility turned his thoughts to Gigot.

"Gigot, how do you get a leader to lead?" Humility asked Gigot as they walked up the mound in the direction of the Great Mount.

Gigot thought about his question and replied, "If you have to get the leader to lead, then you're talking to the wrong person. No one has to get the leader to lead because leaders lead, it's what they do. If they're not leading, they're not leaders."

"Where are you in this journey, Gigot? Are you leading? Because you're supposed to be leading, aren't you? Are you leading this group, or, is someone else?"

"You know I'm leading, but I know that it's been mostly accidental, I'm not sure. Things just happen and I know I haven't been the cause or the first to lead out of a situation. It looks like I don't know what I'm doing and that would be true. No, it is true. I don't know what I'm doing or where I'm going."

"Is that entirely true, Gigot?" Humility had to keep Gigot on the plain of truth because it was becoming evident that Doubt had arisen from some mist in the Valley.

Gigot looked to his right and sure enough, Doubt had appeared walking along the side of him…smiling, like an old friend…just not a good, old friend.

Gigot stopped, looked at Doubt, scrunched his eyebrows with a bit of determination, and said, "Why are you here? Where did you come from?"

"Why, I'm your constant companion, Gigot! You know me." Doubt said smiling, cajoling Gigot with an elbow in his side as though he were being playful.

"You are not my constant companion," Gigot laughed. "Why are you here?"

"I am your comfort, Gigot, your ever-present friend indeed," Doubt replied.

Gigot turned to his left and looked at Humility, tilted his head with a wince of his eye and said, "Get out of here!"

As he immediately turned back to his right, Doubt had vanished in a flash.

Will and Purpose had been walking ahead and as Gigot's conversation had turned to Doubt, they had stopped to see where this was going. When Doubt disappeared, Gigot looked eye to eye with Will and Purpose and asked, "Why are you two leading?"

With no response from the two of them, they parted so that Gigot and Humility could pass through the middle of them. Obedience took to Will's side and Suffering took to Purpose's side and they proceeded towards the Great Mount.

Up and down the grassy mounds, they traveled as they were gradually climbing with each new mound. Gigot wondered at the work they had to do to get to the Great Mount, with the up and down and the up and down, nothing was ever easy.

The approach to the Great Mount was long. It was an upward, continually upward incline that seemed to have no end. Grassy mounds of fields to the right and the left, ever onward, ever upward. Once they got up one mound, they would have a short decline leading to a brief valley and then it was upward again. By the time they had reached the tenth mound, they felt certain they were reaching the peak of the Great Mount.

The higher they traversed the green mounds, the more the green was becoming a darker shade of lavender to purple for they were entering the gateway to the Great Mount by way of the Fields of Lavandula. The flowering plants of the Lavandula covered the mounds leading to the last remaining ascent to the Great Mount. This was the reason why the Great

Mount always looked dark, but it wasn't because it was Dark, it was because it was covered in varying shades of purple.

As they pushed up the long, gradual ascent they brushed through the bushes. Their clothing was becoming quite aromatic of mint, lavender, basil and sage, as well as, turning dark purple from the oils of the over abundant supply of fragrant flowers. It didn't take long for them to realize that they were awashed by the oil in the flowers. Everything about them had turned to dark purple and the only thing on them that wasn't purple was their faces. They reached the pinnacle of the Great Mount and sat to rest.

"I'm tired," said Will, "I suddenly feel like I need a nap or something."

"I'm energized, I'm ready to go!" said Purpose.

"It's the nard at work, Will. Feel refreshed and awake your mind," said Suffering.

A mighty sound of rage was coming from just over the ridge of the Great Mount and so they crawled on their bellies to the edge of the cliff of the Great Mount to see what was happening below. As they continued to crawl through the Fields of Lavandula upwards towards the cliff, their bodies and clothing had become visibly dark purple from the oils so that as they peered through the plants to the gathering below, they were unseen in their seeing. The plants had given them their camouflage, albeit a dark purple hue.

All of a sudden, Will started sneezing from the over abundant supply of fragrance in the oils of the flora.

"Stop that! Immediately!" Gigot demanded in a whisper. "You can't give away our position!"

Obedience shoved Will's arm up into his face and said, "Be done with that!"

Will looked intently at Obedience and said through his arm stuffed in his face, "Ok, already."

"Chew a bit of it and get used to it," Obedience told Will.

Immediately, Will stripped a stalk of the flower and clenched it through his teeth and pulled the stalk through his teeth leaving the flowers in his mouth.

"This tastes sweet," he said to Obedience as purple oily drool flowed from his mouth.

"Not too much of that and chew with your mouth shut," Obedience winked back at Will.

Will used his arm to wipe his mouth and smiled at Obedience revealing an entirely dark purple mouth full of lavender and sage.

As they all peered through the Lavandula at the Thicket of Cadgwith below, they saw a sight that none of them had seen before. They could see the Carb afar off, but to get to the Carb, they had to get down from the Great Mount and go through the raging storm of Mendacium amidst the battling trees of the Thicket of Cadgwith. It was all of this that awaited them.

The Dark clouds rising from the Mendacium rose almost to the pinnacle of the Great Mount as the thousands upon thousands of Mendacium raged their breath awaiting their leader, Ementior. The Mendacium did all that their leader commanded as breath breathed into Dark blackened vapor searching for someplace, any place to light upon anything that might be light and make it Dark.

"You see what Lies before us, Gigot," Suffering said. "We have to get to the Carb to join Faith and Truth at the Atlas, on the Crested Hill side of the Carb. Others are meeting us there, but it is our task to get to the Prominens and take the Carb."

"What others?" Gigot asked.

"The others that those who are with us; that have always been with us, but not shown." Suffering replied. "They are waiting."

Somehow Gigot knew and didn't need to ask any more questions. These were those that had been with him before who had said that they would be with him and yet he had forgotten in the midst of the journey. They had told him that they would not leave him and yet when he did not see them, he believed they had.

"They've been waiting for you to come along side Obedience and Humility. You have traveled enough with me and you've gotten used to me, haven't you?" Suffering said.

Gigot turned his head towards Suffering to his right and said, "You're right. You've led because it's what I desired. Humility's led a way and now it's time for me to walk with Obedience. Are you going to disappear, too, when this is all over?"

Suffering looked through Gigot and said, "Walk together, fight together, abide together."

"Gigot, all of this land that you see is yours, it's always been yours," Suffering added.

A tear came to Gigot's eyes. It was a tear of revelation, a tear of exhilaration and, yet, it was a tear of regret for having to come this far with so much calamity. He knew that what was rightfully his, he had given up over time and now it was time to take it back. Obedience was by his side and he knew he would never fight another fight without him.

They all knew what was before them now as the Dark breath of death of the Mendacium rose to their nostrils in sharp contrast to the oil of the lavender. They gathered their swords about them as they lay upon the earth of the Great Mount washed and hidden by the purple.

"Chew some Lavandula to cover your teeth," Suffering revealed.

As they moved about covered in dripping purple, they looked as tall, waving lavender moving along the brink of the Great Mount to a place where they could slide down the Mount to the Thicket of Cadgwith below. Their plan was to infiltrate the Mendacium undercover and make their way to the Prominens of the Carb by stealth. There, they would set their charge against Ementior and his Mendacium, just before the Carb. They purposed to reverse the field of battle against the totality of the Lie and battle by surprise.

XXV

Anger in the Thicket of Cadgwith

The Dark driving wind that blew up from the depths of the Crevice of Mum's Deep caused the Thicket of Cadgwith to sway turbulently. The trees were so thick there that no one could make it through without getting a bruise, a point, a stab or a death as they made their way through the thicket of trees. What made things worse, was the fierce gales that constantly came up from the Crevice of Mum's Deep that caused the trees to sway and claw at each other as though they were constantly battling for their territorial rights. Only the strongest of the trees survived and hardly ne'er a man ever did when the wind was at its height. The unpredictability of the fierce winds coupled with the swaying of the trees created a fearsome fright for anyone journeying through to the Carb. It was a desolate place that no man wanted and was useless for anything except a hiding place for Darkness. Anything that pertained to the Dark enjoyed its residence there for no one cared to go and meander along that part of the Crevice.

As it was in days gone by, Purpose, who used to go by the name of Ambivalence and having lived on Halfway Boulevard in Middletown, used to play in thickets because he was too afraid to venture afar off from home. The thickets barely hurt him none because he had this unusual and uncanny navigational mind to navigate through a thicket without any harm to himself. It was a gift, he supposed, and as Purpose looked down upon this Thicket of Cadgwith, he was not intimidated in the least by its thickness, rudeness and its overall unpredictability from the gale force winds. In his mind and through his eyes, he could plainly see the trail that led from the bottom of the Great Mount all the way through the Battling Trees on to the entrance to the Carb.

Even though the Dark plumes of breath rose from the Mendacium in the swaying thicket of the trees, he could still make out the white, rocky trail that lay open before him because the trail had been a trail before the thicket had grown into a thicket.

"I see the way," Purpose proposed.

"You see the way?" Gigot inquired. "How do you see the way? How could there even be *a way*?"

"Think through this, Gigot," Suffering said.

"We'll have to stay covered in the Lavandula so as not to be detected," Obedience said. "What do you see?" he asked Purpose.

"I know you may not believe this, but I see a trail, even through all the Dark vapor and the swaying of trees. I see where we need to walk to get to the Carb."

"Tell me what you see, then." Gigot told Purpose.

"You see down to the right in between the two boulders, there is an entrance down there where the rock forms a roof and goes out into the Thicket. The trail starts there."

Unbeknownst to the Echad, this was the place the Mendacium referred to as The Devil's Frying Pan. There the breath of Ementior passes through and hisses back in blueish green sludge as an ocean roaring with foam and histle. The breath of Lies that Ementior breathed were sent out to willing ones ready to receive, but always returned when they were not, so that they may Darken others in need of Darkened Lies ready and willing to obey the Lie.

Purpose continued, "The trail continues and goes in complete curls all the way to the Carb, do you see it?"

"I see it," Humility answered.

"I do, too," Will said.

"And I do, as well," said Suffering.

Gigot looked at Obedience and they both nodded.

"If I hadn't seen it with my own eyes, I wouldn't have believed it, but I see it plain as day, Purpose," Gigot said.

Purpose grinned a very large smile.

"If it's ok with you, I'll lead the way," Purpose asked Gigot.

"Go, we're ready," Gigot responded.

And with that, Purpose led the Echad down the mossy green embankment of the Great Mount down to the bottom where the Mount met the Thicket of the Cagdwith. The Dark smoke from the plumes of breath of the Mendacium billowed upward as the dark purple camouflage provided a double cloak so that they all made it down from the Mount undetected. They met where the two boulders meet with a sliver of stone forming a roof over the entrance. The breath of Ementior was knee deep sludge going in and out of the place. As the breath entered the pass it hissed and howled as it hit upon the rock and then would be pulled out as a tide each time Ementior breathed. They called it the Devil's Frying Pan from the hiss. The breath roared as an ocean when it hit upon the rock and gave the Echad a disturbing tempo to wade through under the pass.

The anger of the Mendacium was brewing strong as Ementior stood on a rock in front of the Prominens at the front of the Carb. He was breathing rage into his clones in preparation for the final battle for Crested Hill. He also knew that whoever took the Carb, took the Hill, but his plan was to simply destroy the Carb, so that there would never again be any movement from the Crested Hill to the rest of the region. Half of his army would move over the Carb and half would stay in the Thicket of the Cadgwith and he would rule it all from the Atlas of the Carb.

Dark anger, born of hate, filled Ementior's rage. He was filled with passion decreeing and declaring all that was about to occur. He believed his words. Ementior bore the signet of the Unbibium with bright bluish green triangles sided with the color of red triangles. His helmet had the resemblance of the Octahedra, with four hexagons of twelve spheres. This signet, he believed, was the foundation of Death and Darkness to rule the Crested Hill and he feigned a caring interest in his clones to aid him in his quest.

"Dark to rule the Dark and Anger to rise from Hate, if it were not for me, there would be no universe," he repeated his mantra over and over despite his knowledge and resentment of the Dodecahedron.

The more he said this, the more enraged the Mendacium became. They breathed in his breath as he spewed out his venom. All breath was Dark matter and it was on this matter that the Mendacium relied. Without the Dark Breath, they would cease to be no more, so they sided with their master for their very breath to breathe to kill and to hate and to rule the region with the Darkness of their existence.

As the Mendacium repeated the mantra of Ementior, they flailed their arms and weapons of war high and shouted, "Dark to rule the Dark and Anger to rise from Hate, if it were not for him, there would be no universe. Cancer to rule this earth and Death to the Light above. Death to the Light within and Darkness to rule them all. All Pain and Sorrow rise to Death. Hate rise to Divorce and cause the Great Divide upon the earth."

The breath of Ementior and the Mendacium formed the Dark vapor rising above the Thicket of the Cadgwith until Darkness completely enveloped the region. The breath bore the Spectre of Cancer upon the land and even the Battling Trees shook with Fear and Fervor awaiting the Death of it all.

"No more Light, no more joy! Death to rule the Day and Death to rule the night," Ementior expounded. "I stand upon the rock of Prominens and upon this rock, I will build a fortress more mighty than any could overcome. Darkness is our friend and the Lie is our Master. Darkness is our life to rule the Land, and the Lie to rule the Heart and the Lie to rule the Mind."

At once, a group of Mongling Mendacium soldiers came out from under the Carb bearing two captives that had been beaten and captured from the Crested Hill. They dragged the beaten captives by their bound arms behind their backs as blood soaked the bags over their heads.

"We have a prize, or two," Ementior laughed as the two bloody captives were thrown at his feet.

It was at this time that the Echad had been making their way in stealth through the Thicket amongst the glaring Mendacium. As rage filled the air, the Echad, covered in dark purple and following Purpose along the trail, watched in horror as the two captives thrown at Ementior's feet were beaten once again with the Rods of Thoughts of who they were not and what they were never to become.

Obedience held the arm of Will as Will attempted to take a step forward and draw his sword from its sheath. Obedience merely shook his head, "No," not saying a word and remaining undetected.

Tears formed in the eyes of Purpose so Humility struck his face with a lock of Lavandula. The tears would have fallen from his eyes upon his face revealing his true identity. Humility looked at Purpose with a shaking head of "No" and that was the end of the tears.

The group had come to a place among the Battling Trees as the raging mocks of the Mendacium being sickened by their Dark breath and the Hate that rose in the Land.

They moved slower now through the raging crowd, one by one, they moved in stealth to get closer and closer to the Prominens where the two captives lay. The Mendacium was focused ahead on Ementior's breath and strove with each other to catch the breath of Death that exuded from Ementior as they were invigorated with each blow upon the heads of the captives.

As they moved closer, they covered their faces up to their eyes so as to not breathe in the Darkened vapor. They had no intention of receiving the breath that seethed Hate and Despair, Lies and Death.

The two captives, though, were another matter. They had no intention themselves to breathe the breath of Ementior, but they had been beaten and mongled by the Monglings that Weakness was beginning to prevail over them. Weakness conjured his spell mixed with Fear and Torture as the two captives were beaten over and over with the Rods of Thoughts by the Monglings.

"You failed. You were not. Your death awaits. You are defeated. Your Cancer is ours to give. You were tricked, duped, deceived and are helpless. Hell is your reward," the Mongles beat the two captives mercilessly.

"Get up on your knees and bow to the one who gives you your life!" another said.

The Monglings pulled the two captives from the bloody ground and brought them up to their knees in front of Ementior.

"Worship your king, worship your king and give him praise," a Mongling said as he struck one of the captives across the top of his head.

The two captives were on their knees, hooded with the bloody bags, with their heads hanging low to the ground. Weakness and Despair came to their sides and wisped their mixtures above them as moths to light.

"Give in, submit and all will be well with you," Despair creeped his cry.

"Don't fight anymore. It's time to give in. Breathe the breath of life, yes, yes, breathe it in," Weakness mimicked breathing, waving his hands towards his own face as he taunted the two who could not see what he was doing, but were influenced by the spell of his words nonetheless.

"Summon Ophis," Ementior motioned with his hand as he sat upon his rock. Ementior looked crazed with tormenting joy as an idea had rushed through his mind. Ementior stood and said, "We have here before you the two captives that matter. They are the only ones who matter. All else is play among the children," he shouted and the Mendacium roared.

He motioned with hands raised high. "Here before you are the two that we have longed for and this day, they are no longer captives, no, no, no, they are no longer beaten, NO! But they are becoming one of us! This day, they shall be we and we shall conquer all that is and all that shall be forevermore!"

The Mendacium shouted and jeered in raging joy stabbing their cohorts in fits of joyful Hate. As quite a few of the Mendacium fell surprised to their deaths, the Echad evaded the spears and the daggers in their midst and acted out the rage themselves so as not to be revealed. Half of the Mendacium fell in those moments and the remaining crowd cheered, raising their daggers and swords as high as they could in praise to Ementior.

Ementior smiled a cruel smile.

Before Ementior an enormous Snake of blue green serpentine slithered into the midst having come up from the Crevice of Mum's Deep. He bore the stripes and the angles of the Octahedra and his skin was that of serpentine, the impregnable stone. Gigot recognized him as Ophis, the great serpent who killed the Tiger. He was the all-powerful lie who Did Not Care and could strike at any moment.

The Snake slithered in front of Ementior as Ementior took a step back on his rock. Ophis rose his head high equal in height to Ementior as Ementior sensing his demeanor of equality rose his right arm with his scepter and pointed it at the Snake.

"Ophis, I give you the two captives," Ementior shouted and jeered his jeering smile.

The Mendacium, who had quieted when Ophis slithered in front of Ementior not knowing what was really going to happen, cheered at Ementior's words.

Ophis slithered closer to Ementior and whispered a thissing hiss towards Ementior's ears and then turned towards the raging crowd, saying, "You give me nothing that I don't already have." He slithered, smiling himself, whipping his tongue around the two captives.

The Mendacium quieted themselves to a small fervor because they knew that Ementior was threatened by Ophis because he Did Not Care and feared no one and bowed to no thing, except the Great One.

"Do your worst," Ementior demanded of Ophis as he looked him square in the eyes, not to be the least bit intimidated. Ementior sat down on the rock to watch Ophis perform his work.

The two captives sat motionless upon their legs on their knees, still bound with their hands behind their backs. The bags on their heads covered their identities as their clothing was soiled black from the breath of the Medacium and the Monglings. Ophis slithered around the two, carving a trench around them in the earth with his forked tongue. The Mendacium was quiet and even the Battling Trees quieted as the wind from the Crevice had ceased. All was quiet as Ophis continued to circle the two, slithering his tongue in and out of his mouth.

"So, who do we have here today, my dear Ementior," Ophis said, looking over to Ementior and then towards the crowd. The crowd of Mendacium did not know who the captives were for it was the Monglings who had gone in as spies and battled their way over time to capture these prized possessions for Ementior. Ophis was certain of the prey that lay before him, and in order for him to do his work, he needed to know for sure who he was dealing with.

"May I?" Ophis slithered his tongue around the bagged head of the one and lifted the front of the bag so that he could see the face of this particular captive. He lifted the bag far up enough so that only he could see the face of the captive.

"Um!" he said as his head flashed back in glee. He slithered his tongue around the second captive with a most desired look on his face presupposing who this next captive might be.

"Oh, let me guess, let me guessss…" he hissed as he raised the bag just slightly from the head of the second captive. His head, once again, flared backwards in glee. His sickening joy made him wiggle in the trench he had made around the two captives. He looked with lust towards Ementior as Ementior smiled his wicked smile.

"We have what we need to rule this world, do we not?" Ementior queried Ophis, standing as he spoke.

"We do, indeed," Ophis said wryly, slithering his tongue before his feast.

"Uh, you know not to kill them, don't you, just harm them in every way possible. We possess this land and it's only good to us as long as they're alive, but under our control." Ementior explained.

"As I said before, you do not give me anything I do not already possesssss," Ophis slithered his tongue, hissing at Ementior challenging his perceived authority.

As the two masters of Darkness seemingly prepared to dual over the lives of the two captives, all of the Mendacium quivered as to who might win the battle. These Mendacium had not seen either one of these Lords of Darkness defeated in this Land and wondered what might be their own demise if Ophis defeated Ementior before their eyes.

Ophis sensed the tension brewing in Ementior as Ementior was preparing a lie from the Deep intended only for Ophis. "Do what you will with these two, then, they are yours to have and to hold until Death comes to part these two from their wicked ways," said Ementior.

Ophis winced at Ementior's remarks knowing that he was the Master of the Lie and believed that all that lie before him was Ementior's. Ophis thought within himself at what he might say to wiggle his way to authority, or if he should just end this thing now with one fell swoop of his fangs into his head. He wiggled a bit more, thought a bit more, slithered his tongue around the two captives one more time and said, "What would you have me do…oh, great Master of the Lie?"

Ementior tilted his head, not believing his ears at what he'd just heard. In the tension of the moment, he raised his scepter towards Ophis and pointed it in the face of the great Snake.

"Do you mock me, you villainous angel of light?" Ementior screeched with teeth gritted in anger.

Ophis slithered up to Ementior's face and face to face, with piercing eyes he said to Ementior, "You know that I bow to no one and no thing." He slithered his tongue around Ementior cradling his scepter with the end of his tongue. Ophis whispered into the ear of Ementior and all around could see Fear wrap himself around Ementior tending to every thought within.

"Do your worst!" Ementior screamed to Ophis.

Ophis flipped around and in one movement had turned and ripped the bags off of the heads of the two captives spitting out the bags from his venomous mouth.

He picked the two captives up with his two fangs by the ropes that had bound their arms behind their backs and swirled them around so that all in the Thicket of the Cadgwith could see who they were.

A frightened shutter fell over the Echad as they were standing not far off from the rock of the Prominens. They held in their gasps as they tightened their grips on their swords, choking on the shock who was hanging before them. The horde of Mendacium fell back a bit in quiet shock and gasps. Then, once the breath of Ementior breathed out before them, they received the breath and cheered in joyous wickedness over the surprise of their captives. They rocked and cheered and poked their swords high in the air. They had won, or, so it seemed to them. They had their prize, the prize of the land and soon, all else would be theirs as well.

XXVI

The Failure Revealed

As the two captives hung by the ropes that bound their hands behind their backs, Ophis peered out into the Darkness to survey the cheers and the jeers of the Mendacium. He smiled his smile and whipped his bifurcated tongue around the dangling legs of the captives as they hung to their lives from his fangs. Ophis' mouth was open wide and as the roar of the torrential rage egged him on to do something…he thought he might just swallow them. But that was not what Ementior wanted and it made sense to him not to swallow them either, for where was the torture in that? As he listened to the rage, Ementior sat on his rock waiting for Ophis to do something spectacular. He was enjoying the mocking and the taunting that was going with these two captives believing that they deserved everything that they had coming to them and more. Ophis and Ementior were both enjoying the power that came with their given authority particularly when the enjoyment was at the expense of someone from the Light.

It was in these distorted moments of obliquity that as Ophis was receiving the praise due his name, he noticed a tiny fraction of the Mendacium having no movement. In fact, the area surveyed was not as Dark as the other areas. He winced as his eyes peered into the distance as the color of the rising vapor seemed to be as purple and the breath of Life emanated from it. He counted the figures below the purple vapor as they had remained motionless. There were six figures standing as one among the horde of Mendacium. He recognized Suffering by the shape of his hat and the thinness of his body.

Ophis raised his head high and as he did, the Mendacium immediately went to quiet. Ementior moved to right himself on the rock and ceased to breathe in anticipation of what Ophis was about to do next. Ophis raised his head even higher than before and reared back with tension on his neck and then flung his head forward tossing the two captives from off of his fangs flinging them into the midst of the Mendacium right at the feet of where the Echad was standing.

Gigot and Obedience stepped back out of the way as the two captives rolled upon the land to their feet. The rest of the Echad stood shocked as the moment of revelation had obviously come.

"Oh, the irony of balance in the world…isn't it just grand?" Ophis seethed with grandeur.

"To have you all here in one place is just too good to be true. Isn't it Ementior?" he continued.

Ementior rose to his feet in astonishment as the Echad brandished their swords and surrounded the two captives. They formed a circle around the two in the midst of the Mendacium as the confused Mendacium looked to their leader as what to do next.

"NO!" Ementior shouted to his league raising his hand to halt any onslaught. Amazed in wonder at this terrific opportunity, he raised his scepter high and said, "I'll finish this! Make a pathway!"

The Echad continued to stand with their swords and shields made ready, waiting for the torrent to come, but Ementior's demand implied for his army to part so that he could get closer to the captured foe.

As Ementior made his way down from his rock and walked slowly towards the Echad, Ophis slithered in behind him peering over his head supposing his authority over Ementior without Ementior knowing what he was doing.

"I know what you're doing Ophis, back off!" Ementior stopped and screamed as he turned around.

"Umph!" Ophis responded sulking back a bit so as to give the impression of submission but slithering nonetheless behind Ementior.

Ementior made his way to the Echad who were ready for anything, but it seemed that Ementior was making ready to talk rather than finish them off quickly. Ementior caught the eye of Will and grinned slightly at the prospect of toying with him, but hesitated, wanting to know exactly who the leader was today.

The Echad made ready and continued their circle around the two captives and grew tighter in. They had nowhere to go and nothing to do but fight to the finish. Gigot knew that things were not to be as they currently were, but he also knew within that all that he had done, or had failed to do, had led up to this point.

"Rest," Gigot commanded.

"But…" Will hesitated, but complied shaking his head back and forth.

Ementior arrived closer to them, speaking to Gigot.

"Yes, yes, indeed, the irony of balance, as our own Ophis has so eloquently surmised," Ementior laughed as he turned to congratulate Ophis on his awareness.

"My, my, my, doesn't purple suit you well, Gigot? And, is that you Suffering?" he said with a chuckle, "It seems that your leader has picked you out to work hard with these buffoons. Obedience, you have failed once again."

Ementior glanced over the tired, but readied group, who were not ready to speak, but readied to fight to the death.

Gigot sucked in his own breath, knowing that the breath of Ementior was lethal to life and that all that came from his lips were lies.

"I want to keep you all around a while, Gigot, Will, Purpose, and look who's come to dinner, well if it isn't Kardio and No`us," he said extending his arms wide to the two captives on the ground.

Kardio and No`us had been sorely beaten with the Rods of Thoughts and had not an ounce of strength left. They lay there on the Land in the Thicket passed out from the beatings of Torture and Fear. They had been overcome as Gigot and Will had been preoccupied with their own troubles. Gigot and Will had not realized that their troubles coincided with the failures of Kardio and No'us. Kardio and No`us had kept Crested Hill intact until the upheaval. They had prevailed in battle after battle and then they didn't.

Who was to blame?

Ementior cast Confusion to breathe his spell of doubt as Ophis cast Accusation, as Accusation breathed into their ears to keep the spell of blame alight.

Will was to blame. Gigot was to blame. Kardio was to blame. No`us was to blame. All shared blame as their heads bowed low.

Each and every little failure along their way amounted to consistent failures and breaches of every kind. The frequency of the failures were purposed to be a slow, pathetic death and a catastrophic downfall that none of them, individually, would see coming. Now, they would reap Death as they had sown carelessness to the influential onslaught of Darkness.

As they stood there against the breath of Ementior and the accusations of Ophis, they knew what Ementior knew and it was all on their faces. They were all to blame for giving in every other time to whatever temptation came their way. And here…here, captivity was the result. The Land had been taken over by one spirit after another and Gigot had shown up too late to make any kind of difference.

"I commend you for your courtesy that you have afforded me during these times of opportunitiesss," Ophis hissed aloud. He slithered closer to Gigot and continued,

"Each time you had a chance to tell me to go, you waited, you hesitated…oh, how you hesitated…you bad, bad boy. You know, I do have to compliment you on something…you are a good listener, aren't you?" he said as he slithered his tongue around the back of Gigot and around his head, removing Gigot's helmet from his head.

"You will not be saved," Ophis whispered into Gigot's ear, "Your Light is nowhere to be found."

"You're supposed to know the Light, why, you're supposed to be the Light and now, look at you…all hidden in disguisssse, disgracccced, annulled, fallen from graccccccce. Are you so certain you were ever His? Are you, my dear…Gigot? I know your name. It was given to you as mine was. The leg of the Lamb…Tsk, tsk, tsk. You needed too much seasoning and you are hard-baked rather than a rare one. All for naught, isn't it? Failures you are and failures you be," Ophis hissed and licked the back of Gigot's head, pushing his head forward in presumed humiliation, as he slithered away and around to the back side of the Echad where Purpose was standing.

"My, my, my Ambivalence, what brought you here? A little here, a little there…oh, yessss, it was your feet, wasn't it? Why, Gigot and Will were riding Faith and Truth and it was you who got them off of their place and onto what you were most comfortable with…a desperate little thicket. You know that I know that you love to walk and to hide in thickets, so I prepared this cove just for the three of you," he said snickering as he slid to Will.

"And Will, Will, Will," he tilted his head to the right as Will refused to make eye contact with him. "Look at me, boy. I said, look at me, boy!" Ophis licked up the chin of Will and held his head up with his tongue as he lowered his own head at eye level with Will's.

He slithered in his tongue and said, "You are the worst of all. Weak. Give in. No fight. WEAK!!!" he screamed at Will and Will dropped his head in shame.

"No, no, this is too easy, too simple, even the Tiger in you had more fight than all of you put together. At least he fought me and tried to conquer me with what he had. His death was your death…but you knew that… didn't you, Will? You're just…just…FAILURES! That's what you are… FAILURES! Failures as one and failures as all."

Ophis sulked away and slithered back behind Ementior in demented ruse. He had the demeanor of being disappointed because he knew he had just won the fight without lifting a scale, but it was all a ploy as it had been with so many others.

"You know I own you," Ementior spoke to the Echad. "I own you and you and you and you and you and you!" he said to each of them as they continued to stand hunched together in their circle. Kardio moaned as No`us rolled over on his back.

"So, what are we to do now? You do know that this is no stalemate. You are defeated. Darkness has come over the land as I have commanded it. Doom, Despair, Depression, Defeat have all joined us here to celebrate your demise. Breathe them in Gigot, breathe them in Will."

Ementior was waving his hands forward as he spoke encouraging each of them to receive him and the breath of Death that he was so willing to give. Darkness covered the Echad in total vapor as Depression and Despair tightened their grip on the east and the west. Defeat and Demise burdened the north and the south and weighted the Darkness over them as a heavy laborious cloud.

"I can't breathe, Gigot," Purpose whispered, worried about what was about to happen.

Delusion arrived in numbers as a family and surrounded the black cloud of Darkness and whispered their whispers of "He does not care for you. He's not here, is He? Breathe in the Death and give us your life."

Delusion was sickening as each of them began to falter to their knees without any air to breathe. Delusion had taken everything that was right and everything that was light and made it seem Dark…very, very Dark.

Ementior smiled. "Failures each and every time you failed, we remember them all. Breathe in the Death, Gigot. It's you that we want. Kardio, No`us and Will are already ours. Purpose never mattered, but you, Gigot, give your life to me and all of this will be over and I promise you, you will live with me forever."

Torrent and the Mendacium had all gotten on their knees to worship and pray to Ementior, their leader and their king. As it seemed to them, the battle was won and they all laid down their arms and bowed on their knees. They bowed and paid homage to their fearful leader. On their knees, they raised their backs up and they bowed their heads down. Up with their backs and down their heads went with their eyes closed and their hands clasped together until they finally bowed once more with their heads to the ground in fearful homage to their king.

No Mendacium dare look up or look out as Fear raged his final rage.

The Echad had no air to breathe in the Darkness, still Suffering stood in the midst of them. Gigot, Will and Purpose could only remain standing as long as Obedience kept them at their swords. He knew that they could not give in to the Dark, they just couldn't. One by one, Gigot, Will and Purpose fell to their knees gasping for air, not knowing what to do or what to say. The entire group was covered in thick suffocating, blackness that none could see through. None of the Echad could see through the clouds of black and none could see into the vast vapor that enveloped them. Gigot, Will and all fell helplessly to the ground expecting to breathe their last breath.

Humility fluttered up above the Darkened cloud and prayed these words, "Father, you are the Great One, my father and Lord of Gigot. I pray for him and these that you have given him that they may be one, even as you and I are one. The little time that Gigot has had, he has followed himself and he has followed you. Make no remembrance of the times when He has failed and throw his failures far away as the east is from the west. He is in your life. He is yours. Keep him in your name as he has submitted his life to you. Strengthen him and these that are with him to say the one thing that needs to be said. Sanctify them by your truth. Your word is truth. May we all be one in you, even as you are One. You in them and them in you. We declare that you alone are the Great One. You alone are Great!"

"Stop it, stop it at once!" Ementior raged at the insult of the name of the Great One and all of the Mendacium rose to their feet. Ophis had become enraged as well by the prayer of Humility and all at once they were ready to pounce on the Echad.

"Kill them all! Kill them every one!" Ementior struck at Humility, but Humility had bowed beneath the blow, back into the covering of Darkness that laid heavy over the Echad.

"Argh!!!" Ementior screamed again. "Kill them! Kill them all!"

With the force of an ocean of hate, Torrent led as the Mendacium flooded into the Darkness covering the Echad with swords flying, daggers pointing and spears jabbing. Bit by bit the Mendacium stabbed, poked and flew their swords and one by one the Mendacium were falling. Wild and raging Fledgling Death was upon the Mendacium in the fight, so they fought all the more slinging their swords aimlessly at anything that moved. One by one, the Mendacium went down in the fight and the battle raged on and on. Bit by bit, with savage butchery, they were meeting their match as they fought and fell by the side out of the cloud of Darkness. Watching this, more of the Mendacium entered the Darkened cloud of the fray as the bodies of the wicked spirits piled high outside the midst of the cloud of Darkness yet the slaughter raged on.

Ophis sat back on his belly and with wincing eyes watched expectantly into the fray until he finally realized that something was amiss. "Ahem," he hissed.

"AHEM!" he hissed again, but no one was listening.

He slithered over to Ementior who was engaged in the battle in his mind and whispered in his ear, "Well, do you think they're dead yet?"

Ementior, irritated at the interruption, gave Ophis a resentful look, yet came to his senses as he observed the dearth of death of the Echad and the multitudinous death of his warriors and shouted, "Cease! Stop! Stop the fighting, stop at once, you imbeciles!"

Ementior ran over to the middle of the dispersed cloud of Darkness searching through the carnage of dead and bludgeoned bodies only to find the stinking and miserable carcasses of the Mendacium, but no remains of the Echad.

"Where are they?" he shouted, "Where have they gone?" he shouted again into the air.

He did not know that the Echad had sunk deep below the Dark cloud and had crawled out beneath the Darkness while Humility was praying and the Mendacium was bowed in homage to their leader. The cloud was so large and so thick that Ementior could not see where they had gone to. He was too preoccupied with his own personal resentment of having to listen to yet another prayer from a Holy One who would pray when the host didn't know what to pray. Now, they've done it to him again!

The Echad had followed Purpose back along the trail where they had followed him before, only this time it was back to the Devil's Pan just beneath the Great Mount. As they were continuing to crawl through the Darkened muck and mire, they were just about to get to the entrance of the two boulders approaching the inflowing flux of breath riding the tide of the nasty breath into the Pan when one of the beleaguered Mendacium spotted them.

"There they are!" the Mendacium shouted as he spotted them floating on the tide of breath into the entrance between the two boulders.

"Catch them, kill them!" another one uttered in rage.

The Mendacium, in mass, trottled through sludge and mire of the Thicket of Cadgwith as the winds began to pick up once again. They lifted their legs high to muddle through the muck of cancerous dead breath which slowed their movement to a slow snarl.

The gale force winds throttled through the dense forest immediately rattling the trees as they had been in the past. In the twinkling of an eye, the winds blew up from the Crevice as a cyclone with tornadoes and gusts that whirled and swirled and licked up the Mendacium throwing them into the Battling Trees. The trees began to battle one another, twisting and turning and being lifted up by their roots, they were crushing the remaining Mendacium as they made chase after the Echad.

The Echad, made it through to the entrance by the flood of the tide of the breath and not even Ementior could retrieve enough breath so as to fight the winds that howled and blew up from the Crevice and back again as a tide being cast out to sea.

Like a man coughing up his cancer, the land began to shift and move with utter violence and an earthquake fell across the Thicket. Everything was moving and all that the Echad could do was move to higher ground, so they proceeded to climb back up the green mossy incline to the Great Mount.

The entire land mass was moving and quaking. The Dark Land was breaking up and the Mendacium had nowhere to hide. Trees were flying, the winds were whipping and howling and the land was splitting at every juncture.

As the Echad climbed up to the middle of the height to the Great Mount, the cords of Death encompassed round about them. The Torrents of ungodliness struck Terror with every movement towards them as the snares of Death confronted them. In their distress, the Echad prayed as one and called upon the Great One in their plight.

Their cry together as one for help before the Great One came into His ears and the whole land shook with continued quakes and the foundation of the mountains were trembling. The hills quaked and were shaken from the anger of the Great One. He bowed the heavens also, and came down shattering the Darkness under His feet.[1] A swift and mighty wind blew over the Great Mount as the Lavandula was blowing everywhere the sweet scent of the nard. The wind was so strong coming from over the Mount that the air turned to purple, the darkest royal purple that ever was. The wind in the air had formed racing clouds of purple that thickened in the moments as the Great One made the purple wind his hiding place and a canopy round about. The Echad could hear the rumbling of something mightier than a rushing wind. It was the rushing and the rumbling of horses' hoofs racing across the wind on the Great Mount as the clouds of purple gave entrance to a blazing and brilliant Light riding over and piercing the Darkness.

XXVII

The Invasion of Light

The Wind and the Great Light flew across the Great Mount with such a force pushing all that Lie before it away from the cliff of the Great Mount. Smoke went up from the Great Light's nostrils and fire from his mouth devoured all that it touched. The turbulent Wind fell over the Thicket and the heat from the fire turned the thicks of the Thicket to burning ashes. The Echad raced back towards the side of the Mount as the undercurrent of purple haze thrust them hard against the side of the Mount. Their backs were pinned against the side of the Mount as the Light rode the Wind over them. The Light pierced the Darkness thrusting itself into the forces of all that was Dark and the Darkness could not overtake it. No Darkness stood against the power of the force of Light as it swept over the Thicket forcing all that was Dark into the Crevice of Mum's Deep. The Wind of the undercurrent thrust the Echad upward in flight against the side of the Mount and carried them up onto the wings of the Wind. Their backs were covered in purple haze of all that was on the Great Mount and they found themselves to be riding the Wind as one behind the Great Light. From the brightness before him, He passed over in thick clouds as his presence thundered a mighty roar. Lightning in abundance was thrust towards the Darkness vanquishing all that it touched. His thick clouds passed with hailstones and coals of fire.[1] (Psalm 18:9-15)

The Mendacium took to flight in running away from the might of the Light. As the Great Light uttered his voice, a lightning storm of arrows flew after them and routed them.

The Wind thundered, "The LORD is great, and our LORD is above all gods. Whatever the LORD pleases he does, in heaven and in earth."[2]

228

The Mendacium were not swift enough to outrun his power. Lightning flashes struck them and their kind with a power they had not seen in that land in time.

"The Great Light has come!" Ementior screamed in horror. He placed his arm over his head to shield his eyes as he stood aghast at the power of the Light. He, too, was forcibly swept away by the power of the Light and the Wind as the Light and the Wind were one dispossessing all that the Darkness had taken.

Nothing Dark could stand against the piercing Light and the Wind that He rode. Faith and Truth were riding in the Wind behind the Light and as they flew, Gigot jumped onto Faith as Will jumped onto Truth as Kardio and No`us flew with the Wind. They rode like the wind in the Wind as the Wind had become their foundation. It forced all that was against them away from them and blew all that was Dark into the Crevice.

Ophis could not withstand the fervor that came against him and as was forcibly thrust, he slithered beneath the Wind as the Wind directed him to fall into the Crevice away from the oncoming force of Light.

All Darkness and Darkened Vapor fled away from the Light as the Battling Trees in the Thicket of Cadgwith were uprooted as though they had never been and were thrust into the Crevice behind the Mendacium and the Monglings. The foundations were laid bare by his presence and all that was of the Darkend Road was thrown into the Crevice.

The power of the Light chased all Darkness into the Crevice and placed a seal on that part of the land so that even the Crevice would fall away. At the Great Light's rebuke, the Crevice of Mum's Deep disappeared away from the Light and it was no more.

Channels of water as in the River of Life took its place filled with Living Water teaming with all types of life from on high.

As the Wind and the Light had thrust all that was unlike itself into the Crevice of Mum's Deep, the Light shed Light onto the Cadgwith of what it truly was and was always meant to be. Green growth sprouted and grew up from the land immediately as a miracle upon the earth and the land was cleansed of its Darkness as all Darkness ceased to be.

The land was free in the Light. The whitened trail that had shown Purpose the way remained as the original path to the Carb as the rock of the Prominens was cleansed of its foreboding Darkness where Ementior had taken his stand. Ementior had believed his own Lie that whoever took the Carb, took the Crested Hill. But he had not taken into consideration that his beliefs were made up of his very particular Lies.

The Carb was never his to take, nor was the Hill. The Carb, the Crested Hill and all that Gigot, Will, and the rest was theirs to surrender to whomever they submitted to. It was by Truth and Faith that they stood and it was to the Light and the Wind that they knew they belonged.

No Battling Tree stood in the Cadgwith as it became a meadow of green and new found growth of color of the azalea, the camelia, the gardenia and the magnolia. The Lavandula had sprouted here and there in splotches of purple as well as all other colors of the flora that had been swept in by the Wind and the Light. The Cadgwith was healed in the Light and all that remained was likened to the Light.

Humility, Suffering and Obedience joined Lortnoc, Sendink and Epaga at the Prominens before the Light and humbled themselves before Him. The Light swallowed the Wind as even the Wind obeyed His every command.

Gigot, Will, Kardio and No`us found themselves at the Prominens to the Carb bowing to the Great Light in all of his glory for he had set their feet on a broad place of peace and rescued them from all of their calamity.

All were speechless and bowed, including Faith and Truth, who came alongside the legs of the Great Light bearing the banner of who he was and had always been. Deliverance was there along with Grace as Grace Walker appeared and bowed as all bowed before their King, the Great One. Innocence, Purity and Charity stood out in appearance as they all bowed before their King.

The Great Light spoke, "The land is cleansed, Gigot. You and all that you are have found a home of life. I give you the friends of Epaga, who is Holy Love. Joy and Peace are as they are as myself and will be in you as you continually abide in Me. I give you the friends of Patience, Sendink, who is Kindness and Goodness to share with those whom you meet as you journey with Will, Kardio, No`us and Purpose to do what I have commanded you to do. And last, I give you Faithfulness, Gentleness and Lortnoc, who is Self-Control, the one you have needed the most. These are friends to hold most close to you so that what I have placed in you can be furthered with Truth and Faith."

The nine friends joined with Gigot as one as they all bowed before the Great One who was and is the Great Light. Gigot and the others prepared to speak before the Great Light who had always been their deliverer and healer of the Land. Gigot knew for certain he had been called unto the Light and to know His voice.

Kardio proclaimed, "We bow before you, our deliverer. I love you, oh Great One, my strength. You are my rock, my fortress and my deliverer. You are my shield, the horn of my salvation, my stronghold. I call upon you for you alone are worthy to be praised. I am saved from all my enemies for all who call upon your name can take refuge in you. You are the Light over any darkness and you alone illumine all my ways. With the merciful, you show yourself merciful; with a blameless man you show yourself blameless; with the pure, you show yourself pure; and with the devious, you show yourself shrewd. You make my feet as hinds' feet and set me upon my high places. You have trained my hands for battle so that my hands can bend a bow of bronze. Your right hand upholds me and your gentleness makes me great. You enlarge my steps under me and my feet have not slipped."

Will shouted, "You have made my enemies to turn their backs against me and as they cried for help, there was none to save. You have delivered me from Contention, from Despair and from all foreign spirits."

Purpose exclaimed, "For who is the Great One, except the LORD? And who is a rock, except our God? It is the Great One who arms me with strength, and makes my way perfect."

Gigot gulped and swallowed his tears of joy exclaiming, "The Great One lives and blessed by my rock. Exalted is He, the God of my Salvation, the One who executes vengeance for me. He subdues all that fall before Him and delivers me from all my enemies."

"You rescued me from the violent man and I will always give thanks to you before all who dwell. You have delivered me from the strivings of the Dark and have lifted me up above those who rise against me. I will sing praises to your name forever and ever and ever."

Gigot bowed in adoration and all of the beauty that the Light had created moved with the breath of the Wind in praise to the Great One in that place.

THE END

With gratitude to King David for Psalm 18

in adoration of the Lord Most High

The Great One

Terry Lursen and TEL Publishing Books

The Treasure Within The Kingdom of God - 366 Christian daily readings concerning the Gospel of Jesus Christ, the Kingdom of God.

Paperback - ISBN - 978-0-9910989-0-3

ebook - ISBN - 978-0-9910989-1-0

The Looking Glass Water: The Water That Woos - a novel about a man whose search for the elusive solution to the many problems that he has created by his poor decisions in life. The lake that holds the key to his dilemma is the same lake that holds the water that woos, the water that heals, the water that brings a man to the brink and tells him all that he is. If a man can drink of this water, then he'll never thirst again...

Paperback ISBN - 978-0-9910989-2-7

ebook ISBN - 978-0-9910989-3-4

www.perspectivesintruth.com

ARTIST
Designer
20
16 COVER ART CH
NC
DESIGNED BY

STEPHEN LURSEN
ARTIST AND INSTRUCTOR
WWW.STEPHENLURSEN.COM

www.ingramcontent.com/pod-product-compliance
Lightning Source LLC
Chambersburg PA
CBHW031236120726
47905CB00002B/612